# 8-BIT CHRISTMAS

# 8-BIT CHRISTMAS

## An '80s Quest for NES

KEVIN JAKUBOWSKI

*8-Bit Christmas* is a work of fiction. Names, characters, places and incidents are the products of the author's imagination or are used fictitiously. Any resemblance to actual events, locales or persons, living or dead, is entirely coincidental.

*Cover design: Jesús Prudencio, carsandfilms.com*
*Book design: editedbycaitlin.com*

2013 DB PRESS FIRST EDITION

Printed in the United States of America

ISBN 978-0-578-13020-0
*Also available in e-book*

kevin-jakubowski.com

To Mom, Dad and Leah

And to Meg, I love you more than Christmas

"For the spirit of Christmas fulfills the greatest hunger of mankind."

—Loring A. Schuler
Editor, *Ladies' Home Journal*

"I feel like eating after I win. Let's go to lunch. Ha, ha, ha!"

—King Hippo
Boxer, *Mike Tyson's Punch-Out!!*

# CHAPTER ONE

Timmy Kleen was not a nice kid. Maybe he grew up to be a nice adult as he got older. Maybe he runs a soup kitchen in Harlem now. I kind of doubt it, though. If I had to guess, I'd say he probably graduated from Harvard, became an investment banker and single-handedly bankrupted half the country. Of course, I don't know that for certain. It's just fun to think about. Maybe he's in jail now.

That would be sweet.

Growing up, Kleen's dad was some kind of vice president for ComEd. He drove a Porsche. I asked my dad once why we didn't have a Porsche and he told me, "Because we have you and your sister instead." Interesting, I thought. Did that mean I was worth half a Porsche? Could we, say, sell my sister for a Suzuki? These were things to consider. Anyway, Mr. Kleen was loaded and he drove a Porsche. He parked it in the family's three-car garage right below their pro-series adjustable basketball hoop, which was directly adjacent to their heated in-ground pool. No one in my town even had an above-ground pool, so being invited to Kleen's was basically like a free trip to Disney World.

For starters, the Kleen house had its very own snack pantry. Not to be confused with their food pantry, the snack pantry's sole purpose was to house and store snacks. I'd never heard of such a thing. Fruit Roll-Ups, Ding Dongs, Ho Hos, Cool Ranch Doritos, Capri Suns and—fun size be damned—*regular*-size Snickers bars. They were all there for the taking. No restrictions, no locks, no health advisories or lectures on hungry Ethiopian children. Just open up the door, turn on the light and enjoy. It made the labors of trick-or-treating seem like some kind of sick joke. The pantry had a gum drawer, for crying out loud. A gum drawer! A drawer with nothing but gum in it! Are you kidding me? Such was the level of kid decadence available at the Kleen house.

The first time I went to Timmy's was for his third grade birthday party. I didn't want to go. My parents made me. Maybe they knew I'd be fed there and might catch a glimpse into the upper-class lifestyle and strive to one day live in a house with an intercom system. Or maybe they just wanted me out of the house for a few hours. Whatever the reason, I went. And after that birthday party my life was never quite the same.

If you grew up in the sixties, you probably remember where you were when you first saw the Beatles or where you were when the astronauts landed on the moon. Well, I grew up in the eighties. There wasn't all that much to remember. The *Challenger* space shuttle disaster? I blocked that out years ago. The Berlin Wall? I'm pretty sure I was at a soccer practice making fart noises out of blades of grass when it went down. So really, my clearest, most vivid memory of the years 1982 to 1989 was watching Timmy Kleen unwrap the town's first Nintendo Entertainment System.

It all started out innocently enough. Unwrapping presents. Timmy plowed through the crap we bought him. What do you get a kid whose parents make ten times more than yours? There were a few He-Man figures (he already had them), a couple of board games (how embarrassing), several Micro Machines. The Grusecki twins gave him a few packs of Donruss baseball cards, which I was pretty sure they'd opened and pilfered from first. Steve Zilinski gave Kleen a Marlboro duffle bag (clearly the spoils of his chain-smoking mother). I gave Kleen the children's book *The Whipping Boy*. A Newberry Medal winner, it told the story of a young servant and a prince, and how the two came to have mutual respect for one another.

"What's it about?" Mrs. Kleen asked.

"It's about a boy who gets whipped," I said, spraying out bits of Twinkie.

That was too violent for Timmy, she said, and threw the book away. Literally threw it away, like she was cleaning food scraps off the table. At the time I didn't think much of it, but looking back, that's messed up, right? If only she'd known the violence that was to come from the next gift, maybe she wouldn't have been so hasty.

With the kid presents opened and discarded, Mr. Kleen plopped down a big one from him and the missus. One of the few universal truths growing up was that when it came to presents, bigger was unquestionably better. Our eyes widened at the possibilities. The box was huge. It was sturdy. Even Kleen didn't seem to know what it was. Weeks of snooping around the attic and his parents' bedroom had yielded no results.

The first rip to the wrapping paper served as a stunner, rendering Kleen unable to proceed in his normal fists-of-fury manner. Through the paper tear we could plainly see onto the box itself. It looked like some kind of space scene about to be uncovered, sort of like looking through the Millennium Falcon windshield right before the jump to hyperspace. What was it? Could this be a new Star Wars toy? Was that even possible? We'd been assured that the next movie wouldn't be finished until the year 1997.

"What is it?" Zilinski quivered.

Kleen wasted no more time. His sickly arms tore in two directions at once, plowing apart the paper at the top of the box. We all leaned forward to have a look . . . And there she was, hovering in outer space, glistening in all her gray plastic glory. A maze of rubber wiring and electronic intelligence so advanced it was deemed not a video game but an 8-bit *Entertainment System*. Equipped with two control pads, a complimentary power gun and a front console home to the all-important on/off button and its savvy counterpart, restart. Within a week there wouldn't be a pair of blistered kid thumbs in the room that didn't feel an instinctive tingle when the word "Nintendo" was mentioned. Timmy Kleen had just hit the jackpot.

We sat there at first, numb with shock. Evan Olsen had already spilled Hi-C on his crotch and was now dripping ice cream down his leg. By the time I came to, I realized I was screaming at the top of my lungs. We all were. We may have been screaming for minutes and not even known it. Kleen tried to lift the box like some kind of title belt above his head and yelled:

"NINTENDO!"

Pandemonium hit the kitchen. Wrapping paper started flying, two kids jumped on the table, the Gruseckis tackled each other in ecstasy, Evan Olsen ran off to the bathroom to relieve himself, and I can never be sure, but I swear I heard Kleen's three-year-old little cousin, Preston, say, "Holy shit" under his breath. This was big. And Batavia, Illinois, would never be the same.

Nintendo had come to town.

# CHAPTER TWO

Batavia, Illinois, is a small, some might say forgettable, suburb about an hour west of Chicago. Not too rich, not too poor. Its claim to fame is that it's the birthplace of Ken Anderson, the losing quarterback of the 1980 Super Bowl. Ever heard of him? Didn't think so. It's also home to the world's second largest atom smasher, Fermilab, which sits on a few thousand acres of prairie just outside of town. No one's exactly sure what it does, but there it remains, billions of tax dollars at work, blasting unseen particles into smithereens in the name of science.

In 1958, an ice skating scene on Batavia's Fox River graced the cover of the *Saturday Evening Post*. It was one of the few covers of the magazine that was *not* painted by Norman Rockwell. Even as a kid I found that hilarious. It seemed the whole world knew that Batavia wasn't quite good enough for someone as iconic as Rockwell. A guy named John Falter painted it. And that's Batavia in a nutshell, really—the poor man's Norman Rockwell.

Nonetheless, in the '80s it was still a nice, quiet, middle-class town. This was before Pottery Barns and Menards Super Stores the size of baseball stadiums started popping up all over Randall Road. In the summer there were cornfields and fireflies, and in the winter, snowmen and central heating. It was a great place to grow up. You could throw rocks at the Fermilab buffalo, maybe even get free pop refills at the Burger King and then bounce around the Whopper Hopper until you puked. Good. Clean. Fun.

Our family lived on Watson Street in a two-story, two-colored, one-hundred-and-twenty-year-old house. We were told it was originally a farmhouse built around the time of the Civil War, but now it could most accurately be described as a construction site. This was thanks to my dad, John Doyle—the dyslexic Bob Vila. Somewhere around 1979 he decided to install a kitchen cabinet and had not stopped since. The place was in a perpetual state of remodeling. It was two colors only because my dad hadn't finished putting up the new green siding on an otherwise blue-sided house. I would be in college before I could accurately say I lived in the green house on Watson Street.

On this particular morning, my dad was walking around our gutted living room in his favorite Saturday attire: bathrobe and tool belt. WGN sports talk radio was playing somewhere in the background.

*"Bottom line, Ditka's gotta stop wussy-footing around and THROW THE FOOTBALL."*

My dad took talk radio literally and considered himself an integral part of the broadcast. He yelled across the room.

"Oh, you can't throw the ball without more pass protection, Pat!"

*"McMahon doesn't have enough time to throw,"* the other on-air guy quipped. *"He doesn't have the pass protection!"*

"Uh-huh. Uh-huh. You see?"

In the adjacent TV room, my mom and sister were doing aerobics to *Jane Fonda's Workout*. The exercise tape would become a staple in the Doyle house, holding prime real estate in the VHS drawer next to *Harry and the Hendersons* and *Crocodile Dundee*—both recorded off TV during the magical two weeks in '88 when we somehow managed to get Showtime.

Dressed from head to toe in leg warmers, my mom huffed and puffed to Fonda. Step for step right next to her was my little sister, Lizzy. She was five going on twenty-five, with a voice so gravely and a vocabulary so sophisticated, it would often stop strangers in the street.

"Work those glutes!" she rasped.

My father popped his head in, chewing on a drywall nail as he often did. He patted Lizzy's Dutch Boy haircut, which held firmly in place.

"Morning, Lizzy."

"Morning, Johnny."

"Uh-huh. What did I say about calling me Dad?"

"Sorry, Daddy."

"Where's Jake at? I need his help."

"He left about an hour ago on his bike," said my mom between leg extensions.

"Where'd he go? Lizzy, where's your brother?"

Not even in first grade yet, Lizzy had already mastered the art of getting me in trouble. Next to My Little Pony and spelling out m-o-n-o-n-u-c-l-e-o-s-i-s for a dollar, it might have been her favorite pastime.

"He's at Timmy Kleen's playing Nintendo. He didn't pick up the dog poop in the backyard either."

.................

In the four months since Timmy Kleen had received his birthday Nintendo, a lot had changed. Jeff Hartwell, for instance, no longer delivered the *Bonnie Buyer* newspaper on Saturday mornings. Instead he dumped his papers in the Mueller Crest Woods so he could get to Kleen's house in time for the nine o'clock Nintendo lineup. This was a system devised by Kleen that allowed a first-come, first-served entrance into his basement to play Nintendo. The line usually began forming sometime before dawn. Only ten lucky kids were let inside for the day, and today, even in the late-November cold, the yard was chock-full of Nintendo hopefuls, including my best friends:

EVAN OLSEN: nervous, allergic to bees, constant Kool-Aid moustache

MATT MAHONEY: tall, loud mouth, great at drawing army guys and lighting things on fire

STEVE ZILINSKI: popular, spike haircut, all-time quarterback, mom's a psycho

RYAN GRUSECKI: chubby, runny nose, smart as a whip, great baseball card collection

TOMMY GRUSECKI: Ryan's twin brother; see above

I was stuck somewhere around the eighth or ninth slot in line, between Mahoney and our sworn enemy, Josh Farmer. The two were already arguing.

"No cutss, no buttss!" lisped Farmer.

"Cool it," said Mahoney.

"No, you cool it."

"No, *you* cool it."

"No, *you* cool it."

"Idiot."

"You're a idiot."

"No, you are."

"No, *you are.*"

And so on and so forth unto eternity.

Lining up this early made even the calmest of us a bit testy. We were also missing quality Saturday-morning cartoon hours. Farmer had started a rumor that Dr. Claw had actually been captured at the end of today's *Inspector Gadget* episode. It had us all whipped up into a dither.

"Impossible," I said.

"You're full of it, Farmer." Mahoney was pushing him now. "Dr. Claw always gets away."

A pathological liar, Josh Farmer had once claimed to have seen and positively identified Randy "Macho Man" Savage in the Batavia Apartments, who had told him, among other things, that WWF wrestling was, in fact, real. The Dr. Claw fib was just one of a myriad of tall tales in his demented repertoire

"It totally happened, I saw it. Dr. Claw gets caught."

"Bull crud."

"Bull true."

"Bull true like how your mom draws all the Garbage Pail Kids? Or how you saw Bigfoot jump off the Wilson school jungle gym?"

"Screw you guys. Dr. Claw totally—"

Farmer was cut short by the sound of high-pitched

barking. The Kleens' dog, Lacey Dog, a five-time contender for Most Annoying Dog of the Year, had just been let outside to do her business. This meant Timmy was about to open up shop.

We all turned to the door. Slowly it opened and Kleen stepped out onto the porch and into the light. Standing high above us in his robe and slippers, he calmly stirred a glass of chocolate milk, surveying the masses like some kind of amused Roman emperor. With a grand gesture, he checked his Swatch watch (both of them): It was nine o'clock. Eight hours of Nintendo to be had.

"Anyone for a little Nintendo?"

"RAAAAAAHHHH!"

The crowd went nuts. Clawing, biting, kicking, scratching, jostling for position. If you were driving by in a car, you'd think zombies were making their way down Cypress Avenue after us. What felt like a hundred and fifty kids for ten spots all swarmed toward the door.

Kleen tallied us up as we rushed through. "One-two-three-four-five-six-seven-eight-nine-ten!"

For the third Saturday in a row I'd made the cut. I was inside, safe and sound. Kleen slammed the door behind him.

"That's ten, that's the cutoff."

Packs of wailing kids banged on walls and windows outside. Ryan Grusecki's little face pressed up against the glass, mouthing unheard pleas to his twin brother, Tommy.

"But my brother's still out there!"

"You know the rules, Grusecki. You can always go back out and join him. It's no skin off my nose."

*No skin off my nose?* That's seriously how Timmy Kleen talked. What kind of a nine-year-old kid talks like that? He barked out more orders as we filed down into the basement.

"Boots off, boots off, watch the carpet. That means you, Farmer."

Lacey Dog yipped incessantly, clawing at our feet and nipping at our crotches. Mahoney casually kicked her in the face.

"Hey! Watch it," Kleen snapped. "She's a purebred Shih Tzu."

"She's a purebred psycho."

"That's it, end of the line!"

"No fair."

"No fair, huh? You wanna be sittin' home next Saturday, playing Sorry! with your sister? I don't think so. End of the line."

Giving the only Nintendo in town to a kid like Kleen had been a real lesson in God's cruelty. I'd already prayed several times to be made part of his family.

Mahoney took his punishment and trudged behind me sadly. The ten of us finished filing down the stairs in numerical order and sat down on the couch to get to business. Kleen gave a customary blow into the *Duck Hunt* cartridge, picked up the gun, scooted himself three inches away from the TV screen, turned and smiled devilishly back at us.

"Winner stays."

Back on Watson Street, Jane Fonda and Co. were in cool-down mode, sipping Tab and Tang respectively, while my dad was outside searching for yet another lost tool in the shed. He was always just one tool away from finishing the house. "Just one tool." As if suddenly locating the missing band saw would miraculously paint the downstairs bathroom and retile the kitchen.

"God bless it! Where the hell is it?"

Pinewood Derby cars, green aluminum siding, old cans of Thompson's WaterSeal all tumbled out onto the lawn. Elwood, our family dog, looked on as he popped a squat in the snow-dusted grass. Two years my senior, Elwood had seen it all. He panted slightly, almost in a half smirk, anytime he watched my dad search for a lost tool. Sometimes I wondered if the dog actually went around burying screwdrivers in the backyard just to watch the old man lose it.

"Where the hell *is* it? How do you lose a nail gun! That's not it . . . What the—? Aha! You dope, Doyle, it's right where you put it."

He walked out of the shed, proudly displaying the nail gun to Elwood.

"You see? Right where I knew it would—"

Blamo. He stepped right in a pile of it. Dog poo. Some of Elwood's finest. If there was one thing John Doyle couldn't stand, it was stepping in dog poo, particularly dog poo in his own backyard.

"JAAAAKE!"

On cue, my sister appeared at the back door and popped her head out.

"He's at Timmy Kleen's. I told you he didn't pick up the dog poo."

Timmy Kleen had now been playing *Duck Hunt* for forty-five minutes straight. He was on level thirty-one, a feat that would be near impossible had he not been pressing the gun *directly* on the screen. He stood in front of the TV, a massive 42-incher, and clicked away, only pausing every once in a while to make obscene gestures to the 8-bit dog that popped up at the end of each level.

"Maybe you should sit a little closer," Mahoney ventured. It was a ploy.

"Maybe you should shut up."

After months of sitting and watching Kleen play to his heart's content, we'd realized the only tactic to get him out of the way so we could play was to antagonize him. He was insanely antagonizable. The word "spaz" comes to mind. Had there been such a thing as ADHD in the 1980s, he most certainly would have had it. Mahoney took great pleasure in riling him up.

"Hey Kleen, has anyone ever told you you look like Molly Ringwald?"

"Shut up, Mahoney. Don't distract me."

"Seriously, like a shorter, dumber Molly Ringwald."

"I said don't distract me!" Kleen fired away at the ducks, missing a few in the exchange.

"Which is weird because Angela Moran looks like Molly Ringwald too, and you're in love with Angela Moran. Does that mean you're in love with yourself? That's really weird. Don't you think that's really—"

"I said SHUT UP!"

The 8-bit dog hopped over the hedge and began his customary laughing fit. Kleen immediately opened fire on him, accidentally letting his shots ring out as misfires on the next level. Before he could register a complaint, the ducks sped off to safety and his game was suddenly over.

"What? WHAAAAT? Those don't count! Those shots don't count!"

"Tough luck, Kleen. Gimme the gun."

"NOOOOOOO!"

Every group of gamers has a kid who can't handle defeat. Ours was definitely Kleen. Casually I slipped Mahoney a high five as we watched him drop to the ground and writhe around in pain, screaming and kicking at nothing in particular. Kleen's tantrums were always extremely amusing to us. Over the years we'd seen him whip baseball bats at Little League umpires and call lunch ladies a plethora of vile names.

"YOU STUPID GAME! YOU STUPID CRUDDY BUTTHEAD GAME!"

"Jesus, Kleen. Take it easy."

"I'M GONNA KILL IT!"

Kleen pounced on the Nintendo and began shaking it violently. In an instant, all ten of us leapt off the couch and tackled him to the ground. Zilinski pressed a pillow to his face, Grusecki threw in a few punches for good measure, and I ripped the console from his hands, carefully backing away from the dog pile. When it came to the safety of the town's only NES, it did not pay to take chances.

"What's going on down there?" Kleen's teenage sister yelled from upstairs.

"NOTHING!" all ten of us shouted back.

"Jake Doyle, are you down there?"

"Yeah?"

"Your dad's on the phone."

Great. We all knew what that meant. There was only one reason for a phone call to a friend's house and it wasn't to ask you what you wanted for dinner.

"He wants you to come home."

"Yeah, yeah . . . "

Nods of sympathy registered within the group. Painfully I trudged up the stairs, already thinking about how happy my departure was going to make Ryan Grusecki or any number of rejects waiting outside, still clinging to hope for a second chance at Nintendo.

# CHAPTER THREE

Elwood was eleven years old—seventy-seven in dog years—and in that time I was convinced he had pooped more times than any other dog in the history of the world. His best work dotted our snowy backyard like chocolate sprinkles on a vanilla cupcake. They were everywhere. And I had to pick up every single one of them. I stood there with a poo-caked shovel and a dumb look on my face as my dad walked by carrying half a hardware store into the shed. I did my best to get out of the chore.

"What's Lizzy doing right now?"

"She's being five years old, Jake. Just pick it up."

"What are you doing?"

Sadly, it wasn't until my high school years that I learned not to ask my father what he was doing.

"What am I doing? Maybe you'd like to drywall the upstairs bathroom."

You mean instead of picking up frozen dog poo? Yeah, sign me up. But all I got out was "Uh . . . "

"You know what I think? I think you've been spending a little too much time over at the Kleens' playing video games."

"Nintendo," I corrected him. There was a big difference.

"That stuff makes you fat, Jake. You can't play outside?"

"It's cold."

"Cold? It's good for you. Take a deep breath."

My dad took a deep breath, soaking in the winter air. I followed suit, slightly.

"Smell that?"

Poo?

"Fresh air. It was all we had and we loved it. Did I ever tell you about the fort my friends and I built in the vacant lot behind Grandma's house when I was your age?"

Only about ten million times. "Yeah, Dad."

"All year round we played out there. Summer, winter, didn't matter. We built booby traps and everything. It was just like in *Swiss Family Robinson*. You remember that movie, right?"

Of course I did. He'd made me watch it every year since I was three. It was his favorite movie growing up. "Yeah, Dad. The one with the pirates and tree forts."

"That's right, *Swiss Family Robinson*. They lived outside all year round and they loved it. Those kids didn't need Nintendo."

"But Dad, didn't they live on a deserted island? Like a hundred years ago? How would they even know about Nintendo?"

"Ah, just forget it," he barked. "Just pick up the poop, will ya?"

He made his way toward the shed, sidestepping landmines. He pointed to a particularly steamy one.

"Do that one last. Let it freeze."

It had become painfully obvious over the course of my birthday and the two months leading up to December that getting a Nintendo in the Doyle household was roughly as probable as Elwood and myself landing the '88 Republican nod for office. My dad thought Nintendo would make me fat, my mom thought it was too violent, not to mention too expensive, and my sister, well, she pretty much only wanted to see me suffer. But as I stood there watching my breath amid the snow and the poo, I made a promise to myself: I would figure out a way to get Nintendo for Christmas. Like Mario's Princess, she was my destiny.

Two hours and two garbage bags of poo later, I was back on my Team Murray BMX bicycle, the sounds of *Excitebike* racing through my head as I pedaled to the one place in the world that could keep my mind off Nintendo: the Bullpen.

The Bullpen was a baseball card store, but it was more than that. It was our mecca, our town hall, our clubhouse—a place where a kid could go to think and chew rock-hard bubble gum. A tiny shop no bigger than a living room, it consisted of five long glass cases filled with cards, a candy counter in the center and, inexplicably, a shelf toward the back that housed porcelain dolls. Yes, porcelain dolls. These dolls were for sale, apparently, but none of us ever saw any of them go anywhere. There was a rumor that Ronnie Dobber had bought one once, but luckily for his sake, it could never be proven. Other than Kleen's house and school, the Bullpen was probably the only indoor place we ever went.

I hopped the curb out front and found Zilinski and the Gruseckis already there, sitting on the bike rack, shuffling through fresh packs of Donruss.

"What are you guys doing here? Why aren't you at Kleen's still?"

"Harwell told Kleen the infinity-lives code for *Contra*. He'll be playing all afternoon."

"Infinity?"

"Yeah, it's like over a hundred."

I sat down next to them to have a look at today's prospects. Although baseball cards had been around almost as long as baseball itself, it wasn't until the mid 1980s that they really took off. Call it capitalism at its best or '80s greed, but once baseball card companies figured out that they could give a monetary value to each card and treat them essentially as stocks, an entire new business was born. Overnight, they went from a hobby to a multimillion-dollar industry. Kids weren't buying cards to stick in their bicycle spokes anymore, they were buying them as an "investment."

Packs of cards served as a roulette of sorts. For fifty cents you could buy an assortment of random players and potentially get a card worth, say, two dollars, thus instantly quadrupling your investment. There wasn't a boy among us who wasn't thoroughly convinced that in twenty years his baseball card collection would finance swimming pools, race cars, futuristic Nintendo systems . . . As such, we had all become hooked on the thrill of the chase.

Ryan and Tommy Grusecki were no exception. Business savvy beyond their years, they were the kind of kids who took pride in rationing their Halloween candy to last till June. That philosophy carried over into baseball cards, slowly building them one of the most valuable collections in town. They were the first to subscribe to the *Beckett*—basically the *Wall Street Journal* of card collecting—and between the two of them there wasn't a card printed in the US that they didn't have a lead on. Tommy scoured his pack, trying to find something of value in it.

"Got it, got it, need it, got it, need it. A Jose Corn-ee-joe?"

"That's Cornejo," Ryan corrected. "Seven cents in mint condition in the *Beckett*."

As usual with Donruss lately, today's packs proved to be duds. Zilinski was almost finished with his jawbreaker, I had a dollar burning a hole in my pocket, so inside we went.

The moment you walked into the Bullpen you were met with a smattering of animosity. The owner, Nick, who hated baseball and didn't like kids, was prone to kicking you out of the store for any infraction he saw fit. Step one to gaining entrance was money. Without it, you were back on the street.

"Lemme see it," Nick barked from behind his tinted Coke-bottle glasses.

I unfolded my dollar bill like a little white flag and walked inside. A sickly looking second grader was standing with his nose to the center glass case, drooling over a Mark McGuire rookie card, but other than him, we were the only customers in the store. Kleen's Nintendo had certainly put a hurt on Nick's business.

If you were lucky enough to get past Nick's first round of demands, you were soon met with a warning sign, the holy decree of baseball card shop owners the world over. Handwritten in red marker, hanging prominently over the cash register, it read:

YOU BEND IT, TWEAK IT, NUDGE IT, NICK IT, SMUDGE IT, DROP IT—YOU BOUGHT IT!

Rumor was, Nick had posted the sign after a kid sneezed on an Ernie Banks card three minutes into his first day of business. It was his lone insurance policy. Slowly I perused the cases. Zilinski and the Gruseckis quietly followed behind me with their eyes to the floor and shirts tucked in, afraid of being kicked out. The sickly second grader tore himself away from the McGuire for a few moments and handed Nick a stack of cards. Nick got out his calculator and pencil and mindlessly shuffled through them. He made a few calculations, pressing the eraser onto the calculator's plastic buttons. He adjusted his glasses and leaned over the counter.

"I'll give you seventy-five cents for the Eric Davis."

The kid wiped his nose with his sleeve in meek protest. "But it's five dollars in the *Beckett*."

"Seventy-five cents, kid."

"But it's going up both ways. It's worth five dollars, Nick."

"Seventy-five cents. It'll buy you another pack . . . "

Nick dangled a new pack of cards over the kid's head like some kind of dog treat. The kid stared up at it longingly, desperately trying to fight the urge. But we all knew what would happen. Millions of government dollars were spent each year to teach us to say no to marijuana, drunk driving, violent television and airplane glue, but boy did they miss the boat on baseball cards. Every birthday penny, shoveled-driveway dollar or grandmother kickback went straight to the fix. Hooked like junkies, strung out on the one-in-nine-hundred chance that Jose Canseco's smiling face might magically appear in a pack—the Bullpen was nothing more than an operation conceived to fuel the gambling addictions of small children.

The kid began scratching himself nervously—still staring at the pack, mouth agape. We probably could have said something like, you know, "Don't do it, kid, Nick's ripping you off," but we didn't want to get kicked out five minutes in. It was obvious the kid was gonna cave. He was too young, too unseasoned, temptation was far too strong. Slowly he nodded yes. Nick took the Davis and tossed him the pack. The kid gave us an anxious smile and scurried out the door to some back alley to get his fix.

Nick immediately put a five-dollar price tag on the Davis and slipped it into a display case. He looked us over. "So, what'll it be, kid? We got a new box of Score, Fleer's been gettin' a lot of good hits."

"Make it two packs of Topps, Nick. It's a cold ride home."

I plopped down my dollar, and he slid two green-and-yellow waxy packages across the counter. I took a deep breath and dove in. The Gruseckis and Zilinski hovered over me to have a look.

Although the "Future Stars" cards in this year's series of Topps ran deep, the boring faux-wood border on each card left a lot to be desired aesthetically. Anything that resembled the wood paneling on my dad's Chrysler minivan was an immediate dislike. Attempts at amusement with the "Did You Know?" section on the back of each card also proved a little weak. Did I know Montreal Expo Jim Wolford "once worked as a life-insurance salesman"? No, I did not. Nor did I give a shit. All I cared about was how much he was worth in the *Beckett*. In Jim's case, that would be three cents. Such began today's packs of Topps.

After Wolford, I shuffled through a series of nobodies

and has-beens. Ed Lynch. Mark Eichhorn. Alvaro Espinoza. Oddibe McDowell. Sparky Anderson—a manager card. Who in God's name wants a manager card? Jim Deshaies. Glenn Wilson. Ken Schrom . . .

"This is the worst pack I've ever seen," observed the Gruseckis, in unison.

"Are you gonna eat your gum?" asked Zilinski. I handed it over and he crunched away. There were only three types of baseball card collectors: the Dealers, the Junkies and those just hanging around for the gum. Zilinski was a Gum Man. You had to hand it to him. He must have saved a fortune over the years.

Quickly I tore into the second pack. Ho-ho! A better start. Darryl Strawberry. *The Straw!* Earlier this year, our teacher Mrs. Hugo had hung up a "Just Say No" poster of Strawberry and his teammate Doc Gooden endorsing the national campaign against drugs. The fact that they were both raging cokeheads at the time apparently went unnoticed by Major League Baseball. Years later, Strawberry and his cousin would be caught by police with two grams of coke and a hooker in the back seat of their car. Allegedly, Strawberry's defense was that his cousin and the hooker had "kidnapped him" and "forced him" to do drugs. Kidnapped by a hooker and your cousin—gotta be one of the best excuses ever.

After Strawberry, next in the pack came Paul Molitor. The future Hall of Famer was one of my favorites, mostly because my uncle Kevin claimed to have hit a homer off of him in Little League, an achievement he would gladly recount after a few summertime Molson Goldens. After Molitor came Tony Armas, then a few no-name pitchers, a pre-Cubs Andre Dawson and then . . . Mike Greenwell.

"I got a Greenwell!"

If you collected baseball cards in the 1980s you know who Mike Greenwell is. The mere mention of the name triggered dollar signs in the eyes of thousands of boys all across America—even though the vast majority of us had never, nor would ever, see him play. He was the perfect example of a baseball card making the player, rather than the other way around. His price, a whopping six dollars in the *Beckett*, was based solely on speculation. And there lay the great mystery of baseball card collecting. Who decided this stuff? Who determined that guys like Greg Jefferies, Eric Anthony or Jerome Walton should be worth more than, say, Tony Gwynn, Barry Bonds or Greg Maddux? You know, guys you'd actually *heard* of? A perennial All-Star like Don Mattingly only went for a buck, but a first-year Mike Greenwell went for six? Next to Jose Canseco's rookie card, this was the most expensive card in the entire Topps set that year. The Gruseckis patted me on the back as if I'd just accomplished something through skill and cunning.

"Good work, man."

"Thanks. I knew it was a good one. I knew it."

Slowly, I took out my retainer and approached the counter. Perhaps today was the day we saw Nick actually pay a fair price. Mike Greenwell was a rare commodity. Proudly, I set the card down before him. He didn't even blink.

"Dollar ten. It'll buy you two more packs."

And that was how I lost my first Mike Greenwell.

# CHAPTER FOUR

It was a well-known fact at HC Wilson Elementary that the true start of the Christmas season rested on the pretty little shoulders of our art teacher, Miss Ciarocci. Once the Thanksgiving decorations had come down and the recess temperatures dropped to proper loogie-hawking levels outside, we all knew we were closing in on the Christmas kickoff. Ciarocci, smiling and steadfast, would sit us down, each of us uniformly dressed in our fathers'-backward-dress-shirt smocks, and lay it on us.

"Good morning, class."

"Good morning, Miss *Cee-ah-roh-cee*."

"Today is a very special day for us. Does anyone know why?"

Could it be? Was today the day? Quickly my hand shot up.

"Yes, Jake Doyle."

"Is it because we're gonna start making our Christmas tree ornaments?"

"Very good, Jake, that's right. Today we start our Christmas ornament projects."

Hell yes! Every year, Ciarocci's announcement was the starter pistol's bang to an entirely new outlook on life, a call to arms that legitimized our collective insanity and excitement over the pending holiday. The ornaments meant there was no denying it anymore. Christmas was here. Officially. Parental threats of canceled Christmases in years past for bad behavior could no longer be deemed worthy of our concern. A teacher had told us to start making Christmas stuff. This was for school. This was for a grade. This was for real. Christmas had begun!

"Now everyone get out your drawing materials. The first step is designing the ornament." She smiled and patted my head as she walked by. Oh man, a head pat from Ciarocci and an announcement that Christmas was here. It was almost too much to handle. I drooled a little bit on my smock as I watched her walk to the front of the class.

I never learned Miss Ciarocci's first name, but I'd like to think it was something cool and groovy, like Sunshine or Gloria. She couldn't have been more than twenty-four. Trapped in an '80s world of yuppie commercialism, she'd clearly been born in the wrong era. Simply put, Miss Ciarocci was a hippie. A grade A, sweet-smiling, no-make-up-necessary, drop-dead gorgeous hippie. Ponytailed red hair, big green eyes and skin the color of peach Crayolas. Where other teachers wore shoulder pads and big ear-rings, Ciarocci wore flowing skirts and hemp necklaces. She smelled of patchouli and paste and I was madly in love with her.

Sweet Ciarocci was probably the only person in the world who could have kept my Nintendo obsession at bay that year. So resolute was my desire to gain her affection that I vowed to create the greatest Christmas ornament ever produced. There was only one small hurdle standing in my way—namely, my utter inability to paint, draw, cut, paste, glue, glitter or otherwise assemble any type of artistic structure not resembling a blob of crud. While marginally creative, I had the fine motor skills of a Muppet. Medical records have since shown, as my sister later pointed to in moments of triumph, that I could not even hop on one foot until the age of ten. But this year I was determined to come up with an ornament masterpiece. It was December 4th. I had twenty-one days until Christmas. The season had officially begun.

Even that night at the family dinner table I could feel the warmth of the holiday spirit seeping in.

"Damn it, Jake! That thing's not a toy!" yelled my father, flicking at my retainer. I was spinning it like a top on the kitchen table, deep in thought.

"But we're about to eat."

"Do you know how much that thing costs? Put it back in."

Reluctantly I popped the retainer back in my mouth. Usually I'd run water over the disgusting hunk of purple plastic (why in God's name had I chosen purple?) before inserting it back in, but when my dad was around it was best to just shove it in there as quickly as possible. The man viewed every second that it was out of my mouth as dollar bills flying out of his wallet.

Lizzy came bounding down the stairs.

"I washed my hands for dinner, Mommy."

"That's very good, Lizzy."

"I know. I bet Jake didn't wash his hands. Did you wash your hands, Jake?"

"Jake, dear, go wash your—"

"Yeah, yeah . . . " I trudged over to the sink.

Oh God, washing your hands . . . For some reason, and I'll never really know why—I don't think any of us will—but when you're a kid there's no task more hated, more loathed at its very sanitary core than washing your hands for dinner. The abhorrence makes no sense. Washing your hands takes about nine seconds. Walk to faucet. Turn on faucet. Slide hands in and out of stream. Turn off faucet. And you're done. That's it. You could even skimp on drying off or using soap if you wanted. I, for one, was constantly pushing the limits of what I could get away with, as if unclean hands were some kind of nine-year-old's badge of honor.

By about the age of seven I'd perfected the single-drip wash. That's one drip, singular. This maneuver required me to turn on the faucet in such a delicate manner that only one drip of water was released. At the millisecond of discharge my hands would dart under the faucet to catch the drip, both rubbing together and shutting off the stream at the same time. No soap. No towel. Total wash time: two-point-eight seconds. I'll show *you* washing hands, Mom and Dad! Sometimes I still catch myself doing it late at night in dive-bar bathrooms.

I hopped down from the kitchen sink stool and shot my sister the evil eye. Chili was being dished out at the table, a sign that it was okay to take out my retainer. Chili was one of the old man's favorites. He poured on the cheese and often favored Tostito chips or Ritz crackers instead of a spoon. Very classy.

"Let's pray, huh," he said, his eyes watering.

We all made the sign of the cross. Never one for correct Catholic wording, my prayer went something like:

"Best that oh Lord for these eye gifts which come out to receive, from somebody, oh Christ our Lord. Amen."

By the time the family was making the closing sign of the cross, my dad already had two mouthfuls of chili in and was starting in on his third. Raised in an Irish/Polish family of eight, he saw prayer only as a deterrent to food. He'd developed a devious dinner prayer shorthand that he conveniently disguised as Latin. Next to driving, praying was probably the fastest thing he did all day. His Sunday post-Eucharist sneak-outs to Smiley's Doughnuts were legendary.

My mom spoke between polite slurps. "You know, Jake, I ran into Steve Zilinski's mom at the Jewel today."

That was never good.

"You know what she said?"

Something that was bound to make my life less fun?

"She mentioned how much you boys have been playing Nintendo. Is that *all* you've been doing over at the Kleens' these past few months?"

Yes. 100%. "No . . . "

"What do his parents say about it?"

"Well, they're not home all that much."

"They're not at home when you're there?"

Quickly I caught myself. "Um, I mean they don't come into the basement all that much, is all."

Lizzy looked up slyly from her chili, waiting to pounce. "This is excellent chili, Mother."

"Thank you, Lizzy."

My dad chimed in. "What your mom is trying to say, Jake, is no more Nintendo."

"What? No way!"

"Just a few hours on the weekends, okay, honey? Mrs. Zilinski read it's been doing all kinds of strange things to children in Japan."

You mean like making them smarter, faster, better at karate? Those things?

"They get so involved, they forget about everything else, school, friends. It's bad for your eyes. One little boy in Tokyo supposedly had a seizure."

Lies.

My dad's bowl had been finished and he was now fully tuned in. "That's why they peddle their techno-junk over here, you know. New Japanese takeover tactics. Reagan won't stand for it, Patty, and neither will I. Jake, no more."

"Mom!"

"Your father's right, honey, just a little bit on weekends. No more during the week. That's final."

Lizzy's smirk was now fully visible. "Nintendo-no-friendo."

This was serious. How was I supposed to convince my parents to get a Nintendo for our own home if they didn't even want me playing it at someone else's?

Later that night, curled up before the gentle glow of our ten-channel Zenith, the gears of my Christmas engine continued to churn. There had to be some way I could get a Nintendo. There had to be. Not even Marc Summers and his messy antics as host of *Family Double Dare* could keep my mind off of it. I had been a fan of the game show for years, regularly envisioning what it might be like if my family was ever plucked from obscurity to compete for valuable prize packages and television glory . . .

*"The Doyle family, ladies and gentlemen! Let's give them a big* Double Dare *round of applause!"*

*The studio audience roared. We stood there before them, team name: "Slime and Punishment" (clearly my sister's idea), half-soaked, covered in ice cream toppings and other various goop-like products, the result of twenty minutes of victorious physical challenges. Of this much I was certain: even if my sister claimed to have the correct answer to any trivia question, John Doyle would still opt for the physical challenge. Being made to look like an idiot in public was something of a Doyle code of honor. Like moths to a flame, Doyle men had a hard time backing down from any dare of physical stupidity. Our backyard had the fireworks scars to prove it.*

*"So, how do you feel about making it to the final round, Mr. Doyle?"*

*"Pretty good, Marc, pretty good. I believe I have a peppermint gumdrop lodged in my ear right now, but I'm confident we can all pull through and get the job done here in sixty seconds or less."*

*"Sounds like a man on a mission. What do you think, Mom?"*

*"I just hope no one gets hurt, Marc."*

*"There you have it, folks. Team Slime and Punishment has sixty seconds or less to grab all eight flags and complete the* Family Double Dare *obstacle course. So tighten up those safety goggles and elbow pads, Doyles, and get ready to get messy. Alright, on my signal . . .* ON YOUR MARK. GET SET. GO!*"*

*Lizzy was off like a shot through the Wringer. Hand cranked by me with enough force to crush her innards, she squirted down the slide and picked up the first orange flag. Summers did the play-by-play, doing his best not to get goop all over his patented jeans-and-sport-coat combo.*

*"That's one down, seven to go, we've got fifty-five seconds left on the clock!"*

*My dad grabbed the flag from Lizzy, thrusting it down his shirt as was bizarrely customary to do. He sprinted straight to an awaiting tricycle, mounted it and fell off three times before he even got foot to pedal. He bashed and slid and muscled his way down the slippery Icy Trike path toward the flag. Chocolate-syrup-covered blood trickled down his face and elbows. You think reality TV shows today are dangerous?* Double Dare *would eat their children.*

*"That's two! Go go go! Forty-five seconds left!"*

*I was next. The Blue Plate Special. Luckily, I had a strategy. I'd noticed on TV on more than one occasion that the flag was never deep inside the waffle on the plate. Instead, it was always poking out somewhere on the perimeter. Throughout the commercial break I had searched for it, slyly, and spotted it. Cheating? Perhaps. But it got us the flag in under three seconds. I think even Summers was impressed.*

*"Jake's got it! Right there! Pass it off! Pass it off!"*

*My mom grabbed the flag and took off toward Pick It!—a plastic nose the size of a Volvo. Somewhere inside one of the nostrils was the flag. You literally had to nose pick it out. I had specifically volunteered my mom for this obstacle, hoping that if she succeeded, the irony of the victory would keep her from scolding me about my own nose-picking tendencies. It was worth a shot.*

*"Dig! Dig! Dig! Find it, Patty! Aaaannnd . . . She's got it!"*

*Covered in synthetic boogers, my mom tossed the flag to my dad, who immediately separated his shoulder sprinting onto the Human Hamster Wheel. WHAM! Down for the count, right on his side. He dismissed the getting-up part and segued directly into crawling his way to the flag, hamster-style. Pain did not exist in my old man's dojo. Neither did dignity.*

*"Oh, they really want it, folks! Look at that! I have never seen it done that way before! Harvey, are you watching this? Twenty-five seconds left! Five down. Three to go!"*

*The sheer determination in my sister's eyes could have leveled a Minnesota Viking. "Outta my way!" BANG! She punched her three-foot frame through the Baked Alaskan Squisher grabbing the sixth flag and passing it to my mom. "Hustle, Patricia! Hustle!"*

*"Ten seconds! Nine! Eight!"*

*Patty Doyle, all ninety-seven pounds of her, dove head-first into the Gak Vat, pulling down fifty gallons of slime and the seventh orange flag.*

*"Seven seconds . . . ! Six . . . ! Five . . . !"*

*It was up to me now. All that stood between us and a prize package of incomprehensible value was Mount Saint Double Dare. Oh no! Not Mount Saint Double Dare! Surely the most feared obstacle in all of Nickelodeon Studios! Frantically I scrambled up the massive faux Nerf volcano. My goggles fogging, my complimentary Reebok tennis shoes holding on for dear life, I was running blind. Gak and slime of all colors and horrible textures spewed forth from the top. I wasn't going to make it.*

*"Four . . . ! Three . . . !"*

*I could hear my family screaming below, my mother's shrieks of encouragement mixed nicely between my father's obscenities. It was now or never. I pushed off and leapt into the slime abyss.*

*"Two . . . One . . . !"*

*My hand clenched something triangular. Cautiously I*

*rose from the goop. Could it be? The clock had stopped and the crowd had reached an eerie silence. Slowly I lifted my hand . . . Through the green chunks, a distinct orange glow shone through.*

*The flag.*

*"He's got it! He's got it! By God, the Doyles did it!"*

*The crowd went berserk. Lizzy jumped into my dad's bloody arms. My mom planted a wet one on Summers' cheek. I did my best Michael Jordan-just-beating-Cleveland jumping fist pump. We did it! We had won it all!*

*"Harvey, tell them what they've won!"*

*"Sure thing, Marc! They've won the gum-ball machine, the Casio keyboard synthesizer, the Nash skateboards, the Speedo exercise attire and leg warmers, the set of Coleman coolers, the Milton Bradley ultimate board game package, the family set of Scott skis, boots and poles, and the Nintendo Entertainment System! A prize package worth over two thousand three—"*

*At the word "Nintendo," my dad quickly reached over and grabbed Summers' microphone.*

*"Oh, sorry, sorry there, Harvey. No, actually we won't be taking the Nintendo. I know, I know, it's just a family rule we have, everybody. We'll be giving the Nintendo to the blue team."*

*What? Hold it right there. Wait a second. In horror I watched my dad hand over the system to our competitors. They were green eyed and redheaded and all had faces that looked exactly like Timmy Kleen's. They were pointing and laughing at me. This couldn't be happening. What was going on? Everything suddenly went into slow motion and I felt myself begin to tumble down Mount Saint Double Dare.*

*"Jake? Jake? Jake . . . "*

Slowly my eyes opened. I'd been asleep for God knows how long in front of the TV. My sister was standing above me, not very gently poking me with a Pound Puppy.

"You were picking your nose in your sleep. And then you started crying."

"Oh." I said. It was all I could muster.

Even in my dreams Nintendo seemed like a stretch.

# CHAPTER FIVE

It had snowed overnight, the first big storm of the season. Flakes started coming down right around bedtime and hadn't stopped since. Waking up to snow was like waking up to a new lease on life. Like a little present just waiting for you outside your bedroom window; tons and tons of the stuff, as far as the eye could see. You could dive in it, climb around in it, slide down it, hurl it at your sister's face with only evaporating consequences, build forts, pretend you were Han Solo saving Luke Skywalker in Hoth—the sky was the limit. In my Nintendo haste I'd actually kind of forgotten how fun it was when it snowed.

"Are we having a snow day, Mom?" I asked, my face pressed up against the kitchen window.

"Don't count on it, dear."

Of course not. Why should I? I often wondered where we'd even heard the term "snow day." TV, maybe? Did snow days really exist? Or was it some kind of urban myth Wisconsinites invented to make Chicagoans look like idiots? Because in all the time I'd been enrolled in the Batavia

Public School System, I'd never had one. Not one single snow day. It was depressing just thinking about it. Nowadays you can't even turn on your computer without reading about some school that's canceled for the day, the week, the month because of weather. There could have been fifty inches and swine flu and we'd still have had to go to school. The policy list of justifications for school cancellation in 1980s Chicagoland must have read something like this:

1. Threat of Soviet attack
2. Snow Tornado
3. Armageddon

So it was off to school I went. I forged ahead into the wind and mush, blocking a path for my little sister behind me. She trudged forth in her lime-green one-piece snowsuit. I pulled up the collar of my JCPenney bomber jacket, careful not to lick the zipper, a mistake I'd learned the hard way last winter.

"Why don't you have your boots on, Jake?"

She knew exactly why I didn't have my boots on.

"Shut up, Lizzy."

"Ooh. You said a swear."

"'Shut up' isn't a swear, alright?"

"I'm gonna tell Mom."

"You do that."

"And I'm gonna tell her you took off your boots too."

There was a reason why I was the only kid in a fifty-mile radius walking to school in his gym shoes. It was a painful reason. One that troubles me even to this day. I wasn't wearing my boots because . . . my boots were *girls' boots*.

Let that sink in for a second. Girls' boots.

Like much of my wardrobe, the boots had been purchased in a TJ Maxx coupon–induced bout of madness by my mother in which all rationale of style, taste, comfort level or gender was thrown out in favor of conquering her ultimate test of motherhood, the closeout sale.

The boots were red with pretty white trim and pretty white zippers and a pretty white logo on the heel that said ESPRIT. A word that I'd later learn was not only synonymous with female fashion but also French. *French!* They were cute and cuddly and a death sentence at school if anyone ever found out. As such, they were now scrunched in my backpack, where I hoped they would stay until I outgrew them and could hand them down to my little cousin Brian. It would be payback for his blatant disregard for water gun fighting rules over the summer. Earth to Brian: You can't use a garden hose in a water gun fight. I don't care what they say up in Minnesota.

"Come on, Lizzy, hurry up, will ya?"

I stood on the corner, about three blocks from school, and squinted. Through the snow and the minivan-lineup exhaust, I could already make out *The Mound*. It had only snowed one night, but already its size sent chills down my spine.

The Mound was really nothing more than a snow pile, but at its February peak it could grow as high as two stories, practically dwarfing the school itself. It was ominous, looming, scary. Because of the school's circular driveway, the city's plows had to dump all excess snow and subsequent gravel in one giant heap next to the jungle gym. The result was the biggest, most dangerous piece of school property in Kane County. And Monday through Friday it was where every boy, K through five, for reasons unknown, would gather before school to have his skull crushed while playing the exceedingly violent knock-out game, King of the Mountain.

I ditched my bag and saddled up next to Olsen and Mahoney at the bottom of the Mound. They were lying in the snow staring up the face of it, the way infantrymen attacking a bunker might. They looked about as scared too.

"Who's on top?" I asked.

"Who do you think?"

It was a stupid question. In my four-plus years in school I had only known one permanent king of the mountain: Dan Delund.

"Whhhhoooaaaaa! Look out!"

Zilinski came crashing down next to us—Delund's first victim of the season.

"I think he just broke my nose. He's really not kidding around up there this year."

We were never quite certain what grade Dan "King of the Mountain" Delund was actually enrolled in, as the vast majority of his time was spent in such foreign districts as the principal's office and the Ben Franklin cigarette counter. He wore Mötley Crüe T-shirts and steel-toed boots and would often give himself pen tattoos of daggers and snakes—or if he was really feeling creative, daggers stabbing snakes. He stood about five foot five, a hundred and twenty pounds. This made him about a foot taller and fifty pounds heavier than anyone else foolishly attempting to knock him from his pedestal. Delund was basically the Andre the Giant of HC Wilson. And he was twice as mean.

Mahoney tapped my arm. "Look at these idiots."

From our vantage point we could see a platoon of second graders try to rush Delund from behind. He spun around and stiff-armed them two at a time. Laughing hysterically, he tossed a few right back down the hill; others, he tackled and whitewashed before discarding their bodies. The defeat of an entire class took about fifteen seconds.

Olsen peered over my shoulder. "I hear he's already got hair under his pits."

A crying second grader crawled up next to us, sans hat and gloves, which were now resting somewhere on the other side of the Mound. A tactic Delund had undoubtedly dreamt up in the off-season.

"He took my gloves! He took my hat! He threw them in a puddle! Why-eeeee?"

"Get yourself together, man!" shouted Mahoney, grabbing the kid by the shoulders. "Don't let him see the fear! You do that and we're all dead!"

Every group of friends growing up has an Army Guy friend. You know the type. Camouflage bedspread, eats GI Joe cereal, actually watches WWII movies with his dad. Mahoney was our Army Guy friend. He got to see *Platoon* at age seven and had since developed a keen sense for war and injustice. A game of laser tag was not just a game of laser tag to Matt Mahoney. It was an exercise in truth.

Up on the Mound, Delund was now hurling down snowballs and insults.

"You babies! Is that all you got? I *said*, is that all you got?"

Mahoney hawked a loogie in disgust. "Somebody's gotta put a stop to this guy. I can't take another year of this. Doyle, are you with me?"

"Right now?"

"Olsen, how 'bout you? Aren't you getting a little sick of this?"

"Uh, I don't know, Matt . . . I got my nice snow pants on . . ."

"We'll attack him head-on. He'll never expect it from the three of us. Goonies never say die, right?"

"Yeah, but—"

"LET'S GET HIM! RRRRRRAAAAAAAHHH!"

Before Olsen and I knew what had hit us, we were charging up the mountain like some kind of Ken Burns documentary, caught up in a moment of sweeping music and freedom. If I'd had a Union flag, I would have been waving it wildly. Delund's eyes locked with Mahoney's. He pushed up his sweatshirt sleeves, exposing a few bleeding snakes, and took off in a dead sprint toward us. The King was not about to go quietly.

"GRRRRAAAAAGHHHH!"

Flanking Mahoney, Olsen and I were immediately close-lined by Delund's outstretched arms. WHACK. WHACK. Mahoney was able to withstand Delund's initial body check, but it didn't matter. In a split second he was met with a roundhouse kick to the face. The next twenty seconds were blurry, but from what I do remember, there were a lot of dead legs and DDTs, followed by some serious retreating. Mahoney's "plan," while brave, was incredibly stupid. We nursed our wounds at the bottom of the hill.

"Almost, fellas, almost."

Olsen checked his snow pants. "I think he stole my milk money."

The ping of the electronic HC Wilson school bell sounded off in the distance. Delund was once again victorious. He trotted down the hill, smiling and gleeking on us as we all filed into the building to face another day.

Ah . . . third grade.

Standing at the door's entrance, sniffling into Kleenex as usual, was our teacher Mrs. Hugo, affectionately known by all of us as Mrs. Huge-Blow. She was sick and perturbed today, as she had been every other day in her fifteen-year career.

"Walk, don't run, children, walk, don't run . . . I said don't run!"

Josh Farmer came galloping up in his moon boots beside us. "Hey. Did you guys hear what the sixth graders are saying yet?"

Was it something like "stop talking to us, Farmer, you're annoying"?

"No, Farmer," Olsen humored him, "what are they saying?"

"Okay . . . So, I'm down at Fun Times Roller Rink, right, hanging out with the sixth graders as usual, you know, no big deal . . . "

More often than not, around Farmer's second sentence I would try to tune out and think of something else. It was the only way to avoid punching him in the mouth. I caught a glimpse of Miss Ciarocci in the Learning Center as we passed by. She was laughing with Mr. Murphy, the fifth grade teacher and a recent Wisconsin transplant. I did not like the way this looked. She was touching the arm of his stupid Green Bay Packer's jacket . . . Screw you, Mr. Murphy. Let's see you make a Christmas tree ornament project of an entire manger scene. (That was my new plan, by they way—manger scene ornament—with donkeys and wise men and all that junk). Ciarocci gave a glance in my direction and flashed a smile. In my head I gave her a cool nod back, but in reality I'm pretty sure I just stared at her with my mouth open.

"Jake. Jake!" Olsen was elbowing me. "Are you listening to this?"

"What?" I asked.

"Farmer says the top Cub Scout wreath seller this year gets a Nintendo."

I stopped dead in my tracks. A Nintendo? From the Cub Scouts? Was that even possible? Every year in Cub Scouts we would have to sell Christmas wreaths. It was a fundraiser for the organization and basically meant giving up a quality Sunday afternoon in front of the TV to traipse around the neighborhood with my dad, trying to get old ladies to place orders. Last year I'd sold a grand total of five, three of them going to my grandparents. I was a horrible salesman. I always chalked it up to a lack of motivation, though. Usually the sales prizes were things like Webelo belt buckles or plastic canteens—basically, junk. But if the top prize was a Nintendo, then this was a whole new ballgame. But this was Farmer we were listening to here, not exactly a reliable source for information.

"Bull crud," I said.

"Bull true," lisped Farmer. "A Nintendo, with games and everything."

"Bull. Crud."

"Bull totally true."

"Totally true like how your dad has a Babe Ruth rookie card?"

"Or totally true like how Murdoch from the A-Team is your uncle?"

"You guys don't have to believe me. I'm gonna win it anyway. I already sold sixty-seven wreaths already."

"To who?"

"People . . . your mom."

"You're full of it, Farmer."

"Says who?"

"Says me."

"Yeah?"

"Yeah."

"Yeah?"

Suddenly a hand shoved a snowball directly in Farmer's mouth.

"*Yeah,*" said Dan Delund, laughing hysterically. We all joined in.

Delund spun around. "Only I laugh."

We all shut up.

# CHAPTER SIX

The humidifier in the corner bubbled and hissed as Mrs. Hugo paced around the classroom, occasionally pulling used Kleenex from her sleeves to blow her nose.

We were all spread out on the hard orange carpet, partaking in another one of her "educational exercises" designed to get us to shut the hell up. We were a terrible class.

Looking back, it wasn't really Huge-Blow's fault. Our class that year would've done any teacher in. We were loud and unruly, a gang of germ-infested, sugar-fueled heathens. And during the Christmas season? Forget it. The class was a time bomb just waiting to go off. It didn't matter that she had us all lying on the carpet listening to a New Age "relaxing" record. Silence and order weren't in the cards for us.

The Relax Records, as they came to be known, seemed like something Ciarocci would've had sitting around her apartment. They were very hippie-esque. You could picture Ciarocci going home, lighting some candles (and whatnot) and making a night of it. Maybe she'd recommended them to Huge-Blow as a way to calm us down. But in an actual classroom setting, with a bunch of nine-year-olds, Huge-Blow was by no means capable of pulling it off.

"We're relaxing, children. Our minds need to be relaxed to think. Now everyone close your eyes"—*nose blow, nose blow*—"and listen to the lady on the"—*sniffle*—"record."

Unfortunately, the lady on the record sounded like a cross between Cyndi Lauper and Eeyore. She wasn't relaxing; she was hilarious.

*"Oooooh kaaaay, nowwwww. Feeeeeeel the waaaaaater. Feeeeeeel it wash away your emmmmmotions."*

Ha! Yes, female hippie Eeyore. Feel it, feel it.

*"The sunnnnnn shines as you drifffffft offfffff down the peaceful blue streeeeeeeeam . . . "*

Down on the carpet things were far from peaceful. Nintendo prize rumors had been circulating like *Mario Bros.* fireballs all morning. With each hour that passed, however unlikely the stories, it became more and more believable that the Cub Scouts might actually be offering an NES to the top seller. Tommy Grusecki whispered the latest.

"Ryan heard first prize comes with a Power Pad. Pass it on."

I rolled over to Zilinski. "First prize comes with a Power Pad. Pass it on."

Huge-Blow hovered above us. "This is quiet time, children. We're relaxing now."

Zilinski rolled over to Olsen. "First prize comes with the Power Pad."

"The Power Pad!"

"RELAX!" yelled Huge-Blow.

*"Together we all breathe in. Then breathe out. We breathe the good in and breathe the bad out. Breeeeeeathe in and breeeeeathe out, breeeeeeeeeathe in, breeeeeeeathe out—"*

BURRRRFFFFTTT. Delund ripped a hard one. Wet and smelly.

"Dan Delund!"

"My butt's gotta breathe too, Mrs. Hugo!"

The class erupted. Delund yelled a late "Door knob!" which under bully rules meant he could now hit whomever he pleased, even if it had in fact been his own fart. You had to hand it to him. He got a few jabs in before Huge-Blow pulled him off and sat him in the "time out chair." Relaxing time was officially over. She strode up to the board and put another check after Delund's name.

"Back in your seats!"

Falling far short of his career average of six checks before lunch, it could only be assumed that Nintendo gossip had sidetracked even Delund.

Lunchtime at HC Wilson was not so much a time to eat as it was a time to do business. Apples for fruit cups, Kudos for Lunchables, PB&J for pop—there was no trade too big, no barter too small. For half an hour a day, every kid in the cafeteria became a hustler. It was cutthroat. If Mike Tuetken accidentally got two Twinkies in his lunch, you better have a line on it and you better show up to his table with fruit snacks or higher, or you weren't getting any. No slouch myself, I'm not ashamed to say that I once lifted a jumbo pack of Extra Winterfresh from Kleen's gum drawer and, stick by stick, managed to get him to trade me his Fruit Roll-Ups everyday for a month. One hundred percent markup. Score, Doyle.

There were two fundamental types of lunch people. You had the "hot lunchers" and the "sack lunchers." Very rarely did you ever have a kid who mixed and matched. You were one or the other. They were like religions, passed down through generations, like Protestant or Catholic. It was in your blood. *You're a sack luncher, son. I don't care how great your friends at school say Taco Day is. Your grandfather didn't sell the family pig and come to this country with negative three cents to see his family turn into a bunch of limp-wristed hot lunchers!*

There were pros and cons to each religion, of course. Sack lunchers had to bow down to the parental gods, who were ill tempered and forgetful and, more often than not, cheap. For years I suffered under the delusion that Cheez Whiz sandwiches were delicious. Cheez Whiz sandwiches, for crying out loud! In what world is a Cheez Whiz sandwich an acceptable meal? Sure, cafeteria food could get a bad rap for being smelly and gross, but at least you knew it had to pass some kind of government nutritional standard. With a sack lunch you were on your own, left to the whims of mom and pop. Sometimes there would be no Butter-Nut bar at the bottom of the sack. Sometimes there would just be a crummy old pear. Sometimes you would end up with your sister's celery sticks. Then what? All you could do was offer them up to the dumpster spirits and hope for grace tomorrow.

Then there was the sack itself. That was reason enough to warrant a hot lunch conversion right there. Sacks were undependable, unpredictable. Condensation, rips, tears, rain, snow, wresting matches—you had to be careful. Five-second rules were hard to apply when your graham crackers were floating in a puddle. You also couldn't trust yourself with a sack lunch. What if you got hungry early? Say, on a bus field trip or on the long walk to school? A little bite of that salami sandwich could get you through it. But one little bite could turn into ten little bites plus a bag of Cheetos, and if you weren't careful you could end up with no lunch *at all* come lunchtime. There was no trading out of that situation.

Sack lunchers had their perks, though. Leftover birthday cake could wind up in a sack lunch. So could last night's Salano's pizza or Aunt Cubby's cookies. But hot lunch had its advantages as well. For starters, it was hot. In the dead of a Chicago February that didn't go unnoticed. Secondly, it wasn't going to get left on the bus or in the fridge at home. It was guaranteed. Third, you didn't have to think about it. No preparation required whatsoever, just get the ticket punched, get the tray, get the spork and dig in. And finally, every Friday at HC Wilson was Spaghetti Friday—with garlic bread. And that garlic bread smelled pretty friggin' good. I'll admit it, I thought about converting to hot lunch several times. In first grade I even took a little nip of Missy Pearson's mashed potatoes on a bet, but ultimately I decided they weren't for me. Despite the occasional Cheez Whiz sandwich, I was a sack-lunch man. It was hereditary.

When we weren't making deals or actually eating, lunchtime conversation usually flowed in question form. Deep, philosophical exchanges that touched on all the current third grade worldviews:

> *Q: Will the Bears win another Super Bowl this year?*
> A: Yes. Without a doubt. It's pointless to even question it.

Q: *Could Duran Duran beat up Wham!?*
A: Huey Lewis could take them both.

Q: *Who's cooler, the California Raisins or the Domino's Noid?*
A: Are you a idiot? The California Raisins. Where are you getting these questions?

Q: *Are you in love with Kleen's sister?*
A: I don't want to talk about it.

Q: *Sox or Cubs?*
A: Cubs. Carlton Fisk is a fatso. Ryne Sandburg is awesome.

Q: *Karate Kid the movie or Karate Kid the cartoon?*
A: Cartoon. There's way more fighting in the cartoon.

Q: *Cosby Show or Family Ties?*
A: Hmm, good one. Gotta go Cosbys.

Q: *Transformers or Gobots?*
A: Gobots.

Q: *Why Gobots?*
A: They're hardcore.

Q: *Optimus Prime is hardcore.*
A: Optimus Prime should be in Wham!, that's how unhardcore he is.

Q: *Okay, Voltron or Gobots?*
A: Gobots.

*Q: Seriously, what's with you and Gobots?*
A: You're not even asking me questions anymore.

*Q: Yes, I am.*
A: No, you're not.

*Q: Yes, I am.*
A: No, you're not.

*Q: Fine. Hi-C or Capri Sun?*
A: Ecto-Coolers do not exist within the Capri Sun family, therefore, Hi-C. In fact I will make that trade with you right now, Evan Olsen. Thank you very much.

Of course, as anyone can tell you, the best part of lunch was recess. What better way to spend the twenty minutes immediately following mass intake of Doritos and pop than running around at full speed in subzero temperatures? Hooray, recess!

We all scrambled to our cubbies in the hall and began putting on the necessary layers. Mysterious lunch ladies bustled around us, zipping up kindergarteners' coats and jamming mittens on fingers. Time was of the essence. If you didn't get outside quick enough, you ran the risk of missing the draft selection for the daily blacktop football game. That was bad. That meant you had to sit in a snowbank and watch, or worse, hang out with girls.

"Jake Doyle."

I turned to find Mrs. Huge-Blow lurking over me. Man, did she ever take a break?

"Is there something you want to tell me, Jake?"

I find it hard to believe that you're employed as a

third grade teacher when you seem to inherently despise children?

"Uh, no . . . "

"You've been disobeying school rules, Jake. Don't think I'm not watching you."

"Uh . . . "

She pointed down at my shoes with a used Kleenex.

"If you go out in the snow once more without wearing boots, your name goes up on the board, with a check. Snow rules. No boots, no recess."

"Boots?"

"Boots. You have boots, right?"

Oh, man . . .

# CHAPTER SEVEN

In 1983, Boy George released a song called "Do You Really Want to Hurt Me?" A catchy little cross-dressing reggae tune, it has since become the soundtrack to my girls' boots nightmare. Whenever it comes on the radio or VH1 plays the video on some celebrities-turned-junkies countdown, I find myself weeping softly. Some guys wince at the memory of dropping a ball in a big high school game, others spend years regretting "the one who got away." Me, hardly a month goes by that I don't wake up at night in a cold sweat to Boy George ringing in my ears and little red Esprits flashing in the darkness.

So it was, that fateful Monday afternoon in December when I finally had to venture out in my girls' boots and face the music.

I did so by standing behind a tree.

Out on the blacktop I could see the teams already being picked for football. As always, Zilinski and Delund were captains. Traditional draft etiquette was usually lost on Delund. He skipped such formalities as taking turns and pretty much just took whomever he wanted. Even if that meant the teams were stacked thirty-seven guys versus Zilinski and four second graders.

"I pick first, I got Padula."

Zilinski tried to counter. "Okay, um, I got—"

"And Schafer and Schmidt. Kramer, Mueller, Nelson, I got you too."

"Hey, no fair, you gotta—"

"The Hussa brothers, Mahoney, Pendrock, DeGemis."

"You can't do it like that, Delund, I have to—"

"Wattendorf, Merlini, Olsen aaand . . . Gubbins."

Ryan Gubbins, a portly fourth grader, trotted over, surprised at his selection.

"I got your gloves, fatso," said Delund, promptly relieving him of his prized Bears receiver's gloves. "You got the rest, Zilinski. You kick."

I watched Zilinski and his team of rejects trot back toward the near end of the blacktop. I could tell he was looking for me. In blacktop football, two complete passes, no matter how short, were enough to warrant a first down. Since it was rare that anyone would ever cover me, I was usually open, and that was the only way Zilinski ever kept the score close: short dump-off passes to Doyle. Team Loser needed me.

"Jake!" Zilinski spotted me behind the tree. "What are you doing over there? We kick off."

Casually, I tried to shoo him away. "I'm, uh, taking a leak. Play without me!"

"Is there a dead squirrel back there again?"

"Uh, yeah. I'm peeing on a dead squirrel. I'll be there in a minute!"

It was no use. Zilinski hustled over with the ball.

"You're peeing on a dead squirrel? What kind of a sick—" He stopped dead in his tracks and looked down. An expression usually reserved for horror movies or broken windows slowly washed over his face.

"Holy . . . shit . . . "

"I know."

"Dude, you're wearing Katie Sorrentino's boots."

"They're mine," I stammered.

"Holy . . . sh . . . "

"I know, alright."

"What are you gonna do?"

"I don't know."

"If Delund sees you he's going to kill you."

"Do you think I don't know that?"

Answering too many math questions correctly, having insufficient cough drops for the taking, these were all grounds for physical retaliation. But girls' boots? Delund had once thrown Ronnie Dobber in a dumpster because there was a rumor going around that his favorite GI Joe was Lady Jaye.

"Hey!" Delund yelled. He was running through the snow toward us. "You're kicking off, Zilinski, let's go."

"I'm coming."

"Is there a dead squirrel back there again? I got dibs on it if its guts are all out and bloody and—"

Delund took one look at my boots and slowed to a halt. Like a hunter coming up on a shotgun-wielding deer in the middle of a clearing, his mind was blown. Completely. He stood there for a moment, not quite sure what to do. Bewilderment and anger had rendered him helpless, as if his bully instincts weren't fully capable of handling such a grave situation.

"What the . . . Boyle? Are those . . . ?"

"Uh, listen, Dan . . . "

I might as well have been inviting him to a My Little Pony sleepover. My mind flipped through the Rolodex of punishment I was sure to endure. Weeks of wedgies, whitewashings, dead legs, dead arms, dead torsos, DDTs, possible Indian burnings, swirlies . . . I took out my retainer in preparation. Zilinski, God bless him, tried to create a distraction.

"Hey, Delund, let's go play some football, huh? We kick."

Delund just stiff-armed him to the ground. "I think we got ourselves a pair of girls' boots here."

"Wait, wait, there's this high schooler, okay," I tried pathetically. "He bet me a hundred bucks I wouldn't wear these boots to school. It's a joke, alright, I—"

"Not buying it, Boyle. You're about to pay up. Big time."

Quickly I went over my options. Running away always looked appealing, but I knew better. That just meant further punishment. Fighting back was just plain stupid. No, the best plan of attack was to take a beating now and be done with it. I closed my eyes and hoped for the best. I could feel Delund's beef-jerky breath on my face as he grabbed me by the coat and lifted me up in the air. But somewhere off in the distance I heard a high-pitched lisp. It was the voice of an angel . . .

"HEY GUYS! HEY, YOU GUYS! CHECK IT OUT!"

Midair, I opened my eyes to see an out-of-breath Farmer sprinting toward us, waving around a green piece of paper like it was the cure for chicken pox.

"I GOT IT! I got it right here. Proof! Proof it's NINTENDO!"

At the word "Nintendo," Delund chucked me into a bush.

"What do you mean, you got proof? Proof of what?"

"Proof that the Cub Scout first prize is a Nintendo. It says so right here, right in the Cub Scout take-home note for today. Look!"

Farmer handed the note to Delund. Delund flipped it over a few times.

"Just a picture of a dumb wreath, so what?"

"You gotta *read* it."

A crowd had now gathered around. I watched quietly from the shrubbery, trying to bury my feet in the snow. This was bigger news than girls' boots any day.

Farmer read from the note. "This year's first prize comes courtesy of Geitner Toys and Books. A perfect addition to any living room. The new Nintendo Entertainment System!"

Delund grabbed the note again and strung the words together. It was there alright, in dotted black computer ink. "The new . . . Nintendo Enter-tain-ment Sys-tem."

By God, little Farmer had struck gold.

A collective cheer went up among us—hugs and high fives all around. Delund went as far as patting Farmer on the back before laughing directly in Kleen's face and shoving him into a tree. And for a brief moment, my girls' boots became a neglected sideshow. It was all I needed. Quietly, and without detection, I scurried off to hide behind the dumpster. No one else had noticed the boots. I was in the clear.

Ecstatic on several levels, I sat there in the stink and the mush and began to contemplate the biggest wreath-selling campaign to ever hit Batavia.

## CHAPTER EIGHT

The problem with having only one Nintendo prize in an already hostile one-Nintendo town is that it makes enemies out of everybody. There was no more "us versus Kleen" mentality. It was now every man for himself. Big or small, smart or dumb, first grade or fourth, it didn't matter anymore. You sold the most wreaths, you won a life of bliss and happiness; it was as simple as that. Plans were already being hatched in notebook margins, and battle lines were being drawn in the snow.

Immediately following the Cub Scout take-home note revelation, Tommy Grusecki faked an earache and was sent home for the rest of the school day, where he was now, no doubt, out on the streets going door to door selling wreaths. It was a gutsy move for a three-hour head start, and I already hated him for it. By 1 p.m., wreath-selling exit strategies were running rampant. Matt Mahoney got caught trying to sneak out of PE, and half the fifth grade gifted program staged an unsuccessful classroom walkout designed as a nuclear-arms protest. The gauntlet had been laid down. If even the smart kids were willing to risk disciplinary action for Nintendo, I had to get my act together.

So I came up with a plan. It was simple but daring just the same. Sometime in the middle of our afternoon quiz on the magic of petrified wood, it started to come to me. I wouldn't sneak out, per se—that had already been proven nearly impossible. At the end of the day I would simply leave faster than everyone else. I only lived about a half mile from school. It was the kid/bully/teacher/bus/minivan traffic jam that always delayed my departure. There were times it took me a good ten minutes just to get outside the building after the final bell. If I could circumvent said traffic jam, then I could be home and selling wreaths almost a full half hour before most other Cub Scouts even got their sales sheets out.

Basically, my plan was this: don't go to my locker, head straight for the fire escape, beat the rush, exit the school and sprint like crazy home. It was a good plan. Straightforward. Clean. The only problem was, it meant I wouldn't have access to such take-home necessities as, you know . . . a coat. No gloves, hat or scarf either. That posed a bit of a problem.

Now, I'd heard of frostbite. I'd seen *Empire Strikes Back*, I knew the dangers of Hoth, but that was the movies. And frankly, Luke Skywalker could be kind of a pussy. I was not a pussy. I was Jake Doyle—Man of Action. I was certainly not afraid of a little frostbite. To me, the term sounded like some kind of Dairy Queen concoction served in miniature batting helmets. *This summer, the Frostbite! With real Snickers! That's coooool!* So what was the worst that could happen? Lose a toe? What's one toe?

Even losing a couple fingers was worth it if it meant getting Nintendo. I could be cold when I was dead.

These were the thoughts racing through my head as I turned in my petrified-wood quiz. Not my best effort. It would later earn me a 26% and a phone call home. Apparently it's not spelled "petra-fried." Huge-Blow was a stickler for spelling. The cold witch.

I sat there in my chair and inconspicuously popped the collar of my imitation Ocean Pacific polo shirt, doing my best to convince myself that this was not a fashion statement but rather a practical maneuver ensuring warmth on the way home. I gave Angela Moran my best Don Johnson look and smiled. I'd always wanted to wear the collar up in school but never had the guts. See? Nintendo was bringing out the best in me already. I watched the clock tick down to two thirty and laced up my Walter Payton KangaRoos . . .

PING. PING—

I leapt out of my seat and bolted out the classroom fire door before the third bell had even registered. Huge-Blow may have noticed, but I was out of disciplinary range before she could say anything. I rounded an icy corner and took off like a shot, my heart pounding at near audible decibels. "Danger Zone" was pumping through my imaginary headphones. I was in the zone. I skidded out toward the sidewalk and kicked it into overdrive.

You know what? This wasn't bad at all. Heck, I wasn't even cold. Not even a little bit. Ha! I raced through the school grounds and dodged a few oncoming station wagons. The crossing guard didn't even have time to look up. I was doing it!

The first block was a blur of houses and mailboxes. I crossed onto the second block and smiled to myself, taking what might have been my first real breath since I'd come outside. I turned the corner onto Jackson Street and—oh my God, this was *terrible*. What the hell was I thinking? My body suddenly began to scream at me. "It's nine degrees out, you fool!" All of a sudden I couldn't feel my legs. My chest was on fire. A wave of panic washed over me. I began panting, wheezing, slowing to a crawl. "Don't stop now, stupid! Keep going!" My hands were turning white. I tucked my thumbs under my forefingers, clenching my fists. The irony of winning a Nintendo now and not having the thumbs to play it was beginning to sink in. Panicking, I looked around. Was I past the halfway point? I was. It was too late to go back. My adrenaline was fading fast. Reality was smacking me in the face. Would I die out here? Could that happen? Maybe Skywalker wasn't such a pussy after all.

Quickly, I hopped over a snowbank and went for the middle of the road. That way, I thought, if I passed out, or died or whatever, while running, then at least a car could come by and see me and take me to a hospital. A part of me thought, well, if I did almost die trying to get a Nintendo, maybe my parents, or some good Samaritan, would actually buy me one for Christmas. "Christ, the kid almost died for this thing, give him the Nintendo, for crying out loud." Yeah, that was it. The thought of a tragic near-death experience perked me up a bit. I dug down deeper and found my footing. Pain did not exist in this dojo.

Nine minutes and thirty-seven seconds after the final bell, I burst into my house, a frozen, crazed wreath salesmen.

"How was school, honey?" my mom asked from the kitchen.

"Blaaaah! Rhaaaah!"

This was no time for pleasantries. I pushed past her and ran directly upstairs, no doubt tracking snow and madness all over the carpet.

Sitting at the kitchen table, Lizzy took note. "He didn't have his coat on. Did you notice that?"

"I did, Lizzy, yes. I'll talk to him."

"If he catches pneumonia, can we get a chameleon?"

"No, Lizzy, we're not getting a chameleon. Drink your hot chocolate."

"Do you know what we learned in school today, Mommy?"

"What's that?"

"We learned about Brazil."

"Really?"

"Yes, it's in South America. They speak Portuguese there. Most people don't know that, but I do. Portuguese comes from Portugal." Lizzy helped herself to a cookie, nibbling thoughtfully as she went in for the kill. "Do you think they have *Cabbage Patch* dolls in Portugal?"

Ah, yes indeed, there were other Christmas plots hatching in the Doyle house.

"Well, Lizzy, I don't really—"

WHOOSH. I came flying back down through the kitchen, buttoning up my Cub Scout uniform and pulling up my long johns. A peculiar itchy feeling was slowly returning to my hands and feet. And the "petra-fried" snot around my nose was beginning to thaw. Looking back, I probably did get frostbite. But screw it. It was worth it.

"Where's the clipboard? The clipboard!" I screamed.

"It's in the junk drawer. Where are you—?"

I was already out the door. Lizzy took another sip of her hot cocoa, unaffected. "They probably don't have

Cabbage Patch dolls in Portugal. Those poor, poor children of Portugal . . . "

It had been only fifteen minutes since school let out and I was already fitted in my dress blues and on my way, secretly envisioning the acres of Alaskan pine forests needed to cover the number of wreaths I was about to sell. I pulled down my Cub Scout stocking cap and threw on my backup gloves. There were no other scouts in sight. The neighborhood was mine. I rushed up the steps of the broken-down yellow house on the corner, poised to make my first sale. I knocked confidently and waited.

Oh, I had the sales pitch all planned out. It was brilliant. I practiced it quietly in my head. "Well, the Cub Scouts have been around for hundreds of years, ma'am. Striving for truth and justice and the overall goodness of America as we know it! Without your help, thousands of boys may become drug addicts and communists before the year 1997. All we need from you is a bit of generosity that can be displayed throughout the holiday season in the form of a marvelous Merry Christmas wreath!"

The door opened, revealing a man who might best be described as dangerous. He wore a wifebeater and a scowl that suggested, to me at least, that he was once in a motorcycle gang. This was not good.

"Whaddya want?"

I stood there, blubbering. "Uh, um, uh . . . "

"Look, kid, they got Ditka on WGN right now tellin' ethnic jokes, what is it?"

"Uh, communists, 1997 . . . "

"*What?*"

Come on, pull it together. "Uh, sir, I . . . "

"Wait a second. You're not trying to sell me something, are ya? Are ya!?"

"Uh, bluhhh . . . "

"Can't you read?" His index finger shot over to a white sign on the door three inches from my face. In big block letters, it read: NO SOLICITORS.

*Solicitors?* Oh no, see, I'm with the Cub Scouts, sir, completely different type of situation here. "But . . . uh, wreaths. You wanna buy a wreath?"

The man looked at me as though I'd just told him Mike Ditka shaved his legs. In disbelief he placed the palm of his hand on the top of my head. Slowly he tilted it upward. Hanging there on his door, a few inches from the NO SOLICITORS sign, was, in fact, a Christmas wreath. I was selling a guy who didn't want to be sold anything something he already had.

"Jeeez-us kid." He shook his head. "You must be retarded."

I stood there with my mouth open slightly and tried to smile.

"Wait a second. You're not really retarded, are you?"

I shook my head no.

"Good." He slammed the door shut, pine needles grazing my nose. This was going to be harder than I thought.

By now, ninety percent of the male population of HC Wilson Elementary was hitting the pavement, hawking wreaths door to door. It was a little astounding when you thought about it. I mean, not even ninety percent of us went door to door trick-or-treating. Nintendo had become the grade school equivalent of the hottest, most popular girl in high school. And this wreath-selling contest was comparable to her winking at each and every one of us in the hallway. It had hypnotized us, infatuated us, given us all false hope. It didn't matter that only one of us could have her. We were all convinced that she would be ours. Nintendo had us in her clutches and we'd do anything to get her.

A whole new level of single-minded madness had taken over. Christmas lists to grandmothers weren't even lists anymore, they'd become declarations—one word on a sheet of notebook paper: *Nintendo*. No backups, no stocking stuffers, no subcategories filled with requests for "Super Bowl Shuffle" cassettes or He-Man accessories. It was Nintendo or nothing. Teddy Ruxpin, pack your bags, my friend, your fifteen minutes were over.

Determined, I walked down Watson Street to Miss Sherman's house. In Chicago Bears terms, if I was quarterback Jim McMahon (which, when wearing my Adidas headband, I often thought I was), Miss Sherman would be my Willie Gault. She was my go-to receiver, an automatic catch, an instant gain of eight yards. Miss Sherman would buy a box of rocks from me as long as I spent a little time with her. She was approximately a hundred and fifty years old, and next to my grandparents, she'd been my only sale the year before. It had taken me an hour and a half inside her cat-infested living room, but she'd bought two wreaths and an order of garland. Certainly, Miss Sherman would start things out right this year.

Optimistically, I rang the doorbell.

"Who is it?" Miss Sherman yelled over the stampede of seven thousand cats.

"It's Jake Doyle from across the street."

"Whooooo?"

"Miss Sherman, it's—"

"Miss Sherman? *I'm* Miss Sherman."

"Yes, I know, Miss Sherman, it's—"

"Who is it?"

"It's Jake—"

"Whoooooo?"

"JAKE DOYLE. FROM ACROSS THE STREET."

"Oh, Jake! Come on in!"

She opened the door. Nine cats jumped on my face. I went inside.

Walking into Miss Sherman's house was a little bit like walking into church. It always smelled like something was burning and you knew you weren't leaving for at least an hour. The place was hairy and unkempt, much like Miss Sherman herself. She stood about four foot eight, a hundred pounds, and as always, was dressed in a bathrobe and slippers. She was a hugger too.

"Oh, it's soooooo good-ta see ya, Jake! What kinda things are they teaching you in school these days?"

"Oh, I don't know, stuff."

"How's your little sister, Lizzy?"

"Okay, I guess."

"You guess? You tell her she needs to come see me. I haven't seen her in ages. She's so cute. And smart as a whip, that one."

"I'll be sure to tell her, Miss Sherman. So, I've got some wreaths to—"

"Would ya like a nice glass of milk?"

"Um . . . "

"And some nice ham sandwiches? You sit down right here and I'll come back with some nice ham sandwiches and some milk and you can tell me all about school."

Sweet.

I swatted away a few cats and settled on the couch. It was at least ninety degrees in there. I was already beginning to sweat through my merit badges. She called back from inside the kitchen.

"I'm gonna warm the milk up for ya! Nice and hot to warm you up!"

"Super."

I glanced around the room. It was WWII-era ancient, the kind of room that looked like it came straight out of *It's a Wonderful Life*, except without any of that Donna Reed cleanliness. Doilies were everywhere, little glass vases, knickknacks, crafts, plates of various American prairie landscapes hung up on the walls. A mound of *Life* magazines rested in the corner, serving both as feline jungle gym and permanent fire hazard. And then there was the kicker—no TV. How could someone live like this? Maybe it was the light fading outside or the shadows in the house, but when you were in there it seriously felt like you'd entered real-life black and white, like you were Dorothy still in Kansas. Or better yet, a POW in *Stalag 17*. There was no escape from Miss Sherman's domicile.

I glanced out the window. Far down the street I could see a few tiny dots of blue on the horizon trudging along the sidewalk. Cub Scouts were already treading onto my turf.

"I'm gonna heat up the sandwiches too, make 'em nice and warm! I just gotta find that grill cheese maker my son sent me. Would you like to see pictures of my son? He lives in Hollywood. He works in the movies."

This was gonna be tricky.

Earlier in the afternoon, I'd run the wreath-selling numbers in the back of my Trapper Keeper. It was a good place to do math, what with the complimentary metric-system conversion table and all. Basically, I figured I'd have to sell at least fifty wreaths to be in the running for first prize. That was just over five wreaths a day, a tall order, especially if I was stuck here in cat land for too much longer. I needed to close this deal and get back out there and sell as quickly as possible.

"Here you go. Some nice sandwiches and some milk."

"Thanks, Miss Sherman."

I took two big bites and a big warm gulp; it was best to get it down fast. Not only did you taste less, but it also looked like you were enjoying it—skills I'd learned from my mother's experimental cooking. In twenty seconds I'd already burned three-fourths of my mouth and polished off half a sandwich.

"My goodness, don't they feed you at home?"

"It's just so good, Miss Sherman. Mmmmmm."

"So, tell me all about school, why-don't-ya?"

"School's fine."

"What are you learning? Tell me all about it."

"Oh, nothing really."

"Nothing? Its gotta be something. Come on, tell me. Come on . . . "

Oh God, seriously? There wasn't much worse than being asked what you were learning in school. It was like getting out of Chino for the night and being asked how it was inside. It sucked, all right. School sucked. We learned about stuff, we ate lunch, we had recess, we learned about more stuff, we went home. Why did adults want us to talk about it so badly? I was a free man right now. I was out of school; why would I want to talk about it? It was bad enough I had to memorize the intricacies of the Dewey Decimal System without having to turn it into interesting conversation.

"I'm not letting you leave until you tell me all about it, Jake."

Sherman wasn't messing around. Casually, I fed a cat a bit of a sandwich under the coffee table, stalling for time. I had to give her something, something educational, something that was engaging enough to satisfy her but also bland enough not to spark a two-hour lecture on the Great Depression or photos of her son. Quickly my mind shifted into salesman mode.

"Actually, we're learning about pine trees right now . . . "

Yes sir, this was going to work.

"Really."

"Yes, it's fascinating stuff. Did you know that the state of Alaska has over a million acres of pine trees alone?"

"I didn't know that."

Probably because I just made it up.

"That's right. Pine trees have a very unique, uh, way to do photo-syn, uh, photo . . . *photosynthesis*, that's it. Did you know that? Photosynthesis? That's why they make such great Christmas trees."

"You're right, they do make good Christmas trees. You know, I need to start putting up my Christmas decorations myself."

"Funny you should mention that, Miss Sherman . . . "

It took another hour inside, but when I came out I'd managed to sell the woman more wreaths than she had doors on her house. God bless you, Miss Sherman. The only problem was, it was now getting dark outside. I only had half an hour before I had to be home for supper. I looked down the street and saw Josh Farmer making his way toward me. The little twerp was even wearing a tie. It matched the smug look on his fat face.

"Heard you ran home without a coat, Doyle."

"What's it to ya?" I snapped.

"Just seems a little desperate, is all."

"You seem a little des . . . perate."

"You don't even know what 'desperate' means."

"No, *you* don't know what it means."

"No, you don't."

"No, *you* don't."

"You don't times a million."

"You don't times a million, times ten. Period. No erasing."

That shut him up.

Farmer gave a nod toward Sherman's house, clicking the multicolor pen in his mittened hand. "Going the old-lady route, eh? Gotta have a good exit strategy to pull that off. Me, I steer clear of old ladies. Too much hassle, not enough profitability."

Who was this guy? Gordon Gekko?

"Whatever, Farmer. You shouldn't be on my block anyway."

"And why's that?"

"Because it's my block. That's the rule."

"You think there are rules here, Doyle? There are no rules. The only rules are gonna be the ones that say you gotta take your shoes off when you come into my mom's house to play my Nintendo."

This was getting ugly now. Did Jake Doyle have to hit a Cub Scout?

"We'll see."

"You bet we will."

We stared each other down for a moment, neither of us flinching. He clicked his pen. I pulled my No. 2 pencil from behind my ear. Somewhere off in the distance a

Metra train piped out an eerie whistle. A plastic Jewel bag turned tumbleweed blew across the sidewalk between us. It was a suburban showdown.

"That Nintendo's mine," I hissed. "You'll never win it."

"Watch me."

With that, Farmer turned and ran up the steps of the house next door to Mrs. Sherman's: the O'Brien house. I'd tried there last year and came up with nothing. He'd never sell them a wreath. They went to Florida every year for Christmas. Sometimes they didn't even bother putting up a tree. Even when they did it was the plastic kind. The house was a total dead end.

"Good luck with that one, dipstick!"

Farmer rang the bell. Mrs. O'Brien answered.

"Yes?"

"Hello, ma'am, my name's Josh. That's a lovely blouse you're wearing."

"Thank you, young man. What can I do for you?"

"Well, ma'am, I just have one question to ask you. Do you love your country?"

Son of a bitch. Farmer was good. Mrs. O'Brien smiled and led him inside. It was obvious I couldn't waste any more time watching this go down. I hustled down the block and got to work. I had less than thirty minutes to get as many houses as I could before Farmer stole them right out from under me.

"Hey, uh, Brett," I said to the five-year-old who answered the door. "Is your mom home?"

"She's at work still. Tiffany the babysitter's here."

"Who is it?" yelled an annoyed Tiffany from somewhere inside.

"It's Jake Doyle from down the street." I leaned down. "Listen, Brett. Here's the deal. How'd you like to play my Nintendo?"

"You got a Nintendo?"

"Not yet. But I'm gonna put you down for two wreaths here. All you have to do is tell your mom that Tiffany said it was okay."

"But Tiffany won't say it's okay."

"Do you like Tiffany?"

"No. She's mean."

"Exactly, Brett, exactly. She'll get fired. You'll get two wreaths to help me win the Nintendo, and I'll let you be the only kindergartener who gets to come over and play it. Deal?"

"Yeah!"

"Good work. See ya next week."

I got through a few more houses in the next twenty minutes. I made a sale to the Garzas and got a promise from Mr. Thompson if I came back later when his wife got home with the checkbook. I had sold close to a dozen wreaths in one afternoon. I was feeling pretty good about myself. The sensation had even returned to my thumbs.

I rounded the corner on Watson and saw my dad's minivan pull into the driveway. I'd even made it home in time for supper. *Take that,* Josh Farmer. But as I trudged up the stairs to my front door, I heard a familiar lisp making an exit.

" . . . and God bless the United States of America. You have yourself a wonderful evening and a Merry Christmas, Mrs. Doyle."

Farmer tiptoed down the stairs and patted me on the

shoulder as he went by. He'd just sold two wreaths to my own mother.

"Suck on that one, Jake."

# CHAPTER NINE

When you really break it down, the entire focus of kid life centers on one specific goal: having fun. All drive and brainpower is dedicated toward the purpose of playing. It's a relentless battle waged against grownups of all shapes and sizes, one that consistently begs the question: How can I, the kid, maximize my ability to play? How can I stretch the parental five-minute warning at Show Biz Pizza into ten minutes? How can I put the least amount of time acceptable into responsibilities so I can play? I just want to play. Can I go play now? Can we go upstairs and play? Can Evan come over and play? Can I go out back and play? Can I play hockey in the street? Can we play football in my room? Is Dad in a better mood now so Lizzy and I can play? Is church over yet? Is Grandpa's story finished? Is dinner done? Is practice over? Can I be excused? On all that is good and holy, I just want to play!

So picture this. You're an eight-year-old kid. You like sports and baseball cards, action figures and TV. Occasionally you get a book out of the library about Bigfoot, but that's pretty much it. But then one day this thing called Nintendo comes along. It speaks to you like nothing has ever spoken to you before. In playing terms, it's off the charts. It's like an arcade that lives in your family room. You don't even need quarters or a birthday excuse to be there. It's better than TV, better than any book at the library because each game is like your own little story that you control. It's filled with magic flutes and airplanes and guys named Piston Honda. Nintendo made Choose Your Own Adventure books seem like finger painting.

Sure, there was Atari before Nintendo, but only weird older second cousins who lived in Indiana, and babysitters' boyfriends, cared about Atari. Atari was boring, the graphics were weak, even the design of the system itself looked hokey. *Frogger* was probably its best game, and the object of that was to not get hit by cars. Seriously? I could do that out on Fabyan Parkway anytime I wanted. Nintendo games were different. Each one was its own new experience.

Take *Super Mario Bros.*, for instance. You're playing along, getting the hang of it, jumping over little mushroom men and smashing blocks with your head, when, out of nowhere, level 2.2 comes along and suddenly you're underwater. Underwater! No way you saw that one coming. Holy cow! What'll they think of next? Look at those graphics! Look at those little bubbles coming out of Mario's mouth! Look at that lobster thing. It looks exactly like a real-life lobster thing! This is amazing!

With books or TV shows, even with your own imagination, results came without any required effort. You want to see what James does with that giant peach of his? Just turn the page and find out. You're not sure how Mr. Belvedere will keep Wesley from being a little asshole this week? All you gotta do is sit in front of the tube for another twenty minutes and watch. But with Nintendo, if you wanted to see what happened next, you had to work for it. Nintendo rewarded *playing*. Sure, winning a game of touch football brought a sense of satisfaction, but beating a level of *Super Mario Bros.* meant you got to lift the curtain on a whole new 8-bit world, filled with what felt like infinite possibility. This was completely different from anything we'd ever experienced before. Nintendo was more than a toy; it was a playing utopia. The only catch was Timmy Kleen working the door.

In the beginning, the games were limited. Kleen's NES came with just the standard dual-game cartridge of *Duck Hunt* and *Super Mario Bros.*, and we played those two until our thumbs were raw and we saw flying turtles in our sleep. It wasn't until Kleen got himself sent to the principal's office for throwing a stapler at a hall monitor that his parents placed him on the decidedly effective Games for Good Behavior program. It was quite possibly the greatest disciplinary action of all time.

Every week that Kleen didn't poke his sister in the eye, every week that he didn't throw his music book at Ms. Powers, every week that he didn't cry at karate lessons, he got a new Nintendo game. It was unbelievable—a carrot on a stick that gave half the school good reason to fess up for crimes we hadn't even committed. We became Kleen cover-up artists and ADD deflectors of the highest order. Who put paste on the carpet? Not Timmy, that's for sure. Who called Lisa Kowalski a stink face? Sure wasn't Timmy. Who knows the answer to number two? That would be Timmy, Mrs. Hugo, because ten of us just whispered it to him. Within three weeks of the Games for Good Behavior program, Timmy Kleen had become the most popular, sociable, well-adjusted kid at HC Wilson. And the spaz didn't even have to lift a finger.

The initial game reward in the Kleen program was *Excitebike*. It lived up to its name and then some. Set in the apparently high-stakes world of Japanese motocross, *Excitebike* tested our reflexes against ramps, pits, straightaways and the clock. It was you versus the computer—three to four other bike racers all hell-bent on knocking you down and making your life miserable. *Excitebike* also introduced us to "power conservation"—a very foreign concept to a nine-year-old. If you went too fast all the time, your excite bike would become overexcited, crapping out and sending you headfirst into the dirt. This was a very difficult idea to grasp. I mean, what nine-year-old boy doesn't want to go fast all the time? Especially a nine-year-old boy who should be on medication? Needless to say, Kleen was not good at *Excitebike*. Both he and the bike spent about ninety percent of each race squarely "in the red." The only reason he didn't smash the cartridge against the wall three rounds in was because we'd usually manage to tackle him to the ground.

After taking the fall for a fogged-up-bus-window drawing of a stick figure picking his nose, Matt Mahoney got Kleen through his second week of the program unscathed. The reward was *RBI Baseball*. It was most definitely a game changer. Made by a company called Tengen, *RBI Baseball* didn't look like a regular Nintendo game. It wasn't gray with grooves on the side; rather, it was black and shaped like the hood of the *Knight Rider* car. At first we weren't even sure if it would work in the NES. But from the first crack-of-the-bat ping, we knew we were in for a treat.

Up until this point, all the games we played were

one-player games. Your competition was the game itself. Sure, *Super Mario Bros.* allowed both Mario and Luigi to play, but that was never at the same time and certainly never against one another. *RBI*, or "Ribbie," as we quickly grew accustomed to calling it, changed all that. Upon the start of the game you were able to select one of eight Major League Baseball clubs as your team and you could go head-to-head with another club of your opponent's choice. You controlled an entire roster of batters, pitchers and fielders, who, despite all looking like the white version of Kirby Puckett, each had their own stats and skill levels. It seems simple now, but back then, to think that a video game could make some batters better home-run hitters than others, or give some pitchers a better curveball, well, that was mind-blowing. Years later, *RBI* would no doubt become instrumental in the popularization of fantasy sports. For if *RBI Baseball* taught us anything, it was that the key to success lay heavily in statistics. As such, we gradually composed a list of Ribbie dos and don'ts. They were:

1. Never throw strikes to Tony Armas. Ever. It doesn't matter that you've never heard of him or that his baseball card is worth seven cents. In *RBI Baseball* he's Babe Ruth.

2. The California Angels suck.

3. Pressing the buttons extra hard directly correlates to extra bases.

4. In the fifth inning Fernando Valenzuela will suddenly start to pitch thirty-seven miles per hour. Remove him immediately.

5. Kent Hrbek is a beast.

6. Ellis Burks should always pinch-hit for Bill Buckner.

7. Vince Coleman is a professional thief. He steals bases.

8. Roger Clemens is an asshole, even in video game form.

9. In *RBI Baseball* sometimes home-run balls go straight through the wall. And sometimes outfield throws get stuck in the bleachers.

10. At the end of the day, the Tengen newspaper never lies.

Down in Kleen's basement, epic round-robin Ribbie tournaments were waged. Athletic attempts normally reserved for Little League failure could now be played out with a little hand–eye coordination and a quick pair of thumbs. We became baseball professionals, turning double plays, hitting sacrifice flies, and throwing wicked knuckleballs. It didn't matter that your batter ran faster to the dugout when tagged out than he did running the bases, *RBI Baseball* felt as real as baseball itself.

But the good times didn't last. The "Pheasant Wood Meltdown," as it later became known, put the Games for Good Behavior program in serious jeopardy. On a Saturday night sometime in September, Timmy Kleen went out to dinner with his family to the St. Charles Country Club, Pheasant Wood. It was a location that none of us had ever been to—a middle-class pipe dream only glimpsed through minivan windows in passing. So Kleen was left to his own devices that night. If there were any other kids dining there, they most certainly had their own Nintendos, because nothing was done to keep Kleen in line. Perhaps in some St. Charles show of superiority, the country-club kids had even encouraged Timmy's spastic behavior just so they could keep the deprived children of Batavia from receiving their precious games. Lousy St. Charles kids. I wouldn't put it past them.

The facts of that night never got out completely, but this much is known. Kleen's hamburger, his mother's plate of linguini, two deckchairs and a teenage waitress were thrown into the Pheasant Wood swimming pool, all compliments of Timmy. Did he not like his burger? Was he upset with the service? Had his sister questioned the styling of his creased dress pants? We were never sure. But the legend of Timmy Kleen's rage had now spread to the far reaches of Kane County, and his parents certainly weren't going to take it lightly. They banned new games for a month. It was a crushing blow to us all.

Over the next few weeks we did our best to get by. We concerned ourselves with getting to the last level in *Super Mario Bros.* and seeing how slow we could make Valenzuela throw through extra innings. The record was nineteen miles per hour—a rate at which a batter could swing three full times before the ball reached the plate. Fascinating stuff.

When we weren't trying to keep Kleen out of trouble, we spent much of our time petitioning him on what game to get next once the ban was lifted. There were plenty to choose from. We'd heard great things about a game called *The Legend of Zelda* from our Tri-City soccer opponents. And Olsen's Canadian penpal had nothing but glowing reviews for *Tecmo Bowl*, *1943: The Battle of Midway* and, of course, *Ice Hockey*. Proving that even Canadians had better access to games than we did. It was decidedly frustrating.

But one sunshiny day during the middle of lunch, Kleen announced the unexpected.

"*Double Dragon*."

"The arcade game?"

"Yep. They turned it into a Nintendo game. It's brand new. My dad's buying it for me on the way home from work. I'm back on the program."

Hell yes! *Double Dragon* was maybe the coolest, and definitely the most violent, arcade game we'd ever come across. And violence, to a nine-year-old American boy, is more addictive than crack. At All Seasons Ice Rink, I'd once taken five dollars from my dad, meant for hot dogs and Cokes for the family, and feverishly spent it on twenty minutes of *Double Dragon* bliss. Pumping in quarter after quarter, I managed to make it all the way to level four, registering electronic immortality with a top-ten score. So incredible was the accomplishment for a novice like myself that I was sure my father would see the value in his five-dollar investment. Sadly, he did not and I was grounded for a week. (It should be noted that denying John Doyle hot dogs was never a good idea.) But it was worth the punishment. As an arcade game, *Double Dragon* had the uncanny ability to suck you in no matter what the consequences, and the NES version ended up being just as addictive.

Whips, aluminum bats, metal pipes, throwing knives—these were all weapons of choice in *Double Dragon*. But the weapons didn't just magically appear as they did in other games. No sir, to get a whip in *Double Dragon*, you had to kill a whip-wielding bad guy first. Actually, come to think of it, it wasn't even a bad *guy* with the whip. It was a *girl*. You had to kill *girls* in *Double Dragon*! With your own bare hands! Once they were dead, then the whip was yours. Then you could kill other bad guys with whips, like slightly Asian-looking bodybuilders and dudes named Lopar, eventually moving up to big rocks and dynamite and so on and so forth, leaving a bloody 8-bit trail of demise behind you. There were no gold coins to gather or enchanted mushrooms to gobble up in *Double Dragon*, just straightforward, unadulterated, two-fisted violence. It was glorious.

So from Halloween through Thanksgiving we gorged ourselves on a steady diet of curveballs and jump kicks. While other new games made their way into the Games for Good Behavior rotation, like *Mega Man*, *Double Dribble* and *John Elway's Quarterback*, *RBI* and *Double Dragon* remained our favorites.

But as the temperature continued to drop outside and Kleen's basement rules became more obsessive, we grew more and more fed up with the situation. The constant grind of standing in line and taking turns was wearing on us all. We wanted our own Nintendos. Badly. Surely the Christmas season would be the answer. Surely Santa Claus or a favorite grandparent would step up to the plate, and Timmy Kleen's Nintendo tyranny would come to an end. It had to.

# CHAPTER TEN

Two raisin eyes stared up at me. They were oozing with Elmer's and loosely attached to a mismanaged tapestry of pipe cleaners. This was my donkey, the shining centerpiece of my art-class manger-scene ornament. The fact that the donkey was three times the size of the manger itself didn't concern me. Nor was I concerned that my ornament project in no way resembled an actual "ornament." These were minor details, trifles in comparison to the masterpiece unfolding before me. Already there were art critics in my head peppering me with baited-breath questions.

*Would you say you're an artistic genius, Jake?*

Genius? Prodigy, maybe. I just create what I feel, you know? But I owe it all to my third grade art teacher, Miss Ciarocci. We're getting married in the autumn, actually.

"What the heck is that?" Mahoney asked, looking over the apparent bomb that had just exploded on my desk.

"It's a manger-scene ornament."

"It looks like my butt."

To the untrained eye, maybe. I brushed him off. "Just wait till it's finished." I didn't have time for the inquiries of common folk. I was on a mission here. Step one: Create genius art project. Step two: Make out with Miss Ciarocci. Step three: Get her to buy me a Nintendo.

All around me kids cut and pasted, while Christmas music played cheerfully in the background. These were the days when you could actually play Christmas music in a public school. Frosty the Snowman and Rudolph the Red-Nosed Reindeer had yet to be deemed dangerous religious icons. It was a simpler time.

In the corner, by the cleanup sink, I could see a group of boys reviewing wreath-selling numbers. In the past week, grades had dipped considerably among Cub Scouts. All academic thinking was now solely focused on selling wreaths. Rumor had it that Josh Farmer was still in the lead, but I wasn't sweating him, because, ladies and gentlemen, as of forty-eight hours ago, Jake Doyle had uncovered a secret weapon.

On the night when my own mother bought two wreaths from my sworn enemy, I'd had a nice little talk with my parents. It went something like this:

"HOW COULD YOU DO THAT TO ME?"

"What's he crying about?" my dad asked, setting down his briefcase.

"Oh, I just bought a few wreaths from the Farmer boy."

"The Farmer boy? I don't trust that kid."

"See!" I yelled. "He's a total dipstick!"

"Watch your mouth," my dad yelled back.

My mother tried to explain. "You always hated selling wreaths, Jake, I didn't even think you were selling them this year. I'm sorry."

"*I* knew he was selling wreaths," Lizzy interjected from the stairs. "It's because the top wreath seller gets a Nin—"

"*Night* in Chicago." I glared at Lizzy. She was one slippery little snot. She must have seen the take-home note. This was going to be tricky. "I—I thought it would be nice for the whole family to go. It's at a hotel or someplace. It's supposed to be expensive."

My mom wasn't buying it. "A night at a hotel? That's a weird prize."

"Yeah, I think the Kleens donated it or something."

"Figures," said my dad, hanging up his coat and immediately switching gears to more-pressing matters. "So, what's for dinner?"

Thirty seconds later I had Lizzy cornered at the kitchen sink as we washed up.

"What the heck are you doing?" I hissed, throwing in a few soapy elbows.

"I don't know what you're talking about."

"You saw the take-home note. I know you did. Why are you trying to tell them about the Nintendo? Don't get me in trouble!"

"You're the one getting yourself in trouble."

I was not amused. "I will seriously tear off the heads of every single one of your Barbies. Don't think I won't do it."

"Go ahead. I'll just tell on you."

"Don't mess with my Nintendo!"

Lizzy shut off the sink and dried her hands. There was something else cooking in that giant brain of hers, I could tell. She looked me straight in the eyes.

"Look, you don't even have it yet, okay? You probably won't even win it."

"So?"

"So I have a way you can do it. A way you can win the Nintendo."

"What is it?"

"You have to help me first."

"With what?"

"Getting a Cabbage Patch. If Santa doesn't get me one, I need Mom and Dad to do it. I can't depend on Santa anymore. He didn't get me Strawberry Shortcake last year like I asked. The system is broken. I want you to help me get one. A redhead one named Dawn."

"How am I gonna do that?"

"Just tell Mom and Dad how much I want one. It looks bad if I say it all the time."

"And what are you gonna do for me?"

"I won't say anything about the Nintendo."

"And?"

"And I have a way to win the Cub Scout contest."

"No, you don't."

"Yes, I do."

"Well, what is it?" I wiped my hands on my pants.

"Every year you sell wreaths to Miss Sherman, right?"

"Yeah."

"She buys a lot, right? 'Cause she's old."

"Uh-huh. Maybe."

"No, definitely 'cause she's old. So what you need is a bunch of other old people to sell to. Ones that are all in the same place so you can go door to door really fast and you don't have to go all over Batavia hunting them down."

"What's your point?"

My mom yelled from across the kitchen. "Dinner's ready!"

"Coming, Mommy," Lizzy called back. Still standing on the stool, she put her hand on my shoulder and laid it on me.

"You need to go to Prairie Pines, Jake. The nursing home. You'll clean up."

*Prairie Pines.* Man, Lizzie was smart. Why didn't I think of that? Why didn't anyone think of that? There must be two hundred lonely old saps up there, easy. Most of them waking up every day just hoping some kid comes by to visit them. They'd all want wreaths. This was genius!

"So, do we have a deal?"

"Yeah," I said, still a little stunned. "We got a deal. Redhead named . . . ?"

"Dawn. With freckles. Don't mess it up."

Prairie Pines Nursing Home had been an institution in "half-dead living"—as my dad put it—for decades. It sat on the corner of Route 31 and Fairview Parkway, an intersection serving as the border between Batavia and neighboring thug town—Geneva. At the edge of the Prairie Pines property stood the prominent, hand-carved "welcome to Batavia" sign, which read, BATAVIA CITY OF ENERGY, an ironic slogan considering the monumental lack of activity that lay directly behind the sign. Not to mention a very loose interpretation of the word "city."

Over the years I'd probably passed Prairie Pines a thousand times, but until that Saturday morning, I'd never been inside the place. As I pedaled my Team Murray up its winding sidewalk, I could already smell that hospital smell. It was something of a cross between hot-lunch vegetables and my great-aunt Bertha. Not a very palatable mix. But it didn't matter. I had work to do. There were only six sales days left in the wreath-selling competition and I was nowhere near the head of the pack. I ditched my bike in the snow, stomped down on the automatic doormat and forged ahead inside.

The first thing you learn as a nine-year-old walking into a nursing home is that you are a very rare commodity. Like a life jacket on a sinking ship or the last brownie at a Phish show; everybody wants a piece. Before I'd even finished telling the nurse at the front desk my story, two elderly men in wheelchairs approached me. They were dead eyed and mush mouthed, smiling and wheezing nonsense. They made the old guys from the Muppets look like New Kids on the Block. To be completely honest, they scared the crap out of me.

"That must be Charlie's grandson!" one of them coughed.

"Look at how big you've gotten!" said the other one, tugging at my arm.

"It's Charlie's grandson!" the same guy coughed again.

"I heard you the first time," said the other guy.

"*What?*"

"I said, I heard you the first—"

"Hey everybody! It's Charlie's grandson!"

And that was how I became Charlie's grandson. I never did meet Charlie, but it didn't matter. I could have been a convicted juvenile delinquent and it wouldn't have mattered to these people. Before I knew what was happening I was surrounded by a dozen drooling half-deads, all smiling and petting me like a puppy. This little trip to Prairie Pines was definitely going to cause a few nightmares in the coming weeks. It reminded me of the time I made the mistake of going through Jaydee's Haunted House alone on a bet. Every molecule in my body was screaming at me to run, but my Nintendo brain kept me locked in position. The time to sell was now.

"Hi, my name's Jake . . . I'm a Cub Scout."

"A little Cub Scout, how wonderful!" a bald lady chirped.

"Charlie's grandson's a Cub Scout!"

"That's right. My grandpa Chuck taught me well."

"I was a Cub Scout before there was such a thing," the guy who was still tugging my arm slobbered. "I could whittle you a canoe!"

"Fascinating, sir."

Another one bellowed out from behind me, "What kind of merit badges have you got, sonny?"

"Only a couple . . . " I paused for effect. "I still have to get my American Business Badge. You know, for selling Christmas wreaths. Do any of you know someone who might like to buy a Christmas wreath?"

Wrinkled hands shot up all around me and cash register bells immediately went off in my head. Or maybe that was just the sound of someone flatlining in the next room. Either way, these people were definitely buying what I was selling.

Yes, they would all like to buy a Christmas wreath, but first I would have to come back to the lounge or the dining room or their living quarters to see pictures of their grandkids and play checkers and hear stories about the Hoover Dam. (What is it about old people and the Hoover Dam?) So that's exactly what I did. I went door to door, I smiled and laughed, I ate stale pieces of fudge. I got schooled in checkers. I gave hugs and handshakes. I listened to stories about FDR and whistled along to Benny Goodman. I took buffalo nickels as gifts. I raised beds. I turned on lights. I lifted spirits.

By lunchtime word had gotten out. There was a nine-year-old boy in the building who had manners and the Christmas spirit. He wasn't selling wreaths; by God, he was selling America! And what war vet or former Depression-era teenager didn't want to buy himself a nice little piece of that? Folks came out of the woodwork. Grumpy old men who hadn't been out of bed in months suddenly found their legs. I was magic tonic. I was Ponce de León. I was Willy Wonka's friggin' golden ticket, dangling over Grandpa Joe's face. I told stories of Pinewood Derby triumphs. I explained the intricacies of the *Star Wars* trilogy. I pledged allegiance to the flag. And I sold wreaths, a truckload of them. I was in Prairie Pines for exactly six hours, and I left with just under three hundred bucks in sales. It was a triumph of Eagle Scout proportions.

Later that night, back at home, I sloshed up the stairs weighed down with dollar bills and change. As I passed Lizzy's room I poked my head in.

"A redhead, right?"

She turned and nodded smugly. "With freckles."

# CHAPTER ELEVEN

Dumpsters make great hiding places for three reasons. One, they're usually readily available. Two, they're almost always tucked to the side somewhere, hidden from view. And three, most importantly, they smell, which keeps whoever you're hiding from at a safe distance. So if you do it right, you don't even have to get into the dumpster itself, you can just hang out behind it, which is precisely what my girls' boots and I had been doing for the past five recesses.

Hiding my boots was actually a lot easier than I thought it would be. The recess bell would ring, I'd take my time putting on my coat and hat, making sure that all the guys were already on their way down the hall. Then I'd slip on my boots, walk past Huge-Blow's room so she was sure to see them, and head for the door. Once I was there, I'd wait for the right moment and then sprint past the jungle gym and dive behind the dumpster. The whole operation took less than fifteen seconds, with only about five or six seconds of actual girl-boot exposure. Those were odds I could live with. And why would anyone pay any attention to me anyway? It was recess, time to play blacktop football and monkey-bar chicken and tag, and whatever the hell it was that girls did out there. Conceivably, I could keep this dumpster thing up well through March.

Sometimes Zilinski would give me a hand or cause a distraction on my way out the door. He was the only one who had first-hand knowledge of my plight. I'd kept my mouth shut about a preschool pants-peeing incident of his for years, so he owed me one. He was the best kind of friend, loyal *and* sneaky. Sometimes he'd even stop by the dumpster for a visit during the football game, just to see how I was doing.

"You see *Temple of Doom* last night?" he asked. We were both propped up on a snowbank, balanced between the wall and the dumpster.

"On a movie channel?"

"Yeah. A guy rips out a guy's heart, right out of his chest. It's great."

"Indiana Jones' heart?"

"No, some loser Indian. You gotta get the movie channels."

"My dad says cable makes you fat."

"Yeah," he contemplated. "I guess. My dad's a pretty big fatso."

Out on the blacktop, Delund was marching his team down the field, changing the rules to suit his needs as he went along. In recent weeks he had grown tired of the lack of physicality in two-hand touching and had resorted to one-armed forearming, usually to your face. Without Zilinski out there, Team Loser was getting massacred. Ronnie Dobber had been given a full-body snowsuit wedgie and was now lying prostrate at midfield. He'd been there for several plays now.

Steve sat up. "I guess I should get back out there. See ya later, Jake."

"Yeah. See ya, Steve."

Zilinski trotted back to the blacktop. I hawked a loogie and watched it drip down the side of the dumpster. I could feel a presence lurking; one that I'd hoped was only my imagination. I was wrong.

"Steve's cool," Conor Stump projected philosophically. He was sitting three feet away from me at the side of the dumpster, where he'd been, conceivably, since August. He was chewing on an icicle. "This dumpster's cool. Sitting back here's cool."

"Uh-huh . . . "

In a word, Conor Stump was weird, the kind of antisocial personality that probably still played with GI Joes in high school. He was a born chewer and overall creepy little kid. He ate eraser heads by the gross, gnawed on *Highlights* magazines, pen caps, the thumbs of his rainbow-patterned Freezy Freakies, whatever he could get his mouth on. His overuse of the word "cool" was also troubling.

"This snow's cool."

And he had nothing better to do than sit behind the dumpster with me.

"We should build a fort back here. A secret Christmas snow fort for Christmas. Christmas is cool."

"Yeah . . . "

But I'd sold a whopping thirty-seven wreaths last week. There was a Nintendo on its way. I could feel it. And when it came, my days in hiding would be a distant memory. I closed my eyes and slowly let my imagination get me through the rest of recess. For there are no dreams bigger than those conjured up behind a dumpster . . .

*Peter Gabriel's "Big Time" blasted from the fifty-pound boom box resting on my shoulder. There was a party going down on 120 N. Watson Street, and it was bumping. I strolled down the stairs in a Rad Racer T-shirt and a sport coat with the sleeves rolled up. Pausing on the landing for effect, I surveyed the Doyles' new, modern Nintendo living room. Big screen TV. Check. Half a dozen beanbag chairs in place of the couch. Check. Nintendo Entertainment System on marble pedestal. Check. Yes indeed, this dream sequence was going to work out nicely. Elwood gave me a fist bump in agreement as he floated by on a hoverboard.*

*The whole crew was in attendance: Mahoney, Olsen, Zilinski, Hartwell, the Gruseckis, even that little kindergartener Brett from down the street. Half the town had come to bask in the glow of my Cub Scout victory. Lizzy was passing out glasses of Tang to Batavians and celebrities alike, who mingled around the house, talking* Zelda *high scores and* Mega Man *strategies. And what was this? Oh-ho! Miss Ciarocci in a red miniskirt, how nice of you to make it. At the moment, she was talking to* Double Dare's *Marc Summers. I didn't like the looks of this. I gave a quick nod to the suit in the corner—Dan Delund, my new head of security. He scurried over and lowered his shades.*

*"Yeah, boss?"*

*"I think we got a problem with Mr. Messy over there. I don't like the way he's talking to the guests. You catch my drift?"*

*"He's already gone, sir."*

*"Good man."*

*As I walked through the crowd, I felt a new sense of pur-*

*pose. There was a bounce in my step, a tingle in my thumbs. I was officially a Nintendo Owner—a man worth talking to. The eighth grader who just yesterday had tossed my lunch in a tree was now tossing me high fives. Perks and benefits, the likes of which I could only dream about before, were suddenly within my grasp.*

*But with great power also came great responsibility. I'd become both Gatekeeper and Key Master to a Nintendo kingdom, and now everybody wanted a turn. I pushed through the crowd of well-wishers and down the red-carpet gauntlet leading toward the TV. Celebrities and pop idols were coming out of the woodwork. I had to pick my spots wisely.*

*No, Mr. Wizard, you can't have next game, I don't care about the volcano experiment you're holding. You, on the other hand, William "the Refrigerator" Perry, yes, I will take one of those Pudding Pops. You and me got a* Tecmo Bowl *date in a half hour. What's up, Max Headroom? Cool, man. Uh-huh. Maybe if you'd just stop stuttering for a second, we can have a conversation. Seriously, you're scaring Spuds MacKenzie. Oh, wow, Alanis from* You Can't Do That on Television? *No way, that's such a coincidence, I think you're super cute too. You should hang out for a while in case this thing with my art teacher doesn't work out. Corey Haim and Corey Feldman! That's seriously how tall you guys are? For real? Tell you what. You see Mike Tyson over there hitting on Mary Lou Retton? If you guys can get him to tell you how to beat King Hippo, I'll give you next game on* Punch-Out!! *For reals.*

*My parents stood in the kitchen doorway, proudly taking it all in. My father put his arm around my mom. "I'm telling you, Patty, that Nintendo Entertainment System is the best thing that's ever happened to this family."*

*"His test scores are up too," she added.*

*I finally made it to the center of the crowd, where the*

*Gruseckis were in the midst of a heated game of* Ice Hockey. *Team Poland was trailing Team USA in the third period.*

*"You know," I said, chomping down on a candy cigarette and exhaling sugar vapor, "some guys go all medium-sized players in* Ice Hockey. *I say mix it up a bit. Me, I like to live on the edge."*

*"Totally, Jake, totally."*

*"When it's your turn to play, I wanna see a team of all fat guys take on a team of all skinnies. You know, really go for it. It's a party." I turned to the crowd. "A Nintendo party!"*

*Thunderous applause.*

*At the door, Delund shook off the cold and gave me a nod. Marc Summers was no longer in the building. Outside, rummaging around in the snow, Josh Farmer and Timmy Kleen could only pick up more poop in the hope that doing my chores would gain them entrance. The two pressed their faces up against the window.*

*"Jake! Let us in, man!"*

*I leaned up against the glass. "Cold out there, eh, Kleen?"*

*"We've been out here for an hour!"*

*"No skin off my nose, is it?"*

*"How much more poo do we gotta clean up?"*

*"Let me ask you a question, Farmer. Do you love your country?"*

*"Yeah."*

*"Then pick it up. All of it."*

*I pulled the curtain shut and turned around. Ciarocci was now standing right in front of me, softly blowing on a* Super Mario Bros. *cartridge.*

*"So, Jake. How 'bout a little two-player?"*

*I popped in another candy cigarette and exhaled. "I'm your Mario, baby."*

"Mario? Like Super Mario?"

"Huh?" I shook off the cobwebs. I'd been off in space for a good ten minutes. The crowds were already heading back inside and lunch ladies were barking out orders. Recess was winding down. Conor Stump had finished off his icicle and was now sucking on the strings of his sweatshirt. He was also seated about three inches from my face.

"Back off a bit, Stump, will ya?"

"I was just watching you stare at your breath. Staring at your breath is cool. It looks like smoke sometimes. Smoke is cool."

"Yeah."

"Are you gonna go back inside?"

"Yeah, I'll be there in a minute."

Conor just sat there, staring.

"So, where'd you get those boots?"

"I don't want to talk about it."

"Those boots are cool."

# CHAPTER TWELVE

Chrysler's 1987 Dodge Grand Caravan was one fine piece of engineering. It was like the Trapper Keeper of cars. There were enough storage compartments and gadgets in that minivan to make any kid want to buy American for the rest of his life. The night my dad brought it home from the dealer's, I cried when my parents wouldn't let me camp out in it overnight. Lizzy and I were fascinated by it. That new car smell, that interior—the car was nicer than our living room. We went from not even knowing what a cup holder was to suddenly having six of them. Six cup holders! Imagine the possibilities! Up to six pops open at the same time, and all comfortably stored throughout the automobile. You could throw a birthday party in there. There was an overhead compartment for the garage-door opener, even one for sunglasses. Cruise control, seat pockets, armrests—it was better than being on a plane. Even Elwood was impressed.

The evening before our first Chrysler road trip, my dad stayed up all night making Steely Dan tapes for the open road that lay ahead, one that he would now, undoubtedly, be cruising in comfort. This was a first for John Doyle. We'd never seen him actually get excited about driving somewhere, at least not in a vehicle with us. The year I was born he'd been forced to put his beloved Triumph TR6 convertible away for good. It was a two-seater and notoriously bad in the snow—not exactly a family car. He'd built a little shed for it in our backyard, and sometimes, late at night, I'd catch him staring at it from his bedroom window. He missed that car.

But it only took one family road trip to Rockford for the Chrysler to lose its magic touch on my dad. Within a few weeks he was back to his old self again: white-knuckled at the wheel, hating traffic, hating construction, hating the weather and hell-bent on getting to his destination as fast as humanly possible. Whoever said getting there was half the fun has never been in a moving vehicle with John Doyle. With our family, getting there was far from fun, it was a seventy-five-mile-per-hour nightmare. My dad needed to drive fast like most other dads needed to watch football on Sunday or go bowling. It kept him sane. Where other parents might place automobile emphasis on seatbelts or antilock brakes, my father's only concern was for speed. The faster the better. And good luck to anyone who got in his way.

You had to hand it to him, though: my dad had a knack for getting from point A to point B. In all the vacations and road trips we'd taken over the years, we'd never once been in an accident or gotten seriously lost. And I'd never seen him get pulled over by the cops either. An early pioneer in fuzz-buster technology, John Doyle always managed to stay one step ahead of the law. Over the years he went through at least a dozen radar detectors, each one supposedly better than the last. The earliest versions were about the size of a VCR. They sat up on the dash, perilously mounted on giant strips of Velcro, constantly chirping and beeping, so much so that the sounds eventually became nothing more than white noise to us. But every so often the thing would reach a blaring frequency, alarming enough to confirm a speed trap, and my dad would slam on the brakes and inconspicuously merge into slower traffic. Chuckling to himself, he'd proudly tally up another point in a decades-long score. "That's Doyle: one-fifty-eight; cops: zero." Those marked the happy moments of our family car trips.

Right now, however, was not one of those moments. Today was our annual Christmas shopping trip into Chicago—hands down my father's least favorite day of the year. It meant getting up early, sitting in traffic, finding parking, shopping, waiting, listening, spending money and driving a minivan—pretty much a grocery list of pain for the man now barreling down the highway.

"God bless it! What the— Come on!" he hollered over the wheel in short bursts of anger, his fury only temporarily cooled by pressing harder on the gas.

My mom was in her normal crash position, bracing herself against the dashboard. Lizzy and I were in the middle and back seats flipping through Sears Wish Book catalogs, doing our best to zone out and think about Christmas. It was nine a.m. on a Saturday, but even the smallest amount of traffic heading into the city was too much for the old man. We were currently on I-88 stuck behind a semi. My dad was tailing it close enough to read the button-sized sticker on its bumper, which read, almost tauntingly:

HOW'S MY DRIVING?

To which my father replied:

"GO EFF YOURSELF!"

"*Honey*. Not in front of the kids." My mom hated it when my dad swore in front of us, even when it was just implied swearing. But reminding him of her disapproval only ever made things worse. My dad was swearing because he was mad. My mom's nagging made him madder, which directly resulted in more swearing. It was a hilarious cycle of escalating tension that they never really seemed to figure out.

"The kids don't need to hear—"

"God bless it! Look at this yahoo! Oh, would ya look at that, Patty? Wisconsin plates. What a shocker. Get the cheese outta your eyes, Oshkosh!"

"Just go around him."

"Go around *him*?" HONK! HONK! "He should be letting *me* pass!"

Some fathers find refuge fishing; others, sanctuary on the golf course. In my father's eyes there was nothing holier than the left-hand lane. Those somehow unaware of his divine right to it were met with a barrage of incessant horn patterns and verbal assaults poetically expressing the dairy idiosyncrasies of Wisconsin. A state, we'd learned, where no one ever used turn signals and often let cattle sit shotgun.

HONK! HONK! Doing his best to lighten the mood, my dad yelled over his shoulder, "Hey Jake? Why'd the doctor from Green Bay send his patient to the nut house?"

"I dunno."

"Because he diagnosed him lactose intolerant. Ha!"

"That means he can't eat cheese," Lizzy explained.

"Oh."

HONK! HONK! "LEFT-HAND LANE! Son of a—"

The truck driver had now confirmed what we'd all known for years: that there was a genuine asshole on his tail. He slowed down to a cool forty miles per hour just to piss my dad off.

"Mother— God BLESS IT!"

"Just go around him, John. There aren't even any other cars on the road."

The odds of my dad giving any vehicle, save maybe the Popemobile, the courtesy of a right-hand pass were about as good as my mom flicking you off. We stayed three inches from the semi's tailgate for another twenty minutes until, thankfully, the driver got off at Harlem Avenue in Oak Park. As we passed by, Lizzy gave him a little apologetic wave, my mom avoided eye contact, and my dad just plowed ahead toward the Sears Tower on the horizon. "Uh-huh. Uh-huh. You see?" He pointed back toward the semi. "Doyle: nine thousand seventy-seven. Wisconsin: zip."

Although we might have an occasional laugh at the expense of a few cheeseheads on I-88, once we reached the outskirts of downtown Chicago, the jokes were over. City driving was a different animal altogether. As soon as we merged off the Eisenhower Expressway onto Congress Avenue, you could feel my father's blood begin to boil. The traffic, the noise, the tourists, the one-way streets— Christmas in Chicago was a virtual biological assault on the old man. The closer we got to Lake Michigan, the higher his threat level rose, usually jumping from orange to red as we made the left past Buckingham Fountain. At that point my mother would turn to us with her index finger firmly pressed to her lips and initiate the "bleeding rule." The rule meant that under no circumstances (unless you were bleeding—hence the name) were you to ask questions, request to go to the bathroom, laugh, cry, talk or otherwise make any noise whatsoever until the car was safely parked. We hated the bleeding rule, but looking back it probably saved lives.

"God bless it! Look at this! Look at this traffic already. I told you we should have left earlier."

"The stores don't even open until ten, John."

"Which street is the turn again? Look on the map, will ya?"

"Um . . . just a second, just a second." My mother, who couldn't find her way downstairs with gravity and a firm push, was for some reason always in charge of navigation. She flipped our ancient city map over and over on her lap, somehow hoping that might help her decode it. "Um . . . I think we make a right."

"On which street?"

"I can't tell."

"Whaddya mean you can't tell?"

"I don't know, John, I don't remember what turn it is. I think we go right."

"If we make a right we're in the lake, for crying out loud!" He grabbed the map, flipping it over and pointing. "See, the lake is east. Right there, the big blue thing. I need to know which street it is. You know the one I'm talking about? The street where I found the spot that one time."

"The spot that one time" was in 1973, and I believed, along with everyone else in the car not named John

Doyle, that it was a figment of his imagination. Apparently, while on a date with my mother back in college, he claimed to have found an unmetered spot on a side street off of Michigan Avenue (spitting distance from Water Tower Place, no less), where he was able to park his car for eight hours at no cost, and a little Italian man had "kept an eye on it for him." He had been searching for the same spot unsuccessfully for almost fifteen years.

"Walnut. I think it was Walnut. Remember? Right by that pizza place."

"They tore that place down, John. Let's just park it in the parking garage."

"A parking garage! For eight dollars? Are you crazy? Kids, keep a lookout for Walnut. We're not parking in a garage. No way in hell."

An hour later, sad and defeated, John Doyle pulled into a parking garage, just like he'd done every year since 1974. The good news, though, was that by this point the drive had taken so much out of him that he wouldn't be much of a problem for the rest of the day. Like a little baby tuckered out from crying so much, he was too tired now to make a fuss. Lizzy, on the other hand, was charged up and chomping at the bit. Her fifty-plus minutes of forced silence was a new record. She shot my mom an evil eye as she hopped down from the minivan.

"That was ridiculous."

"Thank you for being so quiet back there, Lizzy. I'll make it up to you."

"You better, Patricia."

Lizzy had to watch her step, though. Over the past

few weeks her Christmas plight had taken a turn for the worse. Cabbage Patch fever had gripped the nation and stores could hardly keep the orphaned dolls on the shelves. Grandmother riots were breaking out all across the country. It was a nightly news story. The demand got so high that when two disc jockeys in Milwaukee joked on air that a load of the dolls would be dropped from a B-52 bomber over County Stadium, two dozen minivans actually showed up. If Lizzy didn't make some progress with my folks soon, her window of opportunity would be closed for good. So this was an important shopping trip for both of us—a rare hour of sibling solidarity in an otherwise tattletale relationship. We had to be on our best behavior, with our eyes peeled and our sales pitches ready, poised for that perfect moment when we "just happened to" stumble upon a Nintendo display or a stocked Cabbage Patch aisle.

Lizzy and I exchanged game-face glances as we marched through the parking garage. Above us you could hear the sounds of Michigan Avenue: steel drums playing "Silent Night," Santa Clauses ringing Salvation Army bells, and cabbies yelling at tourists. As we emerged and waited for the crosswalk light to change, I watched a man in a Cubs jacket trade smiles with a woman in a White Sox hat. Christmas in Chicago—it was a beautiful thing.

By the time we crossed the street, Lizzy was already sprinting toward the Santa in front of the Water Tower entrance, a reconnaissance mission, no doubt. My mom chased after her, leaving my dad and me to bring up the rear. It was a shopping position we were accustomed to. My dad took a deep breath as we moved through the crowd.

"You smell that, Jake?"

"Hot dogs?"

"Nope. Bum piss. That's why your mom and I moved to the suburbs. Tell me something, you know about yellow snow, right?"

As usual, my dad was about five years late with any kind of helpful advice. And as usual, he picked the strangest moment to dispense it.

"Yeah, Dad. I know about yellow snow."

"Good. Just checking."

Up ahead, Lizzy ran up to Santa, grabbing his bell mid-ring.

"Is this store currently carrying redheaded Cabbage Patch dolls with freckles?"

Santa was slightly taken aback. "Excuse me?"

"Redheaded Cabbage Patch dolls with freckles. Preferably named Marcy May or Dawn Rebecca."

"How old are you, little girl?"

"That's irrelevant, Kringle. Whaddya got in there?"

"Well, uh, I'm not really sure what they carry inside here, Santa doesn't always know what—"

Lizzy cut through the BS and dropped a quarter into the bucket. A bribe. "Cabbage Patch, yes or no. The clock's ticking."

My mom finally caught up to her and scooped her up. "Lizzy, don't run away like that."

"Sorry, Mommy. I wanted to give Santa my allowance. For the poor kids."

"Oh, what a sweet little girl you are."

Lizzy faked a smile to my mom and stared daggers at Santa. Like most bell ringers, this one had not been particularly helpful. My mom carried Lizzy into the building and my dad and I followed. As the palpable wave of shopping-mall hell washed over the old man, I could hear him mutter hopefully, to no one in particular, "I wonder if they put a bar in here yet."

# CHAPTER THIRTEEN

In size and scope, Water Tower Place wasn't much different from any other Midwest shopping mall. It was the atmosphere that set it apart from the rest. Situated as the focal point of the Magnificent Mile a few blocks west of Lake Michigan, Water Tower Place symbolized all that was still classy about Chicago. Escalators ran smoother, robotic elves in window displays somehow looked more elf-like, the Christmas tree was three stories high, stuff like that. People dressed up to go Christmas shopping here. It was an event. From Wheaton to Winnetka, moms dragged their families through its revolving doors to pump cash into a well-oiled Christmas machine. The Doyles were just one of the many thousands of cogs in the wheel.

Even as a kid it was pretty easy to classify me as an anti-shopping guy. Most guys fall under that stereotype, I guess. But it's not necessarily a fair one. It's not that men as a whole don't like shopping, it's that we don't like shopping for crap that we don't want. And we don't like doing it under the rules and standards that are often enforced upon us. Men like to buy friends and loved ones gifts just as much as women do, they're just rarely given an opportunity to do so on their own terms. Heck, if you gave a guy a hundred-dollar bill and a stopwatch and dropped him off at the front of a mall and said, "You have five minutes to buy whatever you want. We're timing you for the record," then shopping might become our new favorite pastime. It's the hours and hours of waiting and walking and choosing and asking opinions and trying things on and looking for better prices that make most men hate it. That's madness. *That's* why guys hate shopping. My dad and I were no exception.

"What about this sweater? It's on sale," my mother shouted over racks of pleated pants.

"Eh." I shrugged. I was slumped over a fourth-floor railing next to my dad, contemplating jumping.

"What do you mean, 'eh'? What's wrong with it?"

"I dunno."

"Don't you think it would go nicely with your green turtleneck?"

"Eh . . . "

Over the years, I'd learned that giving indefinite answers to all apparel questions was the best way to combat the ever-increasing clothes-to-toys gift ratio. It was a strategy my dad also subscribed to, except he feigned even less interest and refused to ever try anything on. To the Doyle man, clothes did not count as a gift; they were more of an anti-gift—a deterrent to getting real gifts like fuzz busters and Nintendos. Our thinking was simple: The more clothing information they got out of us, the more clothes we were sure to get. So you had to be vague and indifferent at all times. Because if it ever got out that you actually *liked* a particular brand or a particular style, then you were sure to receive nothing but clothes for Christmas. And what could possibly be worse than that?

"Jake. Now what am I supposed to tell Grandma Doyle and Aunt Connie when they ask about clothes for you?"

You could tell them to get me *RBI Baseball* for my new Nintendo Entertainment System. That would be a start.

"John, what am I supposed to do here?"

"Eh. I dunno, honey."

After a few agonizing hours in the County Seat and—holy Christ—the goddamn Buster Brown shoe store, we stumbled back into the mall's main foyer to regroup. I had contracted one of my mall headaches—a pain that I was convinced could only be healed with a slice of Sbarro's, which no one would ever buy me. My dad wasn't doing much better. He was comparable to a pack mule by this point, shuffling sadly with the weight of almost a dozen bags. He'd now stopped talking altogether and had taken to closing his eyes whenever he sat down. Lizzy, on the other hand, was acting like a true professional. She'd been remarkably patient so far, humoring my mom with every clothing option she offered up. So when she mentioned maybe heading over to the toy section of Marshall Field's, my mom felt compelled to say yes.

The line in Marshall Field's to pay for a Cabbage Patch Kid stretched from the Frango mints all the way to prenatal care. It looked like something out of a Soviet filmstrip. Serious people with deprived and hardened faces, staring at nothing in particular, standing in line, clutching their dolls like loaves of bread, shuffling forward a few inches every couple of minutes. Security guards patrolled the area, keeping the peace and enforcing the "one Cabbage Patch Kid per customer" rule, conceivably in place to keep the dolls from being resold on the black market.

Right on cue, Lizzy's eyes got misty and she reached for my mom's hand. "Look at all these mommies buying Cabbage Patch dolls. Some girls sure are lucky."

"You know, Cabbage Patch dolls are very expensive, Lizzy."

"Maybe I should ask Santa."

"Why don't you just show me and Dad which kind you want, okay?"

Lizzy quickened her pace and headed to the toy section, passing untouched My Little Ponies and She-Ra action figures. From a distance you could tell that an entire wing of the toy department had been dedicated to Cabbage Patch Kids. A giant cut-out head of one of the dolls marked the area of the store dubbed "The Cabbage Patch." As we approached it, Lizzy began her pitch.

"You know what's most interesting about Cabbage Patch dolls, Daddy?"

My dad was now *walking* with his eyes closed. "What's that, dear?"

"Each one is an individual. Like snowflakes. You don't buy them; you adopt them. They come with their own papers. They even have real belly buttons."

"Yeah," I added. "I bet they'll be collector's items."

Collector's items? Nice one, Jake. Lizzy gave me a look that seemed to suggest I could do better. She continued with her pitch.

"So, the Cabbage Patch I want has red hair and freckles, preferably named Marcy May or Dawn Rebe—" She stopped dead in her tracks. The first Cabbage Patch aisle was completely empty. Four levels of shelves on either side completely bare. We moved to the second aisle—nothing. The third one was the same. Gone. They were all gone. Only one sad Cabbage Patch girl whose arm had been ripped off and three bald-headed boys were left. That was it.

Lizzy stood there with a scowl on her face, teetering between rage and sadness. Marshall Field's had been her last-ditch effort, the only store we'd heard of that still had dolls left in stock. There was nothing else she could do. She punched the one-armed girl in the head and promptly sat down on the floor.

My mother tried to make the best of the situation. "Look at all those nice Care Bears over there, Lizzy. Look how many of those they still have in stock."

"Yippee."

My dad picked her up and gave her a hug. Lizzy rarely ever cried real tears; usually they were prefabricated ones reserved to get me in trouble, but this looked like it might be the real deal. Her mouth quivered for a moment, she held her finger in the air as if to ask for more time, and then began to sob uncontrollably. It was a sob I could relate to, a sob of obsession and disappointment. I gave her a look of encouragement and thought about maybe going over there and patting her on the back or saying something nice. But just as I began to walk toward her, a flash of familiar gray plastic caught my eye . . . *Nintendo.*

Thirty yards away across the store was a state-of-the-art interactive Nintendo display. Blinking sensors and high-tech gadgetry surrounded it, lighting it up like some kind of Japanese Christmas tree. It was beautiful. All the familiar faces were there: Mario, Luigi, Mega Man, Donkey

Kong, Zelda, that midget wizard from *Kung-Fu*—everybody. They were all arranged as cardboard cutouts around a monitor. A crowd of probably twenty kids was gathered around it, chomping on free samples of Nintendo cereal and playing *Double Dragon*. As though pulled in by a tractor beam, I felt myself drifting toward the display. I wanted to yell at the top of my lungs and sprint over there, but I knew better. I had to be smart. I had to act casual about it. If my folks saw how gung-ho I was about the thing, they'd never buy it for me. I could just hear my dad's reaction: "Look how crazy about it he is in the store, for crying out loud! Imagine if he had it at home!"

But a familiar voice called out to me. Looking back, he sounded a lot like Kevin Spacey. It was the Nintendo.

*Hello Jake. How are you feeling?*

Fine.

*I think you're more than fine. I think you're about ready to scream. I think you want to run over here and cradle me in your arms. What are you waiting for?*

I gotta play it cool.

*Play it cool, huh? How's that been working out for you so far? Look into my monitor, Jake . . .*

My eyes began to widen and turn into little pinwheels.

*That's it. Succumb to your emotions.*

Don't mess with me, man, my folks are watching.

*Forget about them, they're worthless. Run over here. Get in line before someone else does . . .*

My arms began to stiffen and outstretch before me. I felt my feet move forward. My mom grabbed me by the shoulder. She hadn't noticed the display. "Jake. We're going to head to the bookstore upstairs. Watch your sister while we're gone."

"Uh-huh."

"Jake, are you listening to me?" She gathered up her bags. My dad still had his eyes closed. "We're going upstairs to buy a book for the Heffernans."

"The Heffernans?" My dad opened his eyes and set Lizzy down. "What the heck for? They never buy us anything."

"That's not the point, honey." My mom tapped her finger on my head like she was ringing a doorbell. "Jake. *Jake.*"

"Yeah?" I was still staring at the monitor.

"We're going upstairs for a few minutes. You can stay down here with the toys. Just watch your sister, okay?"

"Yeah, sure."

I didn't even wait for them to reach the escalator. As soon as they turned their backs I immediately floated toward the Nintendo crowd. Lizzy scurried behind me.

"What about my Cabbage Patch? What about our deal? We need a new plan of attack, Jake. Jake?"

*Pay her no attention, Jake. Come closer. That's it . . .*

Two kids about my age were at the *Double Dragon* controls. They were an odd pair: a preppy white kid in a Hinsdale soccer jacket and a skinny black kid in a Sox hat. Under normal circumstances they probably wouldn't have had anything to do with each other, but here in the toy department of Marshall Field's, they were united in carnage. That was the power of video game violence; it brought us all together. It was kind of heartwarming when you thought about it.

Nevertheless, the South Sider was doing his best to give the Hinsdale kid the business. "Come on, preppy. You gotta use your uppercut there."

"I'm trying." The preppy was having a hard time getting the hang of it.

"What you been playing? *Pac-Man?*"

"This level's hard."

"A girl with green hair is beating you up."

"She's got a whip."

"So kick her in the face!"

The preppy gave his guy a running start and accidentally jump-kicked himself off a third-story balcony. Instant death.

"Sucks to be you, man. Gotta watch out for that."

Now it was the South Sider's turn. He was approaching the cave section at the end of the fourth level. This was a tricky part where two behemoth baldheaded musclemen suddenly appeared at the cave's entrance. To get past them you had to kill them both with your bare hands. Just last week Mahoney had reached this exact spot.

*You know what to do, Jake.*

I called out from the back of the crowd. "Hey, use the backward-elbow move!"

"Huh?"

"Use the backward-elbow move. That's the only move that kills them."

"Elbow move?" The South Sider was jump-kicking back and forth between the men, doing his best not to get tossed around like a rag doll. "Don't bother me, man. You can't punch these guys, you gotta kick 'em."

*Come closer, Jake . . .*

I pushed my way forward. The kid only had a few life hearts left. "I'm serious. You gotta use a backward-elbow move. Get them both on one side of you and press A and the opposite direction."

"An elbow move's not gonna do—" THUD. A muscleman took one to the gut and stumbled backward. "Dang! That stuff works!" The crowd moved in a bit closer.

"Told ya. Just keep doing that for like two minutes or so. It takes a while, but they can't hurt you."

The South Sider slanted a glance toward me. The crowd was getting into it now. When the first muscleman went down for good, they actually clapped. When the second one went down, they flat-out cheered. Most of them had never seen level five before. Someone patted me on the back; another kid gave me a high five.

I pointed to the screen. "Now go in that cave right there. You gotta dodge the falling pointy rock things and kick the purple ninjas without falling into the lava."

"I don't know how to do that, man. I've never been here before."

"You want me to show you?"

"Not on my turn. Just wait till I—" CRUNCH. The crowd gasped as he was crushed by a falling rock.

The South Sider popped in a stick of gum and looked me over curiously. He turned to the preppy. "Take a walk, Bugle Boy. My man with the elbows is in."

"What? No fair. Come on."

"The Oak Brook game ain't gonna cut it downtown anymore."

"Oak Brook? I'm from Hinsdale."

"And I'm sure you got one at home. Go practice. Go on."

The preppy reluctantly handed over his controller. I cracked my knuckles, took out my retainer and dug in. The South Sider gave me a nod.

"You got one life left. Let's see what you got, Elbows."

The most important thing to note when playing *Double Dragon* is that there's a cadence to it, like fly-fishing or skee-ball. Once you got in a rhythm it was imperative that you stayed there. You dodge the first falling rock, you wait a beat, you jump-kick the bad guy, and then you hop over the lava. Dodge, jump-kick, hop over lava. Dodge, jump-kick, hop over lava. One, two-three. One, two-three. One, two-three. Before long I was dancing on 8-bit air. Tossing in elbows and uppercuts like a jazzman jamming out a solo.

"Dang, Elbows. You're in the zone."

The crowd began to grow. Little kids passing by started to drag their parents over to the display. People were craning their necks to see. More boxes of Nintendo cereal were cracked open. All around me I could hear people talking. Kids were making sales pitches and parents were starting to buy into it.

"Look, Mom, look how cool this level is!"

"I don't know, Kevin, this looks pretty violent. Is he throwing a knife?"

"It's just a pretend knife. Dad said Grandpa gave him a real knife when he was ten."

"It was a pocket knife, son."

"Kevin's not getting a pocket knife, honey."

"I don't want a pocket knife. I want a Nintendo. It's way safer. Can I get one, Mom? Pleeeeeaaaase?"

"It does look kind of entertaining, Maureen."

The fathers were coming around. The mothers could be next. It was up to me now. The fates of dozens of boys' Christmas hopes and dreams lay within my grasp. I had to give them a show. I jumped on top of a boulder and scissor-kicked three bad guys into a pit of fire.

"Ooooooh!"

Never before had my thumbs maneuvered with such efficiency. My response time was clicking at an all-star rate. Somehow I knew that if I ever found myself in a dark underground cavern crawling with purple ninjas, I'd now be able to hold my own.

Even Kevin Spacey was getting into it, *Karate Kid*–style.

*You're the best . . . around! Nothing's gonna ever keep you down! You're the best . . . around! Nothing's gonna ever keep you dowwwnn . . .*

"What'd you say your name was, Elbows?"

"I'm Jake. What's yours?"

"Marcus. You got one of these at home?"

"Nope. You?"

"I wish. Man, you're on fire! You're gonna get to level six!"

All other distractions, worries, responsibilities became irrelevant. My senses had reached a higher being. I'd become one with Nintendo. As I roundhouse-kicked two thugs with ponytails, Marcus started a chant.

"When I say, 'elbows,' you say, 'Jake.' Elbows. JAKE! Elbows. JAKE! When I say, 'elbows,' you say, 'Jake.' Elbows. JAKE! Elbows. JAKE!"

Before I knew it, every kid in Field's was chanting my name.

*You see, Jake? You see what Nintendo can do? This is your destiny.*

Beads of sweat ran down my face. My pulse quickened. My tongue wagged out of my mouth Michael Jordan–style. Minutes passed like seconds. I was doing it!

*Your name is Jake Doyle: Nintendo Master. Say it!*

My name is Jake Doyle: Nintendo Master.

*Again!*

My name is Jake Doyle: Nintendo Master!

*Say it out loud, you baby! Say it!*

"My name is Ja—"

"JAKE STEPHAN DOYLE!" It was my mother. She was standing next to me screaming in my ear. She may have been doing so for minutes. "Put that thing down!"

My father was there too. He had gone red in the face—a sign that the dragon had been woken. He grabbed me by the collar and in clear, overenunciated diction, bellowed out the four words most feared by older brothers the world over: "Where. Is. Your. Sister?"

Oh dear God in heaven.

All around me, little boys cringed. The proverbial record had been scratched. Fun time was officially over. I looked to Marcus, who was already backing away, doing his best to distance himself from the horror of horrors that I had apparently just gotten myself into. In the realm of punishable kid offences, losing a little sister ranked somewhere above grand theft auto and just slightly below lighting your grandma on fire.

Where was she? Where was Lizzy? The truth was, the last time I had consciously noticed her presence was all the way back at the Cabbage Patch aisle, maybe half an hour ago. I had no idea where she was! None whatsoever. She could be accepting candy from a stranger at this very moment. She could be in the back seat of a Chevy Malibu next to the kid from *I Know My First Name Is Steven*. She could be jammed in an escalator, metal teeth ripping her from limb to limb. She could be anywhere!

"Where is she, Jake?"

I couldn't get out an answer. I was still clutching the Nintendo controller in my sweaty hands as my body shook violently. "Uh . . . "

It was obvious I had no idea where she was. My dad dropped me like a sack of potatoes and began rushing around the store. My mom had already taken off in another direction, shouting Lizzy's name in a high-pitched shrill. This was serious.

"You're a dead man, bro," were the last words Marcus muttered before he dashed off down an escalator. The entire kid crowd had dispersed for fear of being guilty by association.

For a brief moment (and I'll emphasize *brief*), I considered remaining at the Nintendo display and getting in as much time with the game as possible. The thought being that these might be some of my last hours on earth, so why not make the most of them? But I quickly changed course when I realized where Lizzy could've ended up. If I could get to her before my parents did, there was still hope I would see my tenth birthday.

I took off in a dead sprint toward the Marshall Field's entrance. Under severe duress, moments of clarity often occur. Two such realizations had surfaced. One, allowing my sister to be kidnapped while playing Nintendo might be somewhat detrimental to my chances of receiving the system come Christmas morning. And two, the last thing I'd heard Lizzy talking about were Cabbage Patch Kids and needing a new plan of attack. When all else failed, you always had Santa to turn to. My guess was she was with him right now.

I took a shoulder to the revolving doors and stumbled out onto the Michigan Avenue sidewalk. Sure enough, there was Lizzy, about twenty yards away, chewing the ear off of the same Salvation Army Santa Claus she'd harassed on the way in.

"Lizzy! Lizzy!"

She glanced over and gave a little wave, not so much to say hello as to say, "don't bother me; I'm doing business here." She went right back to questioning Santa.

" . . . and do they speak English at the North Pole?"

"Yes."

"Even the elves?"

"Yes, little girl, even the elves."

"Even the elves that make the Cabbage Patch dolls?"

Santa was seriously reconsidering his role with the Salvation Army by this point. "Yep. Those elves too, kid."

I ran up beside her. "Lizzy! Where were you? Mom and Dad are gonna kill you."

"No. They're gonna kill you. You were supposed to be watching me. Nintendo-no-friendo, Jake."

"Wait a second. Just because I didn't help enough with the Cabbage Patch?"

She smiled coyly. "You probably should tell Mom and Dad I'm out here, don't you think?"

"Stay here. Don't move. Santa, don't let her go anywhere."

Son of bitch, Lizzy was sneaky. Why was she always getting one up on me? I ran back into the mall's entrance and spotted my mom talking to a security guard.

"Mom! Mom! I found her! She's outside. Right out here!"

My mom rushed over, practically knocking me to the ground as she ran through the doors and out onto the sidewalk. By the time I got back out there, she was nearly crying.

"Don't ever do that again, Lizzy. You scared me half to death."

"Sorry, Mommy."

"What are you doing out here?"

"Talking to Santa. They might still have Cabbage Patch dolls at the North Pole! Even ones with red hair! Santa just said so!"

"Lizzy, we told you to stay with Jake."

"He was playing Nintendo."

"We'll talk to him. Where is he?"

I was already hiding behind a garbage can, doing my best to tunnel a hole in the ground. I'd heard Australia was nice this time of year. My dad came barreling out onto the sidewalk and made a beeline for me.

"God bless America, Jake! You play that stuff and your head goes to mush in three minutes!"

"Sorry, Dad. I'm really sorry."

"She's your sister! It's not like losing your retainer, for cripes' sake!"

My retainer . . . Right. Cautiously I ran my tongue over my teeth. Nope. No retainer. I subtly checked my pockets. Wrong again. This was turning out to be quite an afternoon.

My dad took a step closer, smelling the fear. "Open your mouth, Jake."

"Huh?"

"You heard me. Open your mouth."

The actual cost of my retainer had been explained to me in the simple terms of "if you lose it, don't bother coming home." I figured it cost roughly as much as a new car. Carefully, I parted my lips and opened up just enough so you couldn't see my teeth or the roof of my mouth, a slack-jawed look of desperation. I was stalling for time.

"*Open* it, Jake."

"Hey, did you ever find out if they put a bar inside the mall yet?"

"I said open it!"

My mother shuffled over. "John, do you have the Sharper Image bag?"

It was just the distraction I needed. My dad looked

down for a brief second and I took off like a shot down the sidewalk. At first I thought, maybe I'll just run away. You know, for good. Become a hobo in Peoria or something. But then I thought, technically the old man hadn't seen the retainer. He didn't know if it was in my mouth or not, technically at least. If I could find it and get to it before he got to me, I might not be completely destroyed. I took a hard left back into Water Tower Place and began the frantic search for it.

Few truly know the evil that lurks within the plastic mind of a retainer. They're deceitful little objects, far smarter than missing keys or socks. Chances are, if your retainer wasn't in your mouth, it had probably made its way into any one of a number of incomprehensible hiding spots. I'd lost the thing dozens of times before and had stumbled across it everywhere from the pickle jar in the fridge to Elwood's doghouse. It had a mind of its own.

You had to wonder why retainers were removable in the first place. At what drunken dental convention did that sound like a good idea for kids? "I know, Steve, let's give the children the option of taking this gross piece of plastic out of their mouths whenever they see fit! Brilliant!" I'd worn my retainer for over two years now and my teeth still looked like a collection of off-white Legos. So, in my book, retainers were nothing more than an orthodontic ploy calculated to promote ulcers in children. To this day I still don't trust orthodontists.

I galloped up the escalator stairs two at a time, ducking under bags and pushing through packs of shoppers. My guess was that I'd lost the retainer somewhere near the Nintendo display. I didn't dare glance behind me, but I knew my dad was back there somewhere, chasing after me at a competitive jog. This was probably even fun for him, a little excitement in the mall for a change. Once a promising athlete, he relished those moments when he could turn on the old Doyle jets. He was going to catch his son retainerless and take charge of this shopping trip once and for all.

I reached the top of the escalator and scanned the area. A crowd had gathered around the Nintendo again, a fresh crop of boys with no idea of the havoc I'd just caused. They stood around chomping on cereal and genuinely enjoying themselves. Looking up toward the counter, I caught a glimpse of my dad in a surveillance mirror. He was hot on my tail, right at the bottom of the escalator on the opposite side of the Marshall Field's foyer. If I didn't find this thing intact in about ten seconds, I'd be in some serious trouble.

Then I heard it . . .

The sound of plastic scraping tile. It was a sound I was very familiar with. Whenever Dan Delund got bored during bathroom breaks, he would pick me up, tip me over and shake out the contents of my pockets, kicking everything that landed on the floor directly into the girls' bathroom. That sound I was hearing, it was the sound of my retainer being kicked.

I spun around. Sure enough, there it was, thirty yards away, right in the middle of pedestrian traffic, indiscriminately being knocked about by boots and shoes, sliding in the mush, in danger of being squashed at any moment. As expensive as retainers were, they were about as durable as Pixie Stix. They'd crack on a windy day if you weren't careful. All it took was one direct crunch of a boot and it would be all over.

"Jake!"

My dad had spotted me. He was stuck behind a group

of old ladies on the middle of the escalator. Although he couldn't see it, the retainer was lying at an equal distance directly between him and me. It was a father-son standoff. I only had one shot at this. A fire lit deep within me and I made a mad dash for the foyer. Everything else around me went into slow motion. A blur. The only thing I saw was my retainer lying there on the ground. Thirty feet to go . . . I pictured myself charging home plate at Wrigley Field as the crowd roared. Twenty feet to go . . . My legs were pistons pounding under me; my arms cut through the wind with each vaulting step. Ten feet . . . I dove into a headfirst slide, sucking up sludge and dirt, propelling myself under legs and passersby. In one swift motion I scooped up the crud-soaked piece of plastic and popped it into my mouth. Still sliding, I slowed to a stop at my father's feet as he hopped off the escalator. Like an umpire looking for the ball, he pointed to my mouth with authority. I opened wide and smiled a plastic smile.

Safe.

# CHAPTER FOURTEEN

The "Water Tower Fiasco," as it came to be known, blew over relatively easily. My father was dead tired from shopping and from our standoff. My mother was happy with her on-sale purchases, and Lizzy was content with the knowledge that Cabbage Patch Kids were still readily available at the North Pole. So much so that she took mercy on me and decided not to play up my Nintendo obsession as the main culprit behind her disappearance. So, miraculously, I was pretty much in the clear. My dad made great time on the way home; we even made a pit stop for Happy Meals. The Christmas Spirit surely was upon us.

But reality set in again at school the next day. It was the final day of wreath selling and everyone was on pins and needles. The only thing helping me to hold it together was my Christmas ornament project.

Over the past two weeks my "ornament" had grown to such a degree that I was forced to move from my desk in the classroom to the hallway, where I had more room to spread out. Physical constraints should never hinder a true artist.

Recently I had decided to cover my already unusually large donkey in papier-mâché. It was not a wise choice. The donkey was now the size of a small dog, in danger of crushing the manger itself. It looked like Godzilla come to wreak havoc on Bethlehem. The other animals scattered about didn't help matters much. They were all deformed and dripping with glue, sort of an accidental Salvador Dali effect. Furthermore, most of them lacked the ability to stand, so they were all lumped together in a pile next to the manger, as if they'd just been slaughtered. Chickens and horses, and deer for some reason, all piled on top of each other, all overlooking the birth of Christ. The whole thing was a mess. But I was so convinced Ciarocci would love it that I just kept building more and more. Most kids were making paper bells and tiny wreaths with their class pictures on them—you know, *ornaments*. I was building a village with monsters and deformed religious icons.

The three Wise Men were pretty standard. Gumdrop heads and cotton balls for beards. Their bodies were made from hardened macaroni. Mary and Joseph looked about the same, except without the beards. The Baby Jesus was just one single gumdrop with toothpicks sticking out for arms and legs, giving the appearance of some kind of Chinese throwing star. In fact, I'd had to make several versions of him because Delund kept whipping them across the room at Angela Moran's face.

I think he liked her.

The manger itself, though, was the real work of genius. I'd found an old JCPenney shoebox at home and with magic marker turned the J into Jesus and the C into Christ. Pure genius. Then I cut out the front of the box so it looked like an open-faced building of sorts, a manger, if you will. I'd brought some Lincoln Logs in from home, carefully explaining to everyone that, no, I did not play with them anymore, I just happened to have them lying around and used the logs to create an awning across the front of the box. Then I brought in real dirt and grass and crud and packed it inside the box. Some grass I even glued to the outside of the box to make it really authentic. A true masterpiece.

"Jee-zus."

You said it, man, I thought, holding up the gumdrop.

"What a mess."

I turned around to find Mahoney looking over the carnage. Everyone has a friend who tells it like it is. That friend was Mahoney.

"I thought we were supposed to be making ornaments."

"Yeah, so?"

"So this is the biggest ornament I've ever seen. What's with the giant Goat Man?"

"That's a donkey."

"It looks like my butt."

Things were always looking like Mahoney's butt. Zilinski poked his head into the hallway.

"Hey, how'd you get all those gumdrops, Jake? Can I have one?"

Leave it to Zilinski to sniff out stale candy in the middle of cold-and-flu season. I tossed him a rock-hard gumdrop and he popped it in his mouth. Crunching away, he laid it on us.

"So, did you guys hear about Farmer?"

"No. What?"

"A hundred and twenty-nine wreaths."

"No way."

"Way. A hundred and twenty-nine. Even if he's lying and he only sold half of that, that's still like . . . "

"Sixty-four and a half wreaths." Mahoney was also very good at math.

"He's lying. There's no way he has that many."

"Well, how many do you have, Jake?"

This was a very tricky question. The only person who was giving up any information about how many wreaths he'd sold was Josh Farmer. The rest of us were playing it close to the vest. Who was to say that by announcing you'd sold thirty-nine wreaths that someone couldn't just go out and sell one more and beat you just before the final buzzer? It did not pay to take chances this late in the game, and all of HC Wilson was keeping its collective trap shut.

"How many do you have, Zilinski?"

"I'm not telling."

"Well, then I'm not telling either."

"Fine."

"Fine."

"Okay, then."

"Fine."

"*Fine.*"

There was no real retort to "fine" except to repeat it.

"*Fine.*"

"Fine!"

"Will you two shut up. I've sold more wreaths than both of you anyway."

Mahoney was cut short when Miss Ciarocci sauntered out into the hallway. She was wearing her oversized Grateful Dead Summer of 1984 T-shirt as a smock over her blue- and yellow-flower patterned dress. (Not that I was paying attention or anything.) She smiled and patted me on the head. She was always patting me on the head. My God, woman, why must you toy with my emotions!

"Huh-huh, hi, Miss Ciarocci."

"I see you've added more animals to the manger scene, Jake. You must be really passionate about this project."

Yes, I'm a very passionate individual, actually.

"Uh, yeah . . . "

"How come Jake gets to use gumdrops and no one else does?" Zilinski whined.

"Jake had a very ambitious project in mind, and because of that he needed more ambitious materials. Does that make sense, Steve?"

"Not really."

"Well, tell you what, Steve. On our Valentine's Day project coming up, you can use whatever candy you like." She crouched down at eye level to all three of us. "How does that sound?"

"Okay . . . "

The three of us were now flush faced and drooling. Years later I would learn that every boy in Ciarocci's class was in love with her. It kind of made me angry, actually. I'd thought I was the only one.

"I like what you've done with all the foliage, Jake."

Foliage? I stared blankly into her eyes.

"You know, *foliage*. The grass and leaves you put in here. I think many students might make the mistake of putting pine needles for Christmas in manger scenes. But you knew that they didn't have Christmas trees or wreaths in Bethlehem."

Right, right. Actually, speaking of Christmas wreaths . . . "Hey Miss Ciarocci?"

"Yes, Jake?" She stood up and smiled.

"Um . . . would you, uh, would you like to buy a Cub Scout Christmas wreath from me?"

Mahoney and Zilinski looked at me like I had balls of steel. Ciarocci gently pushed her hair back behind her ears and smiled. I was practically melting.

"Oh, how sweet. I'd love to, Jake . . . "

Yes, yes . . .

" . . . but I already bought one from Josh."

# CHAPTER FIFTEEN

The rows and rows of metal folding chairs squeaked uncomfortably beneath us. The cafeteria was pitch black, the only light coming from the waxy candles we held in our hands. Forty-five Cub Scouts sat patiently in the dark, fitted in our dress blues and golden handkerchiefs, each one of us thoroughly convinced that by the end of tonight's meeting we'd be going home with our very own Nintendo.

Our pudgy pack leader, Mr. Halberg, stood at the front of the cafeteria, his Vietnam medals and Jefferson Airplane buttons glistening in the flickering light. He too wore a Cub Scout uniform. That always seemed a little odd to me, much the same way it seemed odd that baseball managers had to wear full baseball uniforms. Why was that? Seeing Halberg in a Cub Scout uniform was like seeing Don Zimmer in tight pants and Yankee pinstripes. There was no need for it.

With the mood now set to his liking, Halberg addressed the pack.

"Gentlemen. As the cub ventures further out on his

own, he realizes more and more the value of his troop. This candle is a symbol of the courage and unity that our pack instills in us. It is the shining beacon of Cub Scout initiative. It is the hope of a better Pinewood Derby. It is the breath of life in your water-safety merit badges. It is the creative enlightenment that guides your shadow puppetry . . . "

Oh, get on with it, Halberg. The man was always making speeches. He was just one example in the long list of letdowns that came with joining the Cub Scouts. Initially, we'd all signed up for the paramilitary kid organization with illusions of dagger-sized pocketknives and big-game safaris west of Rockford. So far, all we had to show for it were a few VFW pancake breakfasts and a campout in Olsen's backyard. The entire experience had been a disappointment, but that was all about to change.

Halberg continued. " . . . Look deeply into the candle's flame. Stare into its dancing light. Make a mental picture of it. Now . . . close your eyes. What do you see?"

Forty-five visions of Nintendo blazed before us. The moment of truth was about to be had. I gave a quick, nervous look around. Conor Stump was sitting next to me, dabbing blindly at the wax of his candle. Sure enough, he took a little bite, burning his tongue.

"You see the flame, gentlemen. It burns even when your eyes are closed. And even when we blow these candles out. The Cub Scout flame will never fade. It will remain with you forever."

Halberg blew out his candle and flicked on the lights. You could tell he was a little choked up about his speech. He pulled out his notebook as we squirmed in our seats. "A lot to go over tonight, gents. The annual chili cook-off; we're marching in the Batavia Loyalty Day parade; uh, the father-son campout is coming up, which unfortunately will be held in the gym again . . . Uh, I've got another great 'Nam poem for you boys, entitled 'A Tie Is Not a Loss.'"

A voice yelled out from the back row. "Get to the wreaths, Halberg!" It was Dan Delund. He'd never been to a Cub Scout meeting before in his life.

Halberg shielded his eyes, trying to decipher who the heck the kid in the Mötley Crüe T-shirt was. "I'm sorry? Who is that back there?"

"The wreaths, fatso."

"I beg your pardon? Are you in this troop?"

"I'm here, ain't I?"

Someone else called out. "Just do the wreaths, Halberg!"

"Yeah, do the wreaths!"

"Yeah, wreaths!"

All forty-five of us began a collective chant-whine. "WREATHS! WREATHS! WREATHS!" Chanting was very big in the Cub Scouts.

"Alright, alright, alright. We can do the wreath prizes first."

"HOORAY!"

Oh, this was it! Anticipation gripped us like a Darth Vader choke hold. Everyone leapt out of their seats and piled into a huddle at the base of the cafeteria stage. Halberg stepped into the janitor's closet and wheeled out a large cart with three sheet-covered prizes on it. They were marked *First*, *Second* and *Third*. First prize looked even bigger than a normal NES system. My mind immediately raced through the possibilities. Maybe it came with a selection of games as well, a Power Pad, a couple boxes of Nintendo cereal—the possibilities were as awesome as they were endless.

"I know you boys have really been selling hard this year. And I wanted to make sure we got the best prizes yet." Halberg cleared his throat and checked his list. "So, without further ado. In third place, with fifty-three wreaths sold . . . "

Yes, yes . . .

"Joshua Farmer!"

A round of applause was met with a smattering of laughter and snickering. Considering Farmer's self-proclaimed wreath totals had reached somewhere in the high hundreds yesterday, this was a delight to us all. Anybody had a chance now.

Farmer trudged up onto the stage to claim his consolation prize. Halberg lifted the sheet, revealing a small box. Farmer cracked the lid and shook out the contents. A postcard fluttered to the floor. He picked it up and read it out loud. "A two-year subscription to *Boys' Life*."

More laughter. A lousy magazine subscription? Oh, the irony. Farmer hopped off the stage, grabbed his coat and walked directly out the door, tossing the card in the trash as he went by. A month's worth of hard work down the drain. I cackled quietly to myself.

Halberg did his best to calm us down. "Okay, okay, quiet down now. In second place, with fifty-five wreaths sold, Conor . . . Conor Stump!"

Applause and shock. Holy cow, Conor Stump! None of us had even seen Stumpty Dumpty outside after school, let alone going door to door selling wreaths. It was the upset of the year. Conor carefully approached the stage, grinning from ear to ear, probably just delighted with the fact that someone actually knew his name. He waved to the crowd.

Halberg lifted the second sheet, revealing a midsized

cardboard box. "Second prize is a globe of the Earth that lights up! Compliments of Bulldog Office Supply." Conor ripped the lid open and gasped when he saw what else was inside. The box was packed full with Styrofoam peanuts.

"Cool."

He wasted no time and popped a few in his mouth, chewing happily as he exited the stage. Man, Conor Stump, what a nut. I'd pay a hundred bucks to know what that guy's up to these days. He's probably running a Fortune 500 company.

"And now, the winner of this year's wreath-selling contest, with a prize compliments of Geitner Toys and Books—with an unbelievable eighty-two wreaths sold . . . Ryan Grusecki!"

Drat! Eighty-two wreaths? That was crazy. I'd tapered off around fifty, but eighty-two? How was that even possible? Ryan Grusecki and his twin brother, Tommy, jumped up and down, screaming at the top of their lungs. It wasn't until later that they revealed their underhanded coalition that combined their individual wreath totals into one lump sum to secure the victory. It was a stroke of genius.

Ryan sprinted up onto the stage, still in shock, gasping for breath like a housewife on *The Price Is Right*. "I did it! I did it!"

The crowd applauded politely as disappointment sunk in. Not winning my own Nintendo was a tough pill to swallow, but at least someone reasonable had won it. No longer would we have to suffer under Timmy Kleen's Nintendo dictatorship. We immediately began vying for position at the Grusecki household.

"Great job, Ryan!"

"Way to go, man!"

"Sweet gym shoes!"

"You're way cooler than your brother!"

Halberg stood behind the massive first prize, holding the sheet between his thumb and forefinger. What other glorious additions to the Nintendo could be under that sheet? What if it came with a TV too? What if every game ever released was under there? What if there was stuff under that sheet that we'd never even heard of before? There was no telling. Grusecki bounced up and down like he had to go to the bathroom really bad. Halberg shushed the pack and laid it on us.

"And this year's first prize, the best we've had in years . . . " He tugged back on the sheet like a magician and spread his arms out wide, unveiling the treasure . . .

"A brand new set of *World Book Encyclopedias!*"

Shock hit Troop 101—horrible, terrible, dog-run-over-by-ice-cream-truck shock. *Encyclopedias?* Forty-five of us stood there under the florescent cafeteria lights unable to move a muscle. I dropped to my knees. My guts felt like they'd been ripped out. The world went black and sound ceased to exist.

When I finally came to, all I could hear was screaming. Apparently, Geitner Toys and Books had noticed the stunning demand for toys over books this Christmas and had modified their donation to encyclopedias instead of a Nintendo.

It was like winning more school.

Dan Delund stood up, punched Tommy Grusecki in the jaw and walked out the fire exit. Swear words not even learned yet fired off in my mind. *Encyclopedias?* How could they? Poor Ryan Grusecki fought off the tears unsuccessfully. And had I known things would only get worse, I might have joined him.

# CHAPTER SIXTEEN

The rest of the Cub Scout meeting was a blur. I couldn't tell you a thing that happened. I don't think anybody could. Eventually Halberg realized we were a broken bunch and let us leave early. We filed out of the school and into the night, numb to the world, each of us finding his own small section of the sidewalk to whimper on in private.

I sat down on the curb and waited for my dad's headlights to make their way up the circular driveway. The air somehow felt colder than usual. There was no socializing tonight, no snowball throwing as we waited for our parents, no ice sliding, no loogie spitting. Troop 101 was in mourning. The Gruseckis sat at the bottom of the jungle gym tearing pages out of their encyclopedias and tossing them into the wind. They went as far as to try to hide the books in the snow when their mom pulled up, but she made them take them home anyway. It was a cruel world.

My dad finally sped up the circle, and I trudged over to the front door and got in.

"What's with you?"

"Nothing."

I sat there fiddling with my yellow handkerchief. The Chicago Blackhawks were playing on the radio. Not even the witty on-air banter of my favorite announcers, Pat Foley and Dale Tallon, were going to cheer me up. And why should they? I was born a Hawks fan, and as such, I was born to lose. Winters with the Hawks, summers with the Cubs, and all of it without a Nintendo. It was a painful existence.

"Hey Dad, did you ever have a Christmas where you didn't get what you wanted?"

"Just a sec, just a sec." He turned up the game. The boys had been on a tear lately, and the old man was in the thick of it. Chicago Stadium was buzzing from the ice to the rafters. Pat Foley's voice danced over the airwaves.

*"A minute left in the power play. Larmer down the near side, back to Savard, over to Wilson, back to Savard . . ."*

"Come on, come on . . . "

*"Back to the point, cross-ice pass to Larmer, fakes the shot, over to Savard, spinarama—he shoots—he SCORES! Denny Savard!"*

"Alright!" The old man banged on the wheel. "Haha! Dipsy-do to you, Lemieux! Would have been nice to catch that one on TV, Wirtz. You putz!"

Every man has his nemesis. My father's was "Dollar Bill" Wirtz, the twisted, money hungry owner of the Chicago Blackhawks. A man so evil that he refused to televise home games in the hopes that it would somehow increase ticket sales. My dad was not so much a Hawks fan as he was a Wirtz enemy. A fact that the pile of smashed-up radios in our garage could attest to.

"You can't run an organization like this, you fathead! Ha-ha!"

*"And Claude Lemieux did not like that goal one bit, partner. He gave Savard a shot right in the back and is still jawing at him."*

"Quit your whining, Claude, you Sally!"

My dad also hated the decidedly *French* Canadian winger/wuss, Claude Lemieux.

"You're all talk, no walk, Lemieux. You hear what I'm saying, Jake?"

"Uh-huh."

"Always remember, a big talker like Lemieux isn't worth a hill of beans. All talk, no walk, worst combination a man can have. Now . . . what do you know about Cabbage Patch dolls?"

Um . . . what? I stared at him blankly.

"Cabbage Patch dolls. What do you know about them?"

"I don't want a Cabbage Patch doll, Dad."

"Yeah, I know, Jake, but you're a kid, you know what they look like, right?"

"I guess."

"Good."

What was going on here? I looked out the window. We weren't on the way home. In fact, we were fast approaching Kirk Road, headed toward neighboring Aurora, the future home of *Wayne's World* and current home to rampant gang-related violence, as seen on the nightly news. Aurora was like that creepy neighbor's yard you never went into, not even if your baseball was lying just over the fence in plain view. It was too dangerous. Josh Farmer said he saw a guy get stabbed in the knee in Aurora once. I was scared of the place.

"Where are we going?"

"To see a guy."

"About what?"

"Cabbage Patch dolls."

"A guy about Cabbage Patch dolls? Dad, I don't wanna—"

"For crying out loud, it's not for you, it's for Lizzy. I need your help. Do you know how hard it is to find one of them at this time of year? Especially one with red hair and freckles?"

"What about Santa?"

My dad struggled with that one a bit.

I'd been well aware of the relationship my parents had with the big man. They had final say over Santa on any gift choices, which is why I was out of luck with a Nintendo, but I couldn't imagine my father having concerns of a doll making you fat.

"Even Santa's having a hard time with Cabbage Patch dolls this year, Jake."

Outside, the houses and picket fences had turned to deserted buildings and dark alleys. Even the Fox River looked scary here in downtown Aurora. My dad turned a few shady corners and pulled to a stop outside of an old factory.

"Alright. This is it. Stay close and let me do the talking."

We got out of the minivan and stood there waiting, for what, I wasn't sure. My dad split a stick of Wrigley's between us, trying his best to look like he knew what he was doing. Born and raised on the South Side of Chicago, John Doyle was not about to have his street cred tarnished by suburban Aurora, even if his reason for being here was, in fact, to purchase a doll for a five-year-old girl.

After what felt like an eternity, a man walked out from the shadows across the street. He wore a Members

Only jacket and tight leather pants. I specifically remember the leather pants because they looked like they would be extremely uncomfortable when it dropped below freezing outside. And it was definitely below freezing right now.

Leather Pants walked up to my dad cautiously—and stiffly because of the pants. As he got closer he outstretched his arms, as though he was about to be cuffed and taken to jail on the spot.

"Alright, alright, officer, what is it this time?"

My dad looked him over. "I'm not a cop."

"You know, if you're a cop, you gotta tell me, right? That's the law."

"Look, pal, I'm not a cop, alright? I got this address from—"

"What about the kid?"

"The kid?" My father was not amused. "Yeah, that's it. The kid's a cop. I got a whole team of 'em down at the station. Ponies and puppy dogs too, undercover ones."

"Alright, alright, just playing it safe, is all, no need to get testy. So, whaddya want?"

My dad tugged at his collar and took a quick look around. He leaned in. "Word is, you've come into a little cabbage."

The man lit a cigarette and smiled. "Step into my office, gentlemen."

He brought us around to a side street and down an adjacent alley to his parked '79 Cutlass. Now, I'd never been down an alley before, so this was very exciting to me. I kept a lookout for Oscar the Grouch and stray cats eating fish bones, but none of them materialized. When we got to his car, he got down to business.

"You got cash on you, right?"

South Side Johnny Doyle was way ahead of him. "Let's see the stuff first."

Leather Pants walked us around to the back of the car.

"I'm gonna need a girl with freckles, you know. Or no deal."

"Not a problem." The man took out his keys and popped the trunk. "Best patch in the Tri-Cities." He pulled off a tarp, revealing what must have been two dozen Cabbage Patch dolls. They were lying neatly in two rows, covered in blankets, with only their heads poking out—almost as if they'd all been tucked into bed for the night in the trunk of the car. It was a little unsettling, actually.

The old man gave me a look. Were these authentic? I leaned in a bit closer and gave them the once over. Real Cabbage Patch Kids, as I'd been told by Lizzy time and time again, could be easily identified by their nose and their smell. Their noses were quite intricate, as these were, and they smelled remarkably like a newborn baby. I took a whiff. Yep, these were the real McCoy. I gave my dad a nod.

"You're sure?"

"Yeah, Dad. But there aren't any freckles on the redhead."

"No," said Leather Pants. "The freckles are on the blonde over there."

"It's gotta be on a redhead, though."

"You got a thing for redheads, kid?"

You got a thing for size-three Walter Paytons up your nose?

"The doll's not for him, it's for his sister."

"Well, I ain't got a redhead with freckles. Not right now, anyway."

"Listen, Mac, I need a redhead with freckles or we don't have a deal."

"Well, this ain't a make-your-own-pizza-pie here, pal. This is all I got."

My dad stood his ground. Leather Pants adjusted his leather pants and tried another route. "Okay, look, I had this lady once, few weeks ago, she was lookin' for a black-haired, green-eyed bit. All I got is a blonde with green eyes. She says she'll just dye the doll's hair . . . badda-bing, badda-bip-bip-boop, she's got a black-haired, green-eyed Cabbage Patch. Eh?"

"That worked?"

"Like a charm."

"How much?"

"A hundred."

"A *hundred*!"

"Where else you gonna find one, man? This close to Christmas? Every store from St. Charles to Schaumburg's out of 'em."

"I'm not paying a hundred dollars for a doll, and that's final. Sixty bucks, maybe."

"Ninety."

"Seventy bucks, and that's as high as I go. I got the name of three Mexican brothers at the train station in West Chicago selling for sixty, and I'll go there right now if I have to."

"The Diaz brothers? You don't want their baldheaded junk anyway. Seventy-five dollars, and that's my final offer."

The old man quivered and rubbed his chin. "Fine. Seventy-five. Maybe you can buy yourself a real pair of pants."

Nice one, Dad.

The old man pulled out the money from his pocket and lifted the doll from under the blanket, only to uncover a shocking revelation.

"What the—?" To our surprise, the Cabbage Patch Kid had no clothes on. None whatsoever. My dad put a hand over my eyes, shielding me from the indecency. "What the hell is this?"

"What?"

"Whaddya mean, what? Where the hell are her clothes?"

"Hey man, you didn't say nothin' about no clothes, clothes are extra, you gotta go see Victor down on Route 31 for clothes."

"Jiminy Cricket! I can't give my daughter a naked doll, for crying out loud! My wife will kill me!"

"I don't do clothes, man. It just complicates things. 'I want this dress, I want that dress. I want a stinking space suit.' No, you want the doll, you get the doll. That's it."

"This is bullshit!"

Yeah. Bullshit.

"What do you want me to do? I ain't got no clothes."

"Sixty bucks, then, or I walk."

"We'll make it seventy. Final offer. Look, I can see how much your boy wants the doll."

"It's not for me! Dad, this is stupid!"

"It's okay, Jake. Sixty dollars. That's all you're gonna get. Yes or no?"

Leather Pants wavered for a moment, then grabbed the money. "Deal."

My dad stuffed the doll in his coat, grabbed me by the shoulders and walked me out of the alley. A small smile made its way onto his face. "Down from a hundred bucks to sixty. You see that, Jake?"

"What about her clothes and her hair?"

"We'll get it all straightened out. Don't you worry. Just keep this whole thing a secret, alright?"

"Alright."

"Your sister's gonna love it."

Of course she would. Like always, Lizzy was going to get exactly what she wanted for Christmas, while I was probably going to get nothing but books and clothes. Somewhere off in the cold distance, a Christmas concerto could be heard. Compliments of Lizzy Doyle, once again playing the parental unit like a fiddle.

## CHAPTER SEVENTEEN

Timmy Kleen may have been a spaz and an asshole, but he was no dummy. He was the only Cub Scout in the cafeteria who smiled when Halberg pulled the sheet back on those encyclopedias. Because that meant his Nintendo had become twice as valuable. This deep into December, there was no way any of us could get our own Nintendos before Christmas now. It was an impossibility, a pipe dream, one that Kleen knew he could capitalize on big time.

The following Saturday morning, the line to get into Kleen's house was no longer a line. It was a mob. Half the school had descended onto his front yard like a swarm of locusts, pushing and shoving and generally trading unpleasantries. Not only did Kleen still have the only Nintendo in town, but word was that he had just gotten the Power Glove as an early Christmas present. This was very big news.

We'd been reading about the Power Glove in *Nintendo Power* magazine for months, staring at pictures, drooling over the technology. Its engineering was revolutionary. It was as though the future had decided to grace the Nintendo Corporation with a gift: a glove that you wore on your hand that allowed you to control the game with a flick of your wrist. The thing made Luke Skywalker's metal hand-replacement look like a Tinkertoy. As far as we were concerned, it was the missing link to humans finally becoming man-robots. And there wasn't a boy among us who wouldn't run over his own family to become a man-robot. That went without saying.

Farmer tapped me on the shoulder. "I heard the Power Glove has a suction cup thing that sticks right into your brain."

"Does not."

"Does too. It makes moves for you before you even think of them. My uncle works for Nintendo."

Of course Josh Farmer's uncle worked for Nintendo. Of course he did.

"Stop talking, Farmer, would ya?"

I was pinned up against the bottom of the porch steps, between a few second graders, trying to figure out what I would offer Kleen as payment to get inside. With the addition of the Power Glove, free admission into his Nintendo lair had gone out the window. You had to pay to play from now on. "One Micro Machine or higher," as he put it. That meant that unless you had at least one Micro Machine to pony up you weren't getting in. I was not a Micro Machine guy myself, so I could only guess at its toy equivalent. I came armed with a couple of M.U.S.C.L.E. Men (small plastic figures of bizarre character) and a shitty paddleball thing I got from my aunt after she went to Mexico. It said something in Spanish on it, I think.

"Hey kid!"

I looked up to see Kurt Marshall skidding up on his bike. His sack of *Kane County Chronicle* newspapers was slung across his shoulders. Kurt was thirteen, with a real job—practically an adult. He had real-world responsibilities and a serious social obligation not to be seen with a bunch of third graders, but it appeared that even he wanted in on this Power Glove action. "How many people do you think this kid's gonna let in today?"

"I dunno, gotta be more than ten this time. Gotta be. What about your papers? Don't you have to deliver them, still?"

"You kidding me? Getting fired's worth it if I get a look at this glove."

The door opened and the crowd forced its way forward. Kleen stepped out onto the porch, his hands stuffed into the pockets of his bathrobe. We all stopped pushing, and a few kids actually kind of bowed down before him. This was getting ridiculous.

"Good morning, children of Batavia!" I'm not kidding, this was seriously how he talked. "I suspect that many of you have heard a rumor regarding an early Christmas present . . . "

You could hear a gumball drop. We leaned forward. Yes? Yes? Did he really have a Power Glove? Was he going to let us use it?

"I'm here to tell you . . . that rumor is true!"

Kleen pulled his right hand from his bathrobe pocket and thrust a clenched fist high into the air. It was the Power Glove, alright. My God, it was even more beautiful in person. Its metallic plastic sparkled in the morning sun. Zilinski shrieked with delight. It was practically a religious experience.

The offers immediately began pouring in.

"Over here, Kleen! Lemme in! I got a Madball for ya!"

"I got a brand-new Cobra Commander!"

"Three Ewoks!

"Take my little brother!"

"I brought my fish!"

Evan Olsen held up his pet goldfish, Rick Sutcliffe, in a Ziplock bag. I couldn't believe it. He loved that fish. Everyone pushed and shoved as Kleen, one by one, had a look at what we had to offer. My paddleball thing and M.U.S.C.L.E. Men didn't seem very promising anymore.

"You there." Kleen pointed his Power Glove at Jeff Hartwell. "What do you got?"

"I got a five-dollar bill from my First Communion."

"Get inside."

Hartwell slapped down the fiver and scurried through the door. The bar had been set. Five bucks. The Grusecki twins got in next with a silver Zippo lighter they'd stolen from their older brother. It had a picture of a naked lady on it, supposedly, but they wouldn't let anyone else see it.

Kurt Marshall ditched his bike and pushed to the front of the line. He'd had enough waiting around.

"Alright, kid, let me inside. I got papers to deliver."

"What did you bring me?"

"Just let me inside. I'm in eighth grade. I want to try this thing out."

"I *said*, what did you bring me?"

"Yeah," said Mahoney, inching forward. "What did you bring him?"

"Listen, little man—"

"No, you listen to us," said Zilinski, pulling off his mittens. "We got rules here."

"Yeah," yelled Evan Olsen, shaking his fish. "Rules."

Jesus, even Evan Olsen was taking a stand.

"I'm thirteen, you dork, what the—"

WHACK. A snowball hit the back of his head.

"Who threw that? Which one of you babies threw that snowball? Which one of you is gonna get—"

WHACK. WHACK. The crowd moved in closer. He was surrounded.

"Hey! I'm older than all of you!"

WHACK. WHACK.

"Lemme inside to see the—ouch—hey. Hey! "

"Get him!"

"Kick him in the groin!"

"Punch his face!"

"Grab his hat!"

"RHAAAAH!"

Before Kurt Marshall knew what was happening, a bunch of nine-year-olds were seriously kicking his ass. His bike got tossed in a bush and his papers were thrown up and down Cypress Avenue. Not even an eighth grader with a job was going to scare us away from our Nintendo. I karate-chopped the back of his thigh with my paddleball thing as he ran away. Mahoney took note.

"What is that thing?"

"It's a paddleball thing from Mexico."

"It looks like my butt."

"Yeah . . . I know."

"I don't think you're gonna get inside today, Jake."

Mahoney was right. Kleen took one look at my Mexican paddleball thing and didn't even bother with the M.U.S.C.L.E. Men.

"Next."

It took a good five minutes for Kleen to weed out the

best loot in the yard, but eventually he found the ten toys he liked most. Mahoney and Olsen were the last two to get in, on the strength of their Hulk Hogan sweatband and pet fish, respectively, and I was stuck sitting out in the cold. I hadn't missed the cut like this in months. A handful of other rejects hung around for a few minutes just in case something went wrong inside, but after a while they all went home too.

I sat down on Kleen's porch and pulled a piece of Trident out of the pouch of my Walter Paytons. At least I could honestly tell my dad I'd spent the morning outside for a change. That would make him happy. I watched my breath in the cold for a bit and pulled up my collar.

I was a little worried that Kurt Marshall might come back and pummel me, but I knew that if I stayed out there long enough I might have a shot at getting back inside. Hartwell always had to go home at noon for lunch. Kleen didn't break until one, so that gave me almost an hour downstairs, and depending on where Hartwell had ended up in the rotation, possibly even a quick game of *Double Dribble*. The slam-dunk graphics alone were worth the wait.

I looked into Kleen's house for any signs of life. I'd heard rumors that his sister would walk around in her underwear from time to time, but I didn't see anything. There used to be two foundation windows with a view into the basement, but too many kids were jumping down into the window wells to watch us play, so Kleen had to board them up with cardboard. Now you couldn't see anything.

I glanced over to their family room. Through the bay window you could see their Christmas tree set up next to the fireplace. It was one of those fake ones, the white kind that looked plastic. I never understood that. Why were rich people so intent on buying fake trees? Wouldn't they want the real ones? Shouldn't it work the way it did with everything else? Like with cologne or sunglasses? You didn't see Donald Trump buying fake Ray-Bans from Wal-Mart. I, for one, was glad it was the other way around with Christmas trees. The real ones went to the working class.

My family always got a real tree. My father wouldn't have it any other way. A plastic Christmas tree to him was an abomination. Both he and my mom took the tree-purchasing process pretty seriously, actually, albeit for decidedly different reasons. My dad's goal was to buy the biggest tree on the lot every year, while my mom's goal was to find the cheapest Christmas tree in the history of Christmas. It was a conflict that caused all kinds of holiday cheer for the Doyle family. The whole procedure, from purchase to decoration, somehow managed to turn John and Patty Doyle, two normally loving and rational people, into a heated, bickering, Midwest version of George's parents on *Seinfeld*. It usually went something like this:

MOM: Hey John, what about that one over there? It's only ten dollars.

DAD: It's brown.

MOM: It just needs a little water.

DAD: It's a dead tree, Patty. That's why it's ten dollars.

MOM: Oh, right, 'cause we're made of money, I forgot.

DAD: So I'm the bad guy here? God forbid I want the kids to have a nice Christmas, God forbid.

MOM: Don't yell at me.

DAD: I'm not yelling!

MOM: Well, we're not getting the fifty-foot one you want, or whatever. It won't even fit in the door. Are you crazy?

DAD: Yes, I'm crazy. I'm an insane person. Nuts, actually.

MOM: Fine. Get whatever tree you want.

DAD: And get that guilt trip? You sound just like your mother. You know that?

MOM: I'm waiting in the car.

DAD: Fine.

MOM: Fine!

DAD: Fine! Jake!

ME: Yeah?

DAD: Help me pick out a medium-sized, cheap-ass tree that no one wants.

But this year's trip to the tree lot had been a little different. For the first time in Doyle family history, my parents had found a compromise: a colossal seven-foot

Douglas fir selling for half-price. It was missing about a hundred branches on one side, but because it was so big and so cheap, neither of them seemed to care. When my sister quite earnestly pointed out that the giant hole in the back would probably have to face the living room window and anyone passing by could easily see it, they both told her to shut up. It was the only thing they'd agree on for the rest of the day.

Unlike my sister, I knew better than to get involved. It was far better to stand back and watch, a lot funnier that way too. Most kids would probably find it troubling when their parents fought, but for some reason, at least when it involved Christmas trees, I found it hilarious.

"You gotta cut it at an angle, kid!" my dad yelled, hovering over the anemic Boy Scout who was using a chainsaw to slice off a fresh layer on the trunk. We were in the parking lot next to Batavia Junior High, where the local Boy Scout troop sold trees every year. It was one of the main reasons I would eventually quit the Cub Scouts. I didn't ever want to move up to selling trees. Wreaths were bad enough.

"If he cuts it at an angle it won't stand up straight," yelled my mom over the noise.

"A slight angle, a *slight* angle, to help take in the water."

"That doesn't make any sense, John."

"You cut it straight on, it doesn't suck up the water because it—oh, never mind. You wouldn't understand. Gimme the saw, kid, you're doing it wrong."

A handful of curse words and a few hundred scratches to the roof of the car later, we were jamming the small forest through our front door, scattering a bed of needles throughout the house that would last until Easter.

"Lift it! Lift it!"

"I'm lifting!"

"You're not lifting, you're pushing. There's a big difference, Patty."

"This tree's too big. I can't grab it!"

"You can't grab it because there's a giant hole back there! Not because it's too big!"

Getting the tree straight on its stand was also quite the ordeal. My dad would scrunch down under the base of it and fidget with the rusted screws as the three of us kept it from falling over. It was like being in one of those silent Charlie Chaplin movies where everything runs at double time and nothing works the way it's supposed to.

"How's it look?"

"It looks okay to me."

"Lizzy?"

Lizzy was buried inside the branches, holding on for dear life. "I can't see."

"Hold it up."

"I'm holding it up!"

"It's wobbling all over the place!"

"Just screw it in, Dad!" I yelled, with sap in my mouth.

"Is it straight or not, Patty? I don't want to get back up there and see that it's crooked again."

"The only reason it would be crooked is because you cut it at an angle."

"No, the only reason it would be crooked is because you won't let me buy a new G-dang tree stand!"

"That tree stand is perfectly fine!"

"This tree stand is a hundred and fifty years old!"

I caught a smirk from my sister through the branches. She was catching on. See? This whole thing was hilarious . . .

I smiled slightly to myself, catching my reflection in Kleen's bay window. I'd been outside for well over an hour, and I was finally starting to get cold. Why did my dad think staying outside was so much fun? This was ridiculous. But just as I was about to grab my bike and hightail it back home, I heard a noise. It sounded like shouting. It was coming from inside. I could barely turn around before—

CREAK-BANG! The door shot open and ten kids tumbled out onto the porch. They looked like they'd seen a ghost.

"Hey. Hey! Where're you going?"

No response whatsoever. A few of them hopped on their bikes, some just took off running. No one bothered to zip up coats or put on hats or anything. Olsen wasn't even wearing his shoes. It was like a fire drill, except for real. Within seconds, all ten boys who had worked so hard to get inside were nowhere to be seen. Poof. Gone. Just like that.

I sat there for a moment thinking about what to do. Clearly, something had gone wrong inside, perhaps something dangerous. But there was still a Nintendo and a Power Glove downstairs. So downstairs I went.

"Hey Kleen? Kleen? I took off my shoes! I'm coming in!"

I called out again as I made my way down the steps. I could see a light flickering in the basement, so I knew he had to be down there. Maybe he just told everyone to beat it. Maybe his dad came home. Maybe there were free pop refills today at Burger King and I didn't know about it. Maybe that's why everyone left. Yeah, that's it. Heh, heh, you can have your free pop refills, fellas, I'm getting me some free Power Glove. I was feeling pretty proud of myself for sticking around, actually. But as I rounded the corner at the bottom of the stairs I knew I was in way over my head.

It was only when I saw her lying there that I realized how odd it had been that Lacey Dog wasn't at the door to bark incessantly when I walked in. She hadn't been on the stairs to nip my heels or hump my leg either. And the reason she hadn't been on the stairs or at the door was because she was currently lying under the weight of a fallen three-hundred-pound, forty-two-inch television set.

"Holy shi . . . "

Shih Tzu is right. The TV had fallen forward on top of her. The dog's hind legs were sticking out, *Wizard of Oz*–style, like the Wicked Witch of the East under Dorothy's house. There was no movement whatsoever. Ding-dong, the dog was dead.

"Holy shi . . . "

I looked over to see Kleen cowering in the corner, biting the fingers of his Power Glove.

A bad report card, swallowed marble, broken stained-glass window—they were a Show Biz Pizza party compared to this. There was glass shattered all over the carpet, There was even a little blood trickling out from under the TV.

Kleen looked up at me, scared out of his tree, desperate for help, something, anything. I stood there for a second frantically trying to think of what to do. All I got out was:

"Trrroubbble . . . "

With that, my kid instincts kicked into gear and I came to my senses. I sprinted right back up the stairs and right out the front door, barely remembering to grab my KangaRoos on the way out. When it came to danger of this magnitude it was always best to run. Always. The ten kids inside earlier knew it as well as I did. I hopped on my bike and pedaled madly away to safety.

About five blocks down the street, I ran into Zilinski, who was still running at a competitive jog. His shoes weren't even tied.

"Zilinski! Zilinski! Slow down."

He stopped for a second and caught his breath.

"Your bike's back at Kleen's, dipstick."

"Oh. Oh yeah. I guess I forgot it."

"What happened back there?"

"The dog. I think it's dead."

"It's definitely dead. What happened?"

"Whaddya think happened?"

"Kleen?"

"Yep."

"Did he go crazy?"

"Yep."

"On what game?"

Zilinski sat down on the curb, still nervously scanning the area.

"It was *Kung-Fu*."

"Oh no . . . "

I knew right away what he meant. For years Timmy Kleen had lived under the fantasy that he was, in fact, a kung-fu master, both in video game form and in real life. He was the only kid we knew who was rich enough to get real karate lessons, and because of this, when agitated, he would often threaten, using vague generalizations, to employ his mysterious powers of Tae Kwon Do. A recess incident usually went something like this:

"Don't touch me, I know Tae Kwon Do!"

"Oh yeah?"

"Yeah."

"Let's see it then."

"I'm not gonna show *you*. It's not worth it."

"Oh yeah?" said Hartwell, pushing him in the chest.

"Don't push me."

PUSH. PUSH. PUSH.

"I said don't push me!"

Under normal circumstances, a kid who took karate lessons would earn himself some instant street cred on the playground, but in Timmy Kleen's case it mostly just made us yell, "GO, KLEEN, GO! TAE KWON DO!" over and over again until we got him mad enough to spaz out.

It usually took about thirty seconds.

"GO, KLEEN, GO! TAE KWON DO!"

"Shut up!"

"GO, KLEEN, GO! TAE KWON DO!"

"Don't make me use my powers!"

"GO, KLEEN, GO!" The whole playground was chanting now. "TAE KWON—"

"ARGHHHHGHH!"

With that, Kleen would begin chopping and kicking the air wildly, spinning and dodging imaginary assailants as he chased after whoever was antagonizing him. The more he chopped and kicked, the louder we laughed and chanted. More often than not, the "fight" would end with him lying on the ground in a heap from exhaustion, without having landed any punches at all. Unfortunately for Lacey Dog, it didn't look like it had gone as peacefully in the basement.

Zilinski continued the story.

"So, Kleen's on the third-to-last level of *Kung-Fu*. The last guys."

"The midgets?"

"No, those elves with the knives."

"I thought they were midgets."

"They aren't midgets, alright, they're kung-fu elves. It says so in the booklet. Anyway, he's on the third-to-last level, standing up, he's wearing his yellow belt on his head, going crazy, yelling at the screen. Lacey Dog is barking all over the place . . . "

"STUPID MIDGETS! WHY WON'T YOU DIE!? DIEEEEEE!"

The other ten kids in the room sat on the couch, waiting for the game to end, carefully passing the naked-lady lighter between them.

"You gotta kick the midgets quicker," Mahoney advised.

"They're not midgets, they're elves," corrected Zilinski.

"WHY WON'T YOU DIEEEEE?"

"Why don't you use some of your karate, Kleen?"

"I don't take karate. I take Tae Kwon Do, idiot."

"Oh, right."

"STUPID GAME! STUPID MIDGETS!"

"Elves. They're elves, I'm telling you. Do you want me to get the book?"

"WHATEVER! THEY'RE TOTALLY STUPID!"

Kleen took a direct hit. Then another. He was losing power. Everyone on the couch sat up a bit. Lacey Dog kept barking and yipping.

"STUPID GAME! STUPID DOG!"

Kleen jumped over a bearded wizard, but when he landed, an elf's knife stabbed him right in the leg.

KLANG-ANG-ANG-ANG-ANG! The death noise in *Kung-Fu* was especially annoying.

Kleen was now out of lives. His turn was over.

"WHHHHHHYYYYY! I DODGED IT! I DODGED IT! STUPID! ARGGGHH!"

He whipped his controller against the couch and began throwing wild kicks in the air. He flailed about the room looking for something to beat on. Evan Olsen clutched his fish protectively. Lacey Dog just kept barking at the TV.

"STUPID KUNG-FU! STUPID GAME!"

Maybe it was because he was bored, or maybe it was because the naked lady on the Zippo distracted him, but it was then that Zilinski yelled the unthinkable.

"GO . . . KLEEN . . . GO! TAE . . . KWON . . . DO!"

Suddenly Kleen centered himself and found his martial arts balance. He chopped the air twice and took off in a dead sprint toward the TV.

"HIIIIIIIIII-YYYYAAAAAA!"

The boys on the couch could only watch in horror as he propelled himself feet first into his father's forty-two-inch RCA, a double-leg jump kick that rocked the set back and forth on its foundation.

"Jesus Christ, Kleen!"

The TV hung in the balance for a brief second. Lacey Dog got out one last vindictive yip and then it came crashing down.

"Lacey Dog! NOOOOO!"

THUMP.

Game. Over.

..................

I handed Steve my last piece of Trident. He chewed it thoughtfully as we walked toward my house.

"We're in some serious shit, Jake."

"Yeah."

"And you know what's worse?"

"What?" What could possibly be worse?

"The Power Glove. It didn't work at all. It sucks."

# CHAPTER EIGHTEEN

It took almost six hours for Timmy's parents to learn of their crushed family dog and destroyed television set. There was a rumor that Timmy had unsuccessfully tried to board a bus to Detroit for a clean getaway, but was apprehended by his sister when he asked her how long it would take him to ride his bike to the bus station. When Kleen's parents finally did see the damage in the basement, they wasted no time finding someone else to blame. They were going all the way to the top of the food chain for this one: Nintendo.

By that night, news of Lacey Dog's violent death at the hands of a video game had spread all across Batavia. My parents grilled me for twenty minutes on my involvement in the incident. I lied through my teeth, quite heroically I might add, and managed to convince them that I was playing snow football at Mueller Crest Park during the time of the accident. After all, I had ten other witnesses who could back that story up. They were the same ten guys who'd made it into Kleen's basement that day. It was Zilinski's idea to get our stories straight. He'd gone house to house that afternoon spreading the word before our parents got to us. Evan Olsen, who had scraped his knee fleeing the scene of the crime, was now brilliantly blaming the injury on the imaginary football game. But it didn't matter. We were doomed anyway. This was worse than getting the blame for something. This was *Nintendo* getting the blame for something. It affected all of us.

The Catholic guilt hung heavy the next morning at Holy Trinity Church. I was an altar boy with the Grusecki twins, and we spent much of the ten a.m. Mass trying to figure out how best to pray to God to get us out of this one. We whispered back and forth at the side of the altar.

"I heard they had to pry Lacey Dog out with a crow bar."

"Father Joe says dogs go to limbo."

"Pass the holy water."

"We're screwed."

Being an altar boy was kind of like being a batboy for God. That's the way I thought of it at least. It got you close to the action and you didn't have to sit in the stands bored out of your mind like the rest of the chumps. I loved being an altar boy. You got to light things on fire (candles and incense), you got to help the priest spray people with water (with the aspergillum-thingy), you even got paid every once in a while (funerals and weddings). Plus, Father Joe was a pretty cool guy. He'd crack jokes all the time and he knew more about the Chicago Bears than anyone I'd ever met. He even called their kicker Kevin Butler "butthead" sometimes. I thought that was hilarious. So if there was one person of authority who would understand our Nintendo Christmas plight, surely it was Father Joe.

He stood before the congregation, calmly adjusting his spectacles. "We ask that these prayers and all the prayers listed in our book of intentions be heard. We ask this through Christ, our Lord. Amen."

Father Joe nodded slightly to have the bread and wine brought up from the back of the church. That was the cue for Tommy to pick up the cross and lead the gift bearers up to the altar. And it was the cue for Ryan and me to come over and wash Father Joe's hands with the holy water. Ryan was on bowl and towel duty, I was in charge of the pitcher—which is the much tougher job, I might add. I took great pride in pouring it slow and steady.

"Lord, please wash away my iniquities and cleanse me from my sins."

When Father Joe pulled his hands up a little bit, that meant to stop pouring. This was my favorite part of Mass. As Father Joe dried off his hands he'd always lean in and have a private word with us. Usually it was a knock-knock joke or something. But as he leaned in, the smile on his face vanished. Today the joke was on us.

"I heard about the dog, gentlemen."

"Uh . . . "

"It wasn't our fault, Father, we—"

"I expect to see the three of you in confession later. No questions asked. Nintendo-no-friendo, lads, Nintendo-nooo-friendo."

Sweet Jesus. This was worse than we thought.

The sign posted outside HC Wilson Elementary the next morning said it all:

EMERGENCY PTA MEETING, 7 p.m. TONIGHT.
VIDEO GAME VIOLENCE MUST STOP!

There was an exclamation point and everything. And I knew that was a big deal, because Mrs. Hugo had repeatedly told us never to use an exclamation point unless it was absolutely necessary. The PTA wasn't screwing around.

I begged my parents not to go.

"The Kleens are crazy, Mom! Nintendo didn't have anything to do with it! He's a spaz!"

"That little dog died, Jake. We have to go. I told you those games were violent."

She was even dragging my dad along. He did not look happy. He hadn't been to a PTA meeting since I was in kindergarten, when he spent the whole time playing H-O-R-S-E with Mr. Grusecki in the gym. He had not been asked back since.

The cafeteria that had held forty-five Cub Scouts just a few days prior was now packed to the gills with parents. The Kleens had recruited some of the most important people in town. Coach Capudo, the high school football coach, was there. So was Mayor Sheehan, along with a few members of city council. There were local newspaper reporters, photographers, even a scientist from Fermilab (and those guys never went anywhere).

Mr. Kleen sat on stage in a tweed jacket and spectacles. Mrs. Kleen was next to him, dressed completely in black, still in mourning. She had on a giant button with a picture of Lacey Dog's face on it, and had generously passed out others to the crowd. She dabbed at her eyes with some of Huge-Blow's Kleenex.

Apparently, before getting his MBA and taking over

his father's wing of ComEd, Mr. Kleen had studied child psychology at Northwestern. Don't ask me why, but he had made it very clear that he was an expert on the subject, even going as far as to list his qualifications at the bottom of tonight's program:

TERRENCE KLEEN
Vice President—Sales, Commonwealth Edison
MBA: University of Chicago
BA: Northwestern University (Child Psychology)
Parent: Batavia, Illinois (15 years)

Our principal, Mrs. Smart, stepped up to the podium. She took crap from no one and smoked approximately seventy-two packs of Winstons a day. You could always tell who had been sent to the principal's office, because they reeked of cigarettes afterwards. It was a well-known fact that if you were ever running from the scene of a crime and caught a whiff of Winstons, chances were you were about to be busted. Which is why, even to this day, I equate the smell of smoke with punishment. It's probably why I never took up cigarettes in the first place.

"Good evening, parents . . . "

The crowd shuffled in their seats, still chattering. Smart wasted no time.

"That means quiet down!"

Everyone shut up. Smart coughed a few cancerous coughs and continued.

"As you all know, tonight is a special meeting of the PTA. I'd like to thank all of the teachers for remaining here at school, on a school night, to discuss your children's well being. The teachers will not, I repeat, will not, be sticking around to talk about little Suzie's and little

Johnny's report cards afterwards. That's what teacher conferences are for, so don't hassle them or you'll deal with me."

Huge-Blow sniffled in solidarity.

Mrs. Smart continued. "Now, tonight's speaker has a degree in child psychology—whatever that is," she muttered under her breath. "And he has asked to talk to you in detail about an incident that affected his family this past weekend. So pay attention. And if there's any Mickey Mousing around in the back row back there, you're outta here. Don't think I'm not watching. So, without further ado, I give you Mr. Kleen."

"Mr. Clean? Heh, heh," my father chuckled, singing the floor-cleaner jingle to himself. "*Mr. Clean. Mr. Clean . . .* "

My mom elbowed him in the ribs.

Mr. Kleen took to the podium.

"Parents of Batavia, thank you all for coming. I would like to start tonight by inviting each and every one of you fine people to ask yourself this very important question. How much do I value the safety of my children? It's an important question. One that I thought was at the very pinnacle of my pyramid of priorities."

The microphone popped with each "p," but you had to hand it to him. Mr. Kleen knew how to speak to a crowd. Everyone was fully tuned in. You could tell where Timmy got his vocabulary, as well as his overall assholeness.

Kleen continued. "I thought I was a great parent. But then one day, I come home from a long day at the office to find my dog crushed to death, my child crying and my forty-two-inch television set in pieces."

"Forty-two inches . . . " My dad was impressed.

"A tragic loss to both the family and the pocketbook. And it was an accident that several of your children took part in. Because of that, Julie and I feel it is important that you see it firsthand."

Kleen clicked a slide-projector remote and a blown-up color image flashed onto the screen. It was a close-up of Lacey Dog's bloodied paw sticking out from beneath the TV.

The crowd gasped.

"Take a good look, people. If you're not careful, this could happen to you. As a parent and as a degree holder in child psychology from Northwestern, and then, uh, subsequently an MBA from the, ahem, University of Chicago, I feel that it is my duty to call you here tonight to discuss this gruesome event. Now, I don't blame your children for Lacey Dog's death, and I most certainly don't blame my son, Timothy, who has been the victim of disabilities his entire life. Imbalances that often cause him to become upset, and on more than one occasion, head butt many of the authority figures in the audience here tonight. But in my professional opinion, last Saturday's incident was not caused by some behavioral problem. I'm afraid it was caused by something much worse. Something that, if you're not careful, may infiltrate your own homes this holiday season. Parents, teachers, there is an evil entertainer in our midst. A social swindler of values, a violent video villain that is snatching up our children's morals and significantly stifling their physical fitness."

"Uh-huh, uh-huh." My dad liked the fitness part.

"This dog-killing crime has a culprit, ladies and gentlemen, and it goes by the name . . . "

The slide changed.

" . . . Nintendo!"

The crowd gasped again.

Projected ten feet high was our beloved Nintendo, splattered in blood and lying on a bed of shattered glass, all juxtaposed against the comfortable backdrop of a suburban basement. It was a gruesome ad campaign if I ever saw one. The Nintendo might as well have been wearing a burglar mask and holding a knife to your daughter.

"Nintendo is the reason for this! And this!"

Another picture. Lacey Dog's dead eyes filled the screen.

"And this!"

A stained and ruined Empire carpet flashed before them.

"And this!"

Timmy Kleen's wailing face filled the frame.

"The question is, are we prepared to do something about it? Are we prepared to do something before it's too late? Dr. Umberto, you're a man of science. What do you think about all of this? What's your professional assessment?"

The Argentinean physicist adjusted his glasses timidly. "Em . . . No es good. No, no. No good. Thanks you very much."

"You see! You see! He can barely speak the language and he knows this is a problem. The smartest man in the room says it's a problem. Mr. Mayor? How about you?"

Mayor Sheehan stood up, adjusting his waistline. "Well, Terry, it's downright frightening, I'll tell you that much. The good children of this fair city should not be subjected to this kind of violence. And as your mayor, I propose we—"

"We should ban it!" Mrs. Zilinski yelled from the front row.

"Yeah. Ban it!"

"Ban it!"

"Japanese take-over tactics!" my dad shouted into the fray.

"Nintendo-no-friendo!"

"I say, no more," Kleen continued. "No more Nintendo. Not in Batavia! Not ever again!"

The crowd roared. A PTA posse was beginning to form. Mrs. Zilinski clutched her umbrella like a burning torch. "The video game killed his dog! We need action!"

"It smashed his TV!"

Officer Masejewski rose from his seat. "No more dogs are dying in my town, God damn it. Who's with me?"

"That's what I'm talking about!" Kleen banged on the podium. "Justice must be served! Our children must be protected!"

Kleen's panicked propaganda continued on well into the night, leaving even the most liberal and skeptical members of the PTA petrified that their television sets might suddenly be jump-kicked onto toddlers, immobile grandparents, Buffalo Springfield record collections. By the end of the meeting there wasn't a parent in the audience who wasn't fully convinced that the devil himself had taken the form of a Super Mario Brother. Poor little Conor Stump, who'd been dragged to the event, sat amid the hysteria and wept openly.

It was virtual Nintendo Armageddon.

# CHAPTER NINETEEN

For the first time in my life I woke up depressed on a Saturday morning. Four days had passed since the infamous PTA witch-hunt, and things had gotten significantly worse. The front page of the *Batavia Republican* on Thursday ran the headline "NINTENDO NO!" with an accompanying story explaining how all local shops and businesses would no longer be selling Nintendo Entertainment Systems this Christmas. I'd sensed it coming for years, but it had finally happened. The grownups had officially gone crazy.

The week leading up to Christmas break was supposed to be the best school week of the year. No homework, happy teachers, classroom parties, videos with no conceivable educational purpose whatsoever, you name it. But our hearts weren't in it anymore. Even watching *How the Grinch Stole Christmas* was painful. All those bratty Whos down in Whoville were getting Jingtinglers and Floobflobbers up the yin-yang, and we weren't getting squat. Screw you, little Cindy Lou Who, I don't care if you're no more than two. That whole "We Are the World" impromptu singing in the square at the end? That was no accident. You knew what you were doing. You knew it would bring the Grinch back down from Mount Crumpit with all your presents. I'm not falling for that crap for a second. I denounce you, Whos! You're all a bunch of Christmas phonies!

My Nintendo depression had gotten to the point where I couldn't even enjoy pizza anymore. The free personal pan pie that was awarded to me for months and months of pretending to read books in the Pizza Hut BOOK IT! program now tasted like cardboard. This was *pizza* we're talking about here, the holy grail of kid food, and I was feeding it to the dog. What kind of parallel universe had I entered?

And it wasn't just me. A black cloud had settled over HC Wilson. Second graders had taken to rushing up the Mound in a continuous stream, kamikaze-style, with no regard for life whatsoever. They didn't care anymore. Delund's once-manic laugh, which had accompanied each kick and wedgie, had turned into a work-like groan. The bleeding-snake pen tattoos on his forearms now dripped despondent tears. Even the most optimistic of us had lost hope. It got so bad that normally devout Jeff Hartwell, who had the lead as Joseph in the church Christmas pageant, ended the play by rising from the manger and exclaiming to parents and clergy alike, "There is no God."

It was enough to make you want to run away.

I tumbled out of bed and made my way downstairs. Lizzy was already awake, planted in front of the TV watching Saturday morning cartoons. Thank God for Saturday morning cartoons. I'd certainly missed them during the months I'd spent lining up in front of Kleen's house. Saturday morning cartoons were a ritual, an '80s and '90s rite of childhood. *GI Joe*, *ThunderCats*, *Teenage Mutant Ninja Turtles*—they would never let you down. Cartoons were like a best friend or a favorite blanket. You could always count on them.

I often wonder if kids today even have Saturday morning cartoons anymore. If they do, do they still have to wake up super early to watch the really good stuff? Or do they just DVR it? Can you imagine what our lives would be like as adults if we could've just watched Saturday morning cartoons at three in the afternoon? We'd be an even lazier generation than we already are.

Saturday morning cartoons, in my opinion, helped to nurture a whole generation of Cold War kids. They introduced a society of little blue men who could exist in harmony with only one little blue woman; a land where turtles and rats could get along; a place where even a smartass like Garfield had friends. Cartoons gave us hope. Not to mention, some of the most important technological advancements of our generation. Don't believe me? Watch *Inspector Gadget* and tell me that Penny's computer book doesn't look a hell of a lot like an iPad. Brain's telephone ear thing? Totally an early version of the Bluetooth. And that berry juice from the *Gummy Bears*? Sure looks like Red Bull to me. Hipsters might still be drinking Tab if it wasn't for cartoons.

I plopped down on the couch above Lizzy. She was on the floor watching *Muppet Babies*. *Muppet Babies* was a sticky subject for us boys. Clearly it was an entertaining show, a Jim Henson creation, and you couldn't argue with that creative pedigree. But you didn't quite know if you could watch it and still keep your masculinity. It was sort of like watching women's tennis. Yes, you were watching a sport, but you probably shouldn't talk about it with your buddies the next day. The show was about *babies*. It was set in a *nursery*: little piggies and froggies and tiny bears wearing diapers, and puppies playing pianos, all whining to a giant-legged nanny when things got tough. That's no *Transformers*, let me tell ya. That's Dan Delund knuckle-sandwich territory. You couple that with a pair of girls' boots and you could wind up in the hospital. So, my policy was just to watch it and never talk about it. Ever. Ironically, it probably ended up becoming my favorite cartoon. It also helped me score points with Lizzy.

"We're watching *GI Joe* after this, Lizzy."

"Yeah, I know."

"You can watch *Muppet Babies,* but we're definitely watching *GI Joe* next."

"Yeah, Jake, I know, jeez."

"Good. Just so we're on the same page here—wow, is Piggy scaling the Eiffel Tower? Ha! How's she gonna—"

"Shh! I'm trying to watch this!"

"Sorry."

Just then the cartoons cut out and a local CBS logo shot up on the screen.

"We interrupt this program to bring you a breaking story from Kane County."

My sister and I looked at each other. They never interrupted cartoons. And they most certainly never interrupted cartoons to go a breaking story in Kane County. Kane County was the most boring county in the greater Chicagoland area. Hands down. Nothing ever happened here. Was it a tornado? It was the middle of December, couldn't be. What the heck was going on?

"Thank you, Walter. We're coming to you live from

the Kane County Courthouse here in Geneva with a fascinating story taking place."

In the background, behind the reporter, you could see dozens of picketers parading around with signs and banners. I couldn't quite make them out.

"The people behind me are all parents who are staging a county-wide petition to ban the popular video game Nintendo."

Oh . . . God. It had made the news.

"An incident in Batavia last week has sparked outrage in parents, citing video game violence as the reason for—well, why don't you explain it to us, Mr. Kleen?"

The camera tracked over, and sure enough, there was Kleen, wearing a "Nintendo" button with a big red circle and line through it like the *Ghostbusters* logo. I took it to mean "No Nintendo."

"What happened exactly, sir?"

"Well, Nintendo killed my dog. Crushed it to death."

"My condolences. That's frightening."

"Yes. Yes, it is. And it can happen to anyone."

"I have to say, though, Mr. Kleen. All these parents here, the impending ban on the sale of, well, essentially a popular children's game right before Christmas—don't you think you folks are taking it a little too far?"

"Tell me something. How would you like to come home from work and find your dog's skull crushed and bleeding on your carpet under the weight of the thousand-dollar television you'd purchased not six months ago?"

"Doesn't sound like a very square deal, I guess."

"You guess? Let me explain something to you and your viewers out there. The people here in Batavia and the Tri-Cities, we have spoken. We will pass this ban. We will pass it and Kane County will never let video games within its borders ever again! Never, ever again! Nintendo-NO! Nintendo-NO! Nintendo—"

I grabbed the remote and quickly changed channels. Lizzy didn't even offer a complaint. She could tell I was about to lose it. A cold sweat washed over me as I frantically searched through the stations. Could I not even watch my Saturday morning cartoons in peace? Was nothing sacred anymore? Suddenly, every show I turned to had an anti-Nintendo message. I was beginning to hallucinate.

CLICK.

MR. T: *I pity the fool who plays Nintendo. I catch that fool, I'll pound him. Pound him to the ground! Pound him till he calls for his mama!*

CLICK.

MAX HEADROOM: *Ni, ni, ni, Nintendo. Ni, ni, ni, Nintendo-no-friendo.*

CLICK.

McGRUFF: *So, remember, kids. A Nintendo house is never a safe house. Get out as fast as you can and tell a grownup. Say no to Nintendo and take a bite out of crime.*

CLICK.

SHIPWRECK: *. . . that's because playing video games turns you into a giant fat-ass.*

SHIPWRECK'S PARROT: *Squawk! Squawk! Giant fat-ass!*

SHIPWRECK: *So now you know. And knowing is half the battle.*

GI JOE SINGERS: *GI Jooooe! A real American Heeeero—!*

CLICK.

STRAWBERRY SHORTCAKE: *La-la-la. Nintendo smells like poop. La-la-la. Poopy-poopy-poop—*

CLICK.

EMPIRE CARPET GUY: *Five-eight-eight . . . two-three-hundred—NO-CHANCE-IN-HELL-YOU'RE-EVER-GETTING-A-NINTENDOOOOOO!*

CLICK

GUY WITH FRYING PAN: *This is your brain . . . This is your brain on Nintendo. Any questions?*

When I came to, Lizzy was offering me a glass of Tang. I gulped it down and wiped my eyes. A hundred and two counties in the Land of Lincoln, and I had to be living in the one that had gone off its collective gourd. Was there no end to this anti-Nintendo madness?

"What am I gonna do, Lizzy?"

My dad came in. He'd been working outside on the house. He'd been doing a lot of that lately. Leave it to him to wait until the dead of winter.

"Jake, Mom told me to remind you to get ready for the Gruseckis' birthday party. It's in an hour. Have you been crying? Lizzy, what's wrong with him?"

"Nothing, Dad. He just has something in his eye."

"Oh, okay." He turned and went back outside.

I looked up at Lizzy. "Thanks."

"A redhead with freckles. Don't forget."

# CHAPTER TWENTY

Birthdays were a tricky thing. Timing was everything. If you didn't time it right, you could end up sharing the limelight. And there was nothing worse than playing second fiddle on your own birthday. Take summer birthdays, for instance. That meant you didn't get to bring treats to school on your real birthday. Instead, you got lumped with all the other summer-birthday losers and had to bring your treats on the last day of school when no one gave a crud. Plus, you had to try to schedule your birthday party during summer vacation, which meant you had to compete with baseball practices and families taking trips to Florida and the Wisconsin Dells to see Tommy Bartlett's Robot World. And good luck trying to compete with robots, even Wisconsin ones—they'll win every time.

Christmastime birthdays were just as bad. Who cares about your birthday when Santa Claus is coming in six days? I certainly don't. Not to mention, if your birthday was too close to Christmas you also ran the risk of receiving the dreaded "double gift"—a single present that lazy grandparents or cheapskate uncles would try to pawn off as being both your birthday gift *and* your Christmas present. The horror!

So, growing up, there was nobody who got screwed harder than Tommy and Ryan Grusecki. Not only did they have to *share* their birthday between them, but they also had to share it with Christmas. They'd been born at 12:30 a.m. on Christmas day. For a while in high school we called them the Jesus Twins just to make light of the situation, but it must've been a nightmare. Their entire kid year was jammed into one twenty-four-hour period. Happy birthday! Merry Christmas! The rest of your year's gonna suck now! Going to bed on Christmas night must have been incredibly depressing. What was there to look forward to after that? Easter? I really felt sorry for Tommy and Ryan. I really did.

The twins were having this year's party at Fun Times Roller Rink. As far as local places of interest went, Fun Times was top notch, sort of like the Six Flags of Kane County. We knew this quite well, since we'd spent a significant amount of time working on our school-assigned Batavia Reports, listing in careful detail all the town's "places of interest." There were about four of them.

1. The Batavia Bellevue Place (aka, the Mary Todd Lincoln Insane Asylum). This was the hospital where Abraham Lincoln's wife went bat-shit crazy after he was assassinated. She lived there against her will for months, slowly growing mad and walking the halls wearing ten pairs of gloves at a time and howling at the moon and whatnot. There was great civic pride in this historic incarceration, as if Batavia had landed the Olympics or won some sort of presidential con-

test by essentially jailing the First Lady. *That's right, Geneva, we're the town where Mary Todd lost her marbles. Not you. Us. We're number one!*

2. The Batavia Museum. This was a museum dedicated to Batavia's rich history, namely the Mary Todd Lincoln Insane Asylum. Inside was a mockup of her hospital room, with pictures of her on the wall looking all puffy and crazy. There was even a pair of her gloves in a glass case, which you were not to touch for fear of being kicked out. Outside the museum was a big red train car that just sat there. You could climb on it and throw woodchips at cyclists riding by on the bike path. And that was pretty much it. That was the whole "museum." One train car and a replica of Mary Todd's nuthouse.

3. The Batavia Windmill. Technically, this windmill wasn't even in Batavia. It was in Geneva, but since Batavia was known as the Windmill City in the 1800s, we still staked claim to it. It was located next to a park on a relatively large hill. Perfect for sledding and, later, tricking girls into making out with you.

4. The Batavia Frank Lloyd Wright house. Definitely the nicest house in town, it was built and designed by the famous architect Frank Lloyd Wright. We figured he must've lost some kind of bet to build a house here. Some rich family lived in it now. They probably had a Nintendo and didn't even tell anybody about it. I envisioned secret parties where the Kleens would go over there to dine on endangered species and swim in vaults of gold coins, Scrooge McDuck–style.

And fifth on the list of Batavia's places of interest was, of course, Fun Times Roller Rink. The pride of the Fox River Valley! The home of DJ Radical! *Come one, come all, and ride the rides—have a ball down at Fun Times!* Fun Times was *the* place to be in Batavia. It was a little too far to ride your bike there in the winter, though, so Olsen, Mahoney and I were getting a lift from my dad. He was doing about seventy on a side street.

"So, what do you guys do at Fun Times besides play more video games?"

Olsen was sitting in the back with his eyes closed, hanging on for dear life.

"They're arcade games, Mr. Doyle," Mahoney corrected. "But there's a roller rink too. This kid, Josh Farmer, said they're building a go-kart track in the back, but I think he's full of it."

"You know, when I was growing up we didn't go to the roller rink to skate, we went ice skating outside. We played hockey on an outdoor rink all winter. The Chicago Park District would flood the baseball fields. When's the last time you guys played outside?"

"The day Timmy killed his dog, Mr. Doyle." Even with his eyes closed, Evan was dutifully sticking to our Nintendo alibi. Well done, Olsen.

"Well, maybe with no more Nintendo you kids will be playing outside a bit more."

"It's too cold, Dad."

"Too cold? If it was up to me I'd make you ride your bikes here. Too cold . . . " He shook his head. "I'll give you too cold."

My dad was always "giving" me things. *I'll give you sorry*. Or, *I'll give you not hungry*. How could you give me "not hungry"? I once asked him about it. He was not amused.

"It's fresh air out there!" he continued. "Your dad would say the same thing, Evan. Matthew, yours too. You kids don't know what you're missing."

By the time we got to the rink, the Grusecki twins were already fighting. I'd been to enough of their parties to know the drill. Three hundred and sixty-four days a year the two got on like gangbusters, but on their birthday they turned into Noel and Liam Gallagher. You couldn't blame them. It's a lot of pressure, sharing your birthday. Who blows out the candles first? Who gets top billing in the birthday song? Just the year before, they'd almost gotten kicked out of Show Biz Pizza when Ryan threw Tommy face-first into the animatronic gorilla piano player. Fighting on your birthday, it was understandable.

I had other friends with siblings who fought all year round. Mahoney and his younger brother, Pete, for instance. Violence straight out of a slasher film. I can't believe neither of them ever died or at least went to jail. I once watched Pete Mahoney try to decapitate Matt with baseball bat during a heated game of home-run derby in their backyard. Literally, bat to neck full swing. To which a shrieking Matthew retaliated by stumbling into the garage and emerging with a tire iron. A good seventy percent of our games ended because they'd start fighting and one of them would gore or stab or maim the other one, and that would set off a tattletale chain reaction that would get both of them, and their Easton aluminum bat, sent inside. But the Gruseckis were different. They always got along. Except, like I said, on their birthday. Currently, they were stomping on each other's shins with roller skates.

"That's my skate! Quit stealing my skate!"

"It's my skate!"

"What difference does it make? We're the same size!"

The two were sitting on a bench overlooking the roller rink. The rink was essentially a big slab of concrete with a metal railing around it. It was painted crimson and gold, Batavia colors. Up in the DJ booth was local favorite and three-hundred-pound disc jockey DJ Radical, better known to us as DJ Fatical. Fatical was enjoying himself immensely as always. A Pepsi the size of a bucket of chicken sat next to the PA microphone, which he would slurp on in between outbursts of "Oooooh yeeeeah!" and "Heeeeeey duuuuude!" Fatical's musical stylings consisted mostly of Wham! and Cyndi Lauper, but ever so often he'd throw in a little Poison just to keep the guys on the floor.

Fatty slobbered into the mic. "Let's give a big birthday shout-out to Tommy and Ryan Grusecki! The big one-zero! Ooooh yeeeeah!"

The Gruseckis paid little attention. They were still fighting over a rental skate.

"Give it!"

"You give it! Mommmm!"

I sat down next to them with my gift.

"Hey guys."

They looked me over.

"Only one gift again, Doyle?"

"Sorry."

"It better not be a book."

It was a book, probably *The Whipping Boy* again. My mom had wrapped it, in Christmas paper of course.

"Yeah, I think it's a book. Sorry."

"Figures."

We looked up to see a bunch of other kids our age walking toward us. They had their shirts tucked in, a good indicator they were from neighboring St. Charles. They looked us over.

"You guys from Batavia?"

"Yeah, what's it to ya?"

"Well, we're from St. Charles."

"Sucks to be you," Mahoney piped up, skating into the conversation. "Don't you guys have your own roller rink to go to?"

It was a ploy. Everyone knew Fun Times was the only roller rink for miles. It was the only category, besides maybe particle accelerators and, later, semi-promiscuous girls, in which Batavia actually had a leg up on St. Charles.

"You know there's no other roller rinks around here."

"So whaddya want, then?"

"We wanna know which one of you buttheads got Nintendo banned."

Buttheads? These were fighting words.

"None of us got it banned," I said. "Only one kid has it and he's a spaz. He kicked his TV and it fell on his dog. And it's not banned in St. Charles, anyway."

"Wanna bet? My parents just took mine away from me. You guys ruined it for everybody! What are we supposed to do now? I was gonna get *Mega Man Two* for Christmas!" The kid was almost crying. One of his crew had to hold him back. "I already saw it hiding under my parents' bed! You guys suck! I hope none of you ever get one ever!"

Then he really did start to cry. He was sobbing right in the middle of Fun Times. We all just sat there, not sure of what to say. It was pretty hard to start a fight when someone was already crying. And the thing of it was, we knew exactly how he felt. We'd just had a little more time to become numb to the pain.

Zilinski stood up. He walked over and put his hand on the kid's shoulder.

"I'm sorry, man. Really."

The crying kid's buddy gave Zilinski a little push.

"Just don't do anything else stupid, like get TV banned. And don't ever come to St. Charles. We see you there and you're dead."

With that, the group walked off toward the arcade games.

"Jee-zus." Mahoney shook his head. "I can't believe they banned it in St. Charles."

Olsen took off his shoes. "Yeah, it's banned in Geneva too. My cousin told me Viking Toys stopped selling it."

"Well, it's not banned in Elmhurst," said Hartwell. "My cousins said they were getting it."

Tommy grabbed his skate from Ryan. "That's because Elmhurst isn't in Kane County. That's DuPage County."

"How do you know?"

Ryan grabbed the skate right back. "Cause we got encyclopedias."

"Oh. Oh yeah. Sorry."

"Let's just get this birthday party over with."

Ryan took to the floor and we all followed. "Walking on Sunshine" blasted over the speakers as we rolled around the rink. It's a funny thing to be completely and utterly depressed while listening to "Walking on Sunshine," especially in a place called Fun Times. Kinda makes you want to kill yourself.

We skated around, weaving in and out of packs of giggling girls and older kids, who were all oblivious to our pain. This really was the end of the Nintendo line, and we could all sense it. It was six days until Christmas. We only had one more day of school before break. Over the past six months, every single attempt at gaining favor with our parents and the community at large in our quest for Nintendo had failed. Miserably. We really weren't going to get Nintendos for Christmas. Defeat had finally set in.

After a while we finished moping around on the rink and got down to birthday business. At the back of Fun Times' main floor was a roped-off cluster of tables where you got to go if you were having a birthday party. They would put a little Fun Times crown made out of roller wheels on the birthday boy—or boys, in this case—and DJ Fatical would trudge over and take a few sweaty pictures with you and your friends. No one ever asked for or wanted these pictures, but they came with the birthday package, so you went along with it.

I felt bad that I'd gotten the twins another book. I was always giving my friends books. I think my mom thought it might somehow balance out the rest of the mindless junk they were sure to get. But the Gruseckis only ever wanted baseball cards. No toys, no clothes, no candy, just cards. You could never have too many. Asking only for cards was actually a very smart move, because even if you ended up with doubles you could always trade one away. Giving baseball cards as a gift was like giving money, except that instead of Abraham Lincoln or George Washington, you had Andre Dawson or Ryne Sandburg. It was like currency with a better personality. You could collect them and save them up for a rainy day, or you could trade them and get something different. Baseball cards were the gift that kept on giving.

"I got a Chris Sabo!" Tommy yelled as he was tearing his way through a pack of Donruss. "And a Ricky Henderson."

"Henderson's worthless." Ryan was plowing through a pack of his own.

"He's not worthless. He's the best base stealer ever."

"Yeah, but his cards are worth zilch."

The twins had waited to open up all their packs at once. They were using *The Whipping Boy* book as a little table between them to stack the packs on, so at least it was useful for something. Everyone had gotten them baseball cards except me. Donruss, Score, Fleer, even a few packs of Topps thrown in for good measure, compliments of Zilinski, who was already eying the gum.

It was in these small moments of excitement that our Nintendo depression subsided, if only briefly. That was the beauty of baseball cards. When someone was opening a pack, nothing else mattered. It was a surprise every time. Anything was possible because you never knew who you were gonna to get.

"I got a Clemens."

"Mark Grace rookie card!"

Zilinski hovered. "Are you gonna eat your gum?"

"I got a Will Clark."

"I got a Mattingly."

"Seriously, are you gonna eat it?"

"I got a Ripken . . . Billy Ripken."

"Who gives a crud about Billy Ripken?"

"'Cause if you're not gonna eat it, I'll—"

"Here. Take the gum, Zilinski, jeez."

Tommy glanced over at his brother, who was still staring at the Ripken.

"It's just a Billy Ripken, Ryan. It's, like, seven cents. Cal's not even worth two bucks in the *Beckett*."

But Ryan just kept staring at the card with his mouth open. It looked like he was witnessing an act of God or something, like one of those Nazis staring at the Ark of the Covenant at the end of *Indiana Jones* just before their faces got melted off. It looked like Ryan's face might go at any moment.

"What is it?"

He could barely get it out. "You guys . . . you guys aren't gonna believe this."

"What?"

We all crowded around to have a look. What could possibly be cool about a Billy Ripken card? He was the mediocre brother of future Hall of Famer Cal Ripken. He had a lifetime batting average of like .247. He looked like a chipmunk. What was the big deal? Was Cal in the card too? Was it an error card? Maybe that was it. Sometimes when a statistic was off, or a number, or the spelling of a last name, it could increase the value of the card by a buck or so. But still, Billy Ripken?

"Right there. On the bottom of his bat, look . . . "

It turns out Ryan Grusecki really was witnessing an act of God. Because there on the bottom of Billy Ripken's Louisville Slugger, tilted slightly toward the heavens, was the single most hypnotizing image any of us had ever seen. Just below the knob of his bat, written in black marker, perhaps as a practical joke by another Ripken, was the word "FUCK." And not just "FUCK." Directly under it was the word "FACE."

FUCK FACE.

It was clear as day. FUCK FACE.

"Holy shi . . . "

We looked around quickly to make sure Grusecki's mom hadn't seen it. DJ Fatical had her cornered at the other end of the table, so we seemed to be in the clear.

There was a swear word on a baseball card. A swear

word! It was almost incomprehensible. This changed everything.

"How could they not see that?"

"This is the biggest error card ever!"

"Lemme see it!"

"Don't nick it!"

We were bouncing in our seats. Olsen patted Ryan on the back. "You're rich, man. You're totally rich! Do you know how much that card's gonna be worth?"

"Nick's gonna lose his mind. I've never seen a card like this!"

Zilinski chomped on another piece. "Maybe he'll even pay a fair price."

Tommy flipped through his *Beckett*. "I bet we could get fifty bucks for that card."

"*We?*"

"You know what I mean. There's never been anything like this. Fleer's gonna pull all the cards from the shelves when they find out. Fifty bucks, easy."

Olsen took another bite of cake. "You're rich, man. Rich."

"Yeah, Ryan, a couple more Billy Ripkens and you can buy your own Nintendo."

And that's when it hit me like an '85 Bears blitz. We didn't need parents or Santa or anybody anymore. We were going to buy our own Nintendo for Christmas. The *A-Team* theme song was already playing in my head. I had a plan . . .

# CHAPTER TWENTY-ONE

When things got hairy in third grade, there was only one place to regroup and reorganize. That was Mueller Crest Park, specifically the woods behind the jungle gym. "Woods" was a loose term. It was more a cluster of trees, probably only a few acres, but it was secluded and mysterious and all ours. This was where we'd play war for days on end and where we'd bet each other during sleepovers to run through without a flashlight. No one had actually done it yet, but it was always fun to talk about. When you "ran away from home" you went to the woods. When you found yourself with some type of contraband, like fireworks or *Playboys*, you brought them there to share. When you had to take a leak in the middle of a football game, you went to the woods to do your business. It was a one-stop shop, an equal opportunity lender, a hideout of Tom Sawyer proportions. So when my Nintendo operation needed the involvement of every boy in third grade, I knew just the place to hold our secret meeting. To the woods!

I stood high atop a tree stump in the cold. Below me gathered the huddled masses of the Nintendo-less third grade class, their breaths cutting through the air in short, pensive puffs. They were expecting a miracle here, one that I had promised to deliver. Months of *Tetris* were finally paying off as I began to fit the intricate pieces of the Nintendo puzzle together. Our jingle bell had yet to toll.

Carefully I searched for the precise words to put my plan into action . . .

"Uh, you guys still want Nintendos for Christmas?"

Delund hawked a loogie at my feet. "What are you, stupid?"

"No, see, it's just, I got this idea—"

"If I gotta sell more wreaths, Boyle, I'm throwing you off the landfill. What are we doing here?"

"I have a way to get our own Nintendo."

Zilinski piped up, "How can we get our own Nintendos now?"

"We can buy our own."

"With what?"

"Our baseball cards. We can sell 'em."

The crowd gasped.

"We can't sell our baseball cards, Jake!"

"Why not?"

Grusecki shook his head. "'Cause they're worth money, duh."

"Who are we gonna sell cards to?"

"We can sell them to Nick."

"Nick? He never buys them for anything close to what they're worth in the *Beckett*. This is stupid."

"Yeah, Jake," Zilinski added. "Even if we do get the money, where are we gonna get a Nintendo anyway? Nobody sells them around here anymore."

"They still sell them in Chicago. We're going there on Monday for the field trip. We can buy one there."

They weren't buying it. Delund was already rolling up his sleeves to pound me. Stump headed for a patch of ice to lick. A few kids began to file out. I was losing them.

"Just hold on a sec and listen. Wait!"

"You're crazy. We can't do it now, we'd get in big trouble," quivered Olsen, always quick to point out his disciplinary concerns.

"Yeah, Jake." Even Mahoney had his reservations. "It's almost Christmas."

"Forget about Christmas! This is serious!"

I hopped down from the stump and pulled the Gruseckis back into the circle. "Don't you guys want to get a Nintendo? This is our last chance. Can't you see that? We can't depend on our parents or Santa or anybody anymore."

Farmer piped up. "Actually, some of the sixth graders told me that Santa isn't a real guy. He's really just your par—"

"Shut up, Farmer!" I dug down deep. "Now's our chance to get our own Nintendo that we can share and not have stupid rules about ten people and taking your shoes off and all that stuff. It'll be just for the third graders, just for us. Our very own Nintendo. Use your imagination!"

Stump stopped licking the ice for a second.

I grabbed Mahoney. "Matt, you've still got that camping generator right? The one your family uses when you go on trips?"

"Yeah. So?"

"So we bring that into the woods. We set up our own little fort. Like a Nintendo fort. Olsen, you bring that TV you've got in your room. We buy a Nintendo and we bring it here. We hook it all up right here in the woods, right under the big willow tree, maybe. We can hide out here after school every day."

Stump wiped his mouth. "Like a secret club?"

Eyes rolled.

"Yeah, Stump, like a secret club, I guess. If we sell enough cards we can get games and—"

"A secret club like in *The Goonies*."

"Yeah, Goonies . . . " Mahoney was coming around.

"Goonies . . . " the Gruseckis chimed in unison.

They were buying it now. The movie reference had done it. A few smiles were registering. Maybe this really was like *The Goonies*. That's what it felt like, at least, like this was our last chance at the rich stuff, our last chance to have an adventure. A real Nintendo adventure.

I looked to Delund. He was the tipping point. If I got his approval, I'd get the rest. "Well, Dan? Whaddya say?"

He snapped a branch over his knee.

"Okay, Boyle. Fine. We're the Goonies. But I get to be Mouth."

"I wanted to be Mouth," whined Farmer.

"You're Chunk, Farmer." Dan pushed his sleeves back down. "Alright, Boyle, what's the plan?"

Less than two hours later, the scene at the Bullpen rivaled a sellout on the floor of the New York Stock Exchange. A surging crowd of nine-year-old traders had overtaken the place, yelling, screaming—flashing hand signals back and forth. Nick could barely pound numbers into his calculator fast enough. The next-door owner of

Scoop's Ice Cream had to come over just to make sure Nick wasn't being robbed and beaten by a prepubescent mob.

But despite the chaos, it was all going according to plan. Our mission was simple: money. Money got us a Nintendo. Cards for cash. It was as straightforward as that. The Gruseckis were in their element here. It was their moment to shine.

"I need the Fleer '84 Puckett! Who's got it?" Ryan called back into the crowd. The twins had taken pole position at the counter, serving as our brokers for the feeding frenzy.

"PUCKETT!" Tommy shouted, flashing eight fingers, then four, then an F for Fleer. Kids began tearing through their shoeboxes and binders filled with cards.

"I got one!" Kramer called out from the back of the crowd. He hustled up to the counter next to us. "It's his rookie card, you know that, right?"

"Yeah, Kramer, we know. That's why we gotta sell it."

Ryan placed the card gently on the counter. "It's mint. Twenty-seven fifty."

Nick lifted his glasses. "Eight bucks."

"Eight bucks?" Kramer yelled. "You gotta be kidding me! It's his rookie card."

Tommy approached the bench. "It's twenty-five bucks in the *Beckett*, Nick. Let's get real here."

"Eight bucks."

"If you think that my brother and I are gonna stand here and sell you a guaranteed future Hall of Famer rookie card for eight bucks, you might as well take those glasses and shove them up your butt. Twenty-two seventy-five."

"Nine dollars."

"Eighteen."

"Nine fifty."

"Sixteen bucks, and that's our final offer. And you're gonna take it, Nick, because this Kirby Puckett is the only card you're missing in that '84 'complete set' of Fleer over there that you've been trying to sell to us for years. Sixteen bucks."

"Fine."

The crowd roared. Nick handed the money over.

Kramer shook his head in disappointment. "It's a twenty-five dollar card, I just . . . "

"It's for a good cause, Kramer. You're a good man."

Kramer moped back into the crowd. Josh Farmer pushed his way forward. We'd been waiting for him for forty-five minutes.

"Where the heck you been, Farmer?"

"Sorry I'm late. I had to help my dad put an ejection seat in our Fiero."

Oh God . . .

"Your dad drives a Buick, Farmer. Gimme a break."

"Nuh-uh, we just got a new Fiero, a red one with a turbo fuel inject—"

"Okay, fine, whatever, let's see your cards."

Farmer handed over a rubber-banded stack. We shuffled through them. He'd promised us some real blue chips.

"Chuck Cottier, Bob Dernier, Jody Davis, Leon 'Bip' Roberts? This collection is awful. Where's the mint-condition Hank Aaron?"

"Couldn't find it."

Tommy continued through the stack. "Hector Villanueva, Dan Quisenberry, Kent Tekulve?"

Conor Stump's head popped up from out of nowhere. "Kent Tekulve's cool," he said, sucking on a Lego.

"Stump, do you even have any baseball cards?"

"Oh no. I collect bottle caps. Do you need any bottle caps?"

"Get outta here, Stump."

Without anything good from Farmer, we were still running about fifty bucks short of our goal. I'd sold five of my best cards already. It was time to pull out the big gun. I gave a nod to Tommy. He knew what to do. He turned to his brother.

"I think it's time, Ryan. Nick's only got a few more buys in him, he's getting nervous. Just look at him."

"Stand back from that counter!" Nick yelled at Delund, who, incidentally, had been stealing Lemonheads a handful at a time for the better part of an hour. "I said stand back!"

"I didn't do nothing."

"I'm watching you, kid!"

Tommy continued with his brother. "Fifty bucks more and we can pretty much get all the games we want, Ryan—the Power Pad too, maybe. You gotta bring out the Ripken."

Nick pounded on the counter as he scanned the back of the shop. The scene was starting to turn ugly. A few kids were now jumping on windowsills, making fart noises with their mouths on the glass, all hopped up on Topps gum and Nintendo fever. This was turning into Nick's worst nightmare.

"Alright! That's it! All of you, I want you all out of here unless you're gonna buy something! I want you all gone!"

Ryan took a deep breath and pulled out a heavy plastic case from his pocket. He stepped up to the counter. Old Fuck-Face was ready to throw down.

"One more trade, Nick."

"No. No more trades today. You're tearing up my store."

"I think you're gonna change your mind." Ryan slid the card across the counter.

"A Billy Ripken? Why do you have it in hard plastic, this is a common—holy cow . . . " Nick lifted his glasses and looked closer. "Did you write that?"

"Nope. It's an error card. Nobody even knows about it yet. They'll probably start taking packs off the shelves."

Nick swallowed hard and wiped his brow. "I'll give you thirty bucks for it."

"Don't insult me, Nicholas."

"Thirty-five."

"There's a swear word on a baseball card, Nick. This isn't a spelling mess-up here. Come on."

"Forty bucks."

Grusecki shook his head. "I'll sell this thing to Grand Slam Sports this afternoon if I have to. I'll ride my bike all the way to St. Charles right now. Don't think I won't do it."

"Fifty dollars. That's my final offer, kid. Take it or leave it."

A hush fell over the store. Ryan Grusecki tightened his gaze and stared into Nick's Coke-bottle glasses. Like Michael J. Fox ordering a keg of beer, his Teen Wolf was about to come out.

"Sixty bucks," he growled. "Or none of us here ever buys a card from you ever again."

And that's how we finally got a fair deal at the Bullpen.

# CHAPTER TWENTY-TWO

There's something magical about getting into mischief. It's a very distinct feeling. Part fear, part excitement, in many ways it's the essence of being a kid. I could barely sleep the night before the field trip. I lay there in the dark shuffling through the cash from the great baseball card sellout. Two hundred and sixteen dollars, we'd ended up with. A fortune. It was now tucked safely inside the Velcro flap of my Trapper Keeper.

Nods of solidarity shot my way as I walked down the halls of HC Wilson on Monday morning. In a few hours I was going to ditch out on the field trip in the middle of downtown Chicago, head for the nearest toy store and buy us a Nintendo. Our moment had come. This was all really happening.

But first, there was some secret business to attend to with Miss Ciarocci. I had a Christmas present to give her.

I walked up to the common area outside the classrooms. Our Christmas ornament projects were lying there on desks and chairs, drying off to be brought home today. However improbable, my "ornament" had grown even bigger over the past week. It now took up the entire table at the center of the room.

At the last minute, I had decided that a star was needed, one that could guide my macaroni Wise Men to Bethlehem. That one star turned into many stars and then a solar system of sorts. So now, sticking out of the shoebox manger on wire hangers, dangling dangerously over the Baby Jesus, were a cluster of a bell- and star-shaped Jingles cookies. They were one of the old man's favorite Christmas treats, and it had taken some sneaking around to get the cookies out of the house undetected. But it was worth it. I was now staring at a masterpiece, a work of art—a true creation of the Christmas spirit. I was already planning on inquiring about space for it at the Art Institute of Chicago later this afternoon.

My plan was to find Ciarocci and let her know that my entire creation was for her. It was hers to take home and admire for the next two weeks while we were apart, no doubt convincing her of my talents and cementing our romantic relationship. I had specifically asked for breath mints in my stocking this year to get ready for the first day back at school in January.

The trickiest part about this whole gift thing, though, and the thing that I was most nervous about, was anyone else catching wind of it. Male elementary-school behavior is bizarre when it comes to girls. You can't like them. Ever. You can't like boys either, obviously, but you most certainly can't like girls. Instead, you were supposed to operate in some kind of strange neutral zone, one that rewarded disinterest and, whenever possible, cruelty. So, let's say you really liked a girl. The best course of action was to push her down the stairs or shove gum in her hair, thus proving that you didn't like her. I wasn't doing that here. I wasn't mouthing off to Miss Ciarocci, or acting out in class. I was giving her a gift. I was crossing the line into confirmed heterosexuality and overall niceness. If caught, this was an offense punishable by years of torment and ridicule from my peers. I really had to watch my step.

"I'm eating your Jingles, Boyle."

I looked up to see Delund pawing at my solar system. This was not good.

"Hey, quit it."

He plucked up a few bells, tossing them in his mouth.

"Come on, quit it."

"Make me."

"That's my ornament project, Dan."

Over the past week, Delund and I had developed enough of a relationship for me to start calling him Dan. Or at least that's what I thought.

He hit me in the arm and we were back to square one again.

"I don't give a crud." He snatched another cookie. "We already got our grades, what do you care?"

"I'm giving it as a gift."

"To who?"

"Uh, nobody."

"Nobody?"

He had me now. It would be years before any of us would learn not to give "nobody" or "nothing" as an excuse. It always backfired.

"Who is it?" He crunched away.

"Nobody, alright?

"A *girl?*"

"No. Shut up."

"Oooh. Boyle's got a girlfriend. Boyle's got a girrrllfriend. Boyle's got a girrrllfriend!"

He was singing now. This was getting serious.

"A girrrllfriend. A girrrllfriend!"

"I do not. It's just a gift. I don't even like it. I just gotta bring it home."

Just then, Miss Ciarocci rounded the corner at the far end of the hall. My face went red as I looked up. She waved to us. Delund put two and two together.

"You're in love with Ciarocci, aren't you?"

"Am not."

"Are too. That's why you're always asking her questions and stuff. Holy cow, you love her!"

"I do not!"

Delund called out down the hall. "Jake Doyle's in love with you, Miss Ciarocci!"

Luckily, she hadn't heard. She was still too far away. I watched her duck into a classroom. How could Delund know I was in love with her? Was it that obvious?

"You want to marry her!"

"SHUT UP! I don't like her! She's stupid! This whole project is stupid. I hate it!"

My face was burning now. Ciarocci exited the classroom and was now heading straight toward us.

"I'm gonna tell her you're in love with her, Boyle."

"No. Don't. I hate her."

"Gimme your Trapper Keeper."

"No way."

"Give it to me or I tell her you want to marry her."

"It's got all the money in it."

"I know. Your plan's stupid. I'm in charge now. I'm buying the Nintendo. Give it to me."

Delund snatched the binder from my hands and dangled it over my head.

"Give it back!"

"No way. I'm telling her you love her."

Ciarocci was seconds away.

"Don't say anything. I don't like her at all. She's gross. I hate her."

"You gotta tell her that, then."

"No!"

"Tell her you hate her. Or I'm gonna tell her you love her."

I could feel my stomach churning. I was sweating. This was the most scared I'd ever been in my entire life. Ciarocci floated over to us, as cheerful and sweet as ever in her Christmas sweaterdress.

"Good morning, boys. Isn't Jake's project great?"

Delund nudged me and stared me down.

"It's stupid," I heard myself say.

"Why would you say that? I think it's great. It's very creative."

"Jake has something he wants to tell you, Miss Ciarocci."

"No, I don't."

I couldn't even look at her. I kept my head down and just stared at the pipe-cleaner donkey next to the manger. Even the donkey seemed to sense the severity of the situation. His two little raisin eyes looked up at me in desperation.

Delund wasn't backing down. "Go on, Jake. Tell her what you were going to tell her, or I'm gonna tell her."

"What is it, Jake?"

"I... hate you," I whispered.

"What?" Miss Ciarocci bent down.

"I hate you, Miss Ciarocci."

Pain registered on her face, the pain of a young teacher not fully grasping the code of honor between nine-year-old boys. Suddenly I hated everything. Delund, school, Nintendo, field trips, being embarrassed, liking a woman twenty years older than me, the barnyard animals and their stupid gumdrop heads, everything.

"Jake, why would you say—"

And then I lost it.

"I hate this whole stupid thing! I hate it!"

WHACK. I kicked the table. SMACK. I hit the manger to the ground. CRASH. I splattered the Wise Men and the animals all across the floor. I stomped on the Baby Jesus's head. I threw Mary and Joseph into the wall. I went bonkers.

"Jake! Stop! Stop it!"

"I hate it! I hate it!" Before I knew it, I was on the ground, screaming and banging my fists on the floor.

Miss Ciarocci grabbed me and picked me up. I was shaking. Delund's smirk was gone. My art project was in ruins.

"What's wrong? Why would you do that?"

I started to cry—thick, heaving, snotty sobs—the kind of tears that won't let you catch your breath. Kid tears.

"Dan, go to your classroom. Right now."

"But I—"

"Now."

Delund left. Down the hall, kids were already putting on their coats and lining up for the bus to Chicago. I watched my Trapper Keeper round the corner, and then it was gone. It was all over. All my months of hard work had been ruined in the span of seconds. No money, no girl, no genius art project, it had all gone to pot. Miss Ciarocci wiped my face with the sleeve of her sweater and waited patiently for me to regain my composure.

"What's wrong, Jake? You can tell me?"

"I'm sorry, Miss Ciarocci. I'm really sorry. I, I . . . "

"What's going on here?" It was Huge-Blow. She was standing over the mess. "What in God's name happened here? Jake Doyle, did you do this?"

Ciarocci stood up. "Everything's fine, Mrs. Hugo. Jake just had a little moment, that's all. Everything's fi-ne."

"Well, we're leaving for the field trip now, so I want this mess cleaned up immediately. He's got a check after his name today. No excuses."

Great. A check. Now I'd have to stay after school on the last day before Christmas vacation. I'd probably have to take down Christmas decorations or clean up Huge-Blow's Kleenex or do some other soul-crushing chore. Could things possibly get any worse?

"And Jake."

"Yes, Mrs. Hugo?"

"Don't even think about forgetting your boots this time. No boots, no field trip."

Son of a bitch.

# CHAPTER TWENTY-THREE

I'd always been fascinated with pirate movies as a kid. Particularly those that involved walking the plank. It was the ritual of it all. There was no need to go such lengths to kill someone unless you were kind of excited about it. I mean, why not just throw the guy overboard? Why blindfold him? Why make him walk so slowly? Because it was a delightfully fun experience for the torturers, that's why. Except for every once in a while when it backfired. Like when Jabba the Hut tried to do it to Luke Skywalker in *Return of the Jedi* and Luke bounced his way to safety. That was the best part about the plank—if you were smart enough, there was usually a way to escape from it.

But there was no escaping this one. It was only about twenty feet from the school's front doors to the awaiting bus, but in my girls' boots it felt like the longest plank walk in history. Slowly I trudged forward, shackled at the ankles in pretty white trim and French cuffs. There was no Jedi mind trick that could get me out of this one. I was walking into certain death.

The smell hit me as soon as I got to the top of the steps. A school bus's smell in the winter is unmistakable. Heat, gas, condensation, vinyl and sweat all mixing together to form a generally foul stench. They say smell is the sense most closely linked to memory, and they're not kidding. To this day, whenever I ride public transportation in the winter, I'm reminded of that school-bus smell and it sends me into a panic. It has become my fight-or-flight trigger. Vietnam vets have napalm and burnt human hair. I have diesel fumes and soggy sack lunches.

As I walked down the aisle, the first person to notice my boots was Katie Sorrentino. I'm pretty sure it was because she was wearing the exact same pair. She looked at me like I had antennas sprouting out of my head.

"What are you *doing*?"

She was kind of a snot, Katie Sorrentino.

"Getting on the *bus*," I shot back. Not the right move.

"Hey everybody!" she called out. "Jake Doyle is wearing the same boots as me!"And that was the end of that. I was stuck in the middle of the aisle with every eye on the Esprits and every finger pointed at my face. Recurring nightmares of Freddy Kruger and the '84 Cubs' collapse quickly took a back seat to this moment. I had a new bad dream to haunt me now.

"Sweet boots, Doyle!"

"Where's your dress?"

"You idiot!"

"How 'bout a Rainbow Brite for Christmas, Jake?"

Little Nate Pellettieri was laughing so hard, he fell right out of his seat. I had to step over him as I made my way to the back of the bus. I caught Delund's eye. He was not pleased.

"Hey, I forgot all about those. You really are a little girl, Boyle. Did your girlfriend, Ciarocci, buy those for you?"

"Shut up."

"He's in love with Miss Ciarocci! He was just crying! I saw him!"

Delund stood up in front of me, blocking the aisle. I tried my best to get by him.

"Where do you think you're gong? You're not sitting back here with those boots."

"Lemme get by."

"What are you gonna do? Hit me with your purse? Go sit in the front with the girls. I'm in charge now."

"Jake Doyle! Find a seat!" Huge-Blow called out from the front of the bus. It was useless trying to get past Delund. I turned around and made my way back toward the front. There was only one seat open and of course, it was right beside Conor Stump. I had no other choice but to sit down next to him.

"Those boots are cool."

"Shut up, Stump."

It only takes about fifty minutes to get from Batavia to Chicago, but those were the longest fifty minutes of my life. I sat there staring out the window, wondering how we'd ever pull this heist off now that Dan Delund was calling the shots. None of my friends came to my aid either. I guess I couldn't blame them. It's tough to stick up for a guy in girls' boots, especially one who'd been called out for being in love with his own teacher.

I passed the time trying to think about happier Christmases. There was the fish tank I'd gotten a few years ago—that was a good Christmas. Sure, all the fish died because I never fed them, but at least I got the present I'd asked for. Then there was the Christmas when I got my Walter Payton football uniform and spent all of Christmas morning freezing my butt off in the backyard, dodging dog poo as my dad sent me out on elaborate passing patterns. That was a pretty good Christmas too. They'd all been pretty good Christmases, actually. So why did this one have to suck so hard?

The bus rattled down I-90 and toward the outskirts of the city. Conor Stump was singing happily to himself. He'd been doing so the entire trip.

"*When you're heading into first and you feel a juicy burst, diarrhea. Diarrhea.*"

Ah yes, the old diarrhea song, a real fan favorite. I looked over at him. He was bobbing to his own music, carefree as a canary, footloose and fancy free. How could a guy like Conor Stump be so goddamn happy? All he did all day long was get dumped on. What was his problem?

"*When you're sliding into third and you* . . . uh, *when you're sliding into third and you feel*, uh . . . " He'd skipped second base altogether and was now having a little trouble with what happened on third.

"*You feel a juicy turd*," I forced myself to say.

His face lit up. "Oh yeah! *When you're sliding into third and you feel a juicy turd, diarrhea! Diarrhea!*"

Was this how it was going to be from now on? Me and Conor Stump together forever, singing poo songs? The bus turned a corner onto Michigan Avenue. It was bumper-to-bumper holiday traffic. We were in familiar territory now. It had taken some phonebook reconnaissance and a little help from the Gruseckis' encyclopedias, but we had pinpointed this area as the place to enact Operation Nintendo. Water Tower Place was just a few blocks away. I looked back toward Zilinski and locked eyes with him. It was now or never.

Zilinski ran up beside me, careful not to be seen out of his seat by Huge-Blow. "What's the deal?"

"Delund stole my Trapper Keeper. He says he's the one who's gonna buy it now."

"Does he even know how to get to the toy store? Does he know we're almost there?"

I looked back at Delund. He was just sitting there counting the money.

"I don't know. Just go ahead with the plan. I'll talk to him. Wait for my signal."

"Got it, Jake. Good luck."

"You too."

Zilinski hustled up to the front of the bus. Our plan was to implement a fake-puke distraction that would give me enough time to hop off the back of the bus undetected. Zilinski was a hell of a fake puker. He had this thing where he'd hide a cup of Mott's applesauce in his sleeve and hold his hand to his mouth and squeeze it out. It was brilliant. Ferris Bueller had nothing on Zilinski. He was definitely the man for the job.

But now that Delund had all the money, our whole plan was in jeopardy. I waited a few seconds for the right moment and then I ran back toward him.

"This is the spot, Dan."

"The spot for what?"

"The spot for the plan. Steve's about to puke."

Up at the front of the bus Zilinski was putting it into action.

"Mrs. Hugo . . . "

"What are you doing out of your seat, Steve? Get back to your seat this instant."

"I don't feel good . . . "

But Delund just sat there. He had his feet propped

up and his hand was resting comfortably on my Trapper Keeper.

"I told you before, Boyle, your plan's stupid. Don't worry. I'll hold onto the money."

"But—"

"I *said*, I'll hold onto the money."

What was he doing? This was ridiculous. Frantically, I heard myself squeak, "Are you chickening out?"

"What did you say?" He rose from his seat. Half the bus was watching now. "Your plan's stupid. I'm not doing it. Now get outta here." He pulled back and socked me in the arm. "Go back and make out with Stump. You girls deserve each other."

I looked around. All eyes were on me. For the second time that day I felt like crying. I started to make my way back to my seat when I made eye contact with Conor. He was smiling slightly, like he was in on his own private joke. His nose was running a little bit still, but it didn't seem to bother him. Nothing seemed to bother him. Not his rainbow mittens, not his purple sweatpants, not his cowlick or lack of friends. He was perfectly content sitting there by himself.

"Don't worry about him, Jake," he said with his mitten half in his mouth. "Delund's not worth it."

And that's when it hit me. Conor Stump was the only kid at HC Wilson who had it all figured out. His dumb face and runny nose were suddenly speaking volumes to me. Conor Stump wasn't a dork. He wasn't a loser or a wimp. He was a rebel. He did whatever he wanted and he didn't give a crud about the consequences. He wasn't scared of Dan Delund. He wasn't scared of anybody. So why should I be? Nintendo or not, Delund had been king of the mountain for too long. I needed to do something about it.

I turned around and walked right back up to him. "Hey! Dipstick!" I shouted.

The bus went silent.

"What did you call me?"

"You heard me. You're all talk, no walk, Delund."

"What's that supposed to mean?"

Without even thinking, I slammed my girls' boot directly into his chest, pinning him to the seat. In my best Indiana Jones voice, I laid it on him. "It means, give me the Trapper Keeper, you heavy-metal hair on an elephant's butt."

Shock. Complete shock. Jaws were dropping all around me.

"*Now.*"

Delund just sat there dumbfounded.

Conor Stump looked on, quietly nodding his head with conviction.

Up at the front of the bus, Steve must have sensed the change in mood, because the bus quickly came to a halt.

"Uggghhh! I'm gonna puke, Mrs. Hugo . . . "

"Open the door. Driver! Open the door!"

I jammed my foot down harder, the sole of my boot practically tattooing ESPRIT on Delund's neck. "Give it to me!"

Cautiously he reached for the Trapper Keeper and, without a word, handed it over. Even the girls in the front row were watching us now. Out on the sidewalk, Steve was letting the Mott's fly, "puking" his guts out as Huge-Blow watched over him. It was now or never.

"Let's do this."

The Gruseckis leapt out of their seats and forged a path toward the emergency exit. Olsen and Mahoney mashed their coats on the alarm buzzer. Ryan pulled the handle, Tommy turned the latch, and before I knew it, I was jumping out the back door onto the cold streets of Chicago.

My feet landed square on the pavement. It took me a second to collect my bearings, but when I did I took off like a shot. Zilinski hopped back onto the bus, and within moments it pulled out into traffic again. As I sprinted down the sidewalk, the bus rounded the corner right alongside me, lurching forward in traffic. We were neck and neck heading down the Magnificent Mile. Kids pressed their faces to windows and doors, silently cheering me on. I was doing it!

"Go get 'em, Jake," whispered Stump.

"Look at him run," gasped Olsen.

"Those boots sure are gay," lisped Farmer.

Never one to weigh the consequences, Mahoney stuck his head out the window and screamed at the top of his lungs. "Goonies never say die, Doyle!"

From the front seat, Zilinski faked another puke and I rushed past the bus for good, disappearing into the crowd. There was no turning back now.

I could barely keep my feet on the ground as I pushed through the doors at Water Tower Place. I'd never been so jacked up before in my life. I was on my own, completely alone for the first time in the adult world. Under any other circumstances I probably would have been a nervous wreck. Just last year I'd gotten separated from my parents at the Kane County Fair for a few minutes and I almost peed myself. But this was different. I had a reason to be here. There were kids depending on me. I was not about to let them down.

But once inside the mall, paranoia started to set in.

Being out in the real world during school hours was a very peculiar feeling, one that you only ever caught a glimpse of when you stayed home sick or had to go to a funeral or something. It was almost like you were seeing behind the curtain. As I walked through the mall, it felt like every grownup in the building was staring at me, as if they all knew I was ditching school. I envisioned Chicago's finest cuffing me at any moment and dragging me away to juvie. But I pressed forward. I made my way to the escalator stairs and followed the scratch-and-sniff sticker smells up to the toy section of Marshall Field's.

At the top of the stairs, I caught a glimpse of my old friend, Nintendo. He looked different now without a crowd of kids around him, almost lonely. I scurried across the floor, still clutching my Trapper Keeper, and stood before the display, where a familiar voice greeted me.

*I knew you'd come.*

I missed you, Nintendo.

*I know you did, Jake. I know you did. How 'bout a quick game of* Double Dragon *for old times' sake?*

I don't think I have time.

*You had time to put on Katie Sorrentino's boots, I see.*

Very funny.

*Just keeping you on your toes. Now, go do what you've got to do. You were born for this moment, Jake. Remember that.*

Thanks, Nintendo.

*Go make me proud.*

I took off down the aisle, and he called after me, his voice almost quivering with delight. *Nintendo is your friend-o, Jake! Nintendo is your friend-o!*

Three minutes later, I was standing in line at the checkout counter, teetering under the weight of an NES, five game cartridges and thirty yards of orange extension cord. Choosing games had been the trickiest part. We still weren't sure what the fallout with Kleen's games might be. Even if we were able to salvage his collection, we were pretty sure that meant we'd have to let him play, which defeated the whole purpose of buying our own system in the first place. So it was imperative that we purchased the right balance of games, not just ones we hadn't played before. It had to be the perfect mix of classics and recent releases. I'd settled on the following:

1. *Double Dragon*. We still hadn't beaten the guy with the machine gun at the end and I was determined to finish the job.

2. *RBI Baseball*. It never got boring.

3. *Excitebike*. You always need a good racing game.

4. *Mega Man 2*. We'd heard great things about this one.

5. *Captain Skyhawk*. My wild card. Sometimes you've just got to go with the picture on the front of the box. And this one looked really cool.

Every grownup in line was staring me down, nervously chattering to each other about the kid in the back of the line by himself. I just smiled and did my best to act natural.

"They got some real good deals here, huh," I said to the guy in front of me, who was looking me over through an armful of board games.

"How old are you?"

"Nine. How old are you?"

"Cute, kid. Where are your parents?"

"They're waiting in the car, couldn't find a parking spot. You know how it is. You got Enchanted Forest, huh? Great game. Lots of magic."

"Your parents just let you pick out your own presents?"

"Yeah, you know, it's a lot easier that way. They say everyone should do it like that."

"Next in line, please." The girl behind the counter was waving the guy in front of me forward. I hadn't really noticed her before. She was probably about eighteen, thin, cute, big eyes, pretty smile . . . Uh oh. Hold on a second here, she was super hot. Good Lord, she was amazing. This was going to be a problem . . .

Even as a nine-year-old, I knew I did not function well in high-stress situations when a cute girl was involved. Girls had been taking my milk money for years. They would prove to be my downfall throughout adolescence, culminating in a pathetic 1080 SAT score in high school, when I had to take the test sitting next to Megan Paparo. You try to concentrate on geometry multiple-choice questions with her legs in the way. I had to retake the thing twice just to get into college.

I watched the guy in front of me pay for his board games and then it was my turn to approach the cash register. I had to stand on my tiptoes and let the extension cords and games fall from the top of the Nintendo box onto the counter. It was the only way I could reach. A few games slid off onto the floor. Not a good start.

"Sorry."

"That's okay. Let me help you with that."

The girl leaned over and touched my arm. Oh man . . .

"Are you here by yourself?"

Act cool. Say something smart.

"Uh . . . Nintendo's fun . . . "

You retard.

"What?"

"I mean, yeah. I'm here alone. I drove in with some friends."

Nice one, Jake. Keep it together, buddy.

"I see. I like your hat. What's your name?"

Is it hot in here? Am I sweating? I'm sweating, aren't I?

"Uh, thanks. It's Jake."

"I'm Terri. Nice to meet you. How old are you?"

"Nine."

"What's that, fourth grade?"

"Third."

"Man, I remember when I was in third grade. My parents would've never let me go shopping alone."

"Yeah, they're pretty cool."

"Do you live around here?"

This was seriously heating up.

"No."

"Do you live in Batavia?"

"How do you know that?"

"It's written on your hat."

I'd been wearing my obnoxious red and yellow Batavia Bulldogs hat all winter.

"Oh, yeah. Batavia. It's next to Aurora in Kane—"

I caught myself. Wait a second . . . Was she about to bust me? Was this all a ploy to get me to say where I was from?

She batted her pretty eyes. "Batavia's in Kane County. I know. There's a ban on Nintendo there."

Damn you, hot woman!

"I can't sell this to you unless your parents are with you. I'll lose my job. You're the second kid from Kane County this week who's tried to buy a Nintendo himself."

"But, but . . . I've got all the money. Look."

"I can't do it. I'm sorry. It's store policy. All the stores here agreed to it."

"Can't you just do it just this once? I won't tell anybody."

"I'll lose my job, Jake. I'm really sorry. I can sell you the extension cord, though."

Great, maybe I'll hang myself with it.

"How about some nice GI Joes or He-Men?"

"Forget it."

I gathered up my money and stormed off. I couldn't even look at the Nintendo display on the way out. I was too ashamed.

Getting a cab on Michigan Avenue as a nine-year-old proved to be a little harder than I thought. Eventually a saxophone-playing Santa on the corner took pity on me and flagged one down. I hopped into the back seat, still clutching my Trapper Keeper.

"Where to, chief?"

"Art Institute."

The cabbie looked me over from the rearview, a little concerned.

"So what gives?"

"I got money, don't worry."

"No, I mean why the long face? What gives?"

Great. Seven hundred cab drivers in the Loop alone,

and I have to get the one who speaks English. I looked up to the rearview and caught his reflection. He was an older guy but spry. White hair and stubble, the kind of cab driver who could probably get you to O'Hare from downtown in twenty minutes. A real pro.

"You're not running away, are you? Where are your parents? Come on, kid, you can tell me. What's wrong?"

"I don't want to talk about it."

"Come on. Everybody talks in my cab. Them's the rules. Are you on Christmas vacation?"

"Yeah, almost."

"Then you should be happy. Go on, tell me what the problem is."

I looked out the window at all the happy shoppers passing by, all the lights and joyful decorations. Okay, fine . . . "I'm not going to get what I want for Christmas," I said. "Nobody is."

"Yeah, that's a tough one. No two ways about it." He rubbed his stubble thoughtfully. "You know, one year when I was a kid, I wanted a horse. Can you believe that? We lived eight blocks from Comiskey and I wanted a horse. All November, all December that's all I talked about. He'd sleep behind the garage, I'd feed him carrots, I'd give people rides in Grant Park, you know, stuff like that. My grandparents, my parents, they all ask me, 'Chester, what do you want for Christmas this year?' A horse, I says, over and over, a horse. That's it, nothing else. Everybody tells me, 'Chester, we can't get a horse and that's final.' I don't listen to 'em and I spend all Christmas waiting for the horse, worrying about the horse, figuring out how to get the stinking horse. And then you know what happened Christmas morning?"

"You got the horse?"

"Nope. I don't even remember what I got that Christmas, but it sure wasn't a horse. A few years later I realized something, though. I'd wasted a whole Christmas. I let a perfectly good Christmas pass me by, worrying about something that didn't really even matter anyway."

A BMW pulled out in front of us, cutting us off. The cabbie just swerved around him without losing speed. The guy was good.

"You see that? Come January, I'd have called that yuppie every name in the book. But right now, well, it's Christmas. You only got so many of 'em and you gotta make 'em count. You know what I mean? Like with you. I betcha you haven't even told somebody Merry Christmas yet this year, have you?"

"I don't know."

The cabbie pulled off onto a side street. I could tell we were approaching the Art Institute. Those big lion statues sat out front, wearing huge Christmas wreaths around their necks.

"Who are you meeting here? Your parents?"

"My class. We're on a field trip and I kind of left. I'll probably get held back now. How much do I owe you?"

The cabbie chuckled. "Hold on there. You cut out on a field trip?"

"Yeah."

"You got some cojones on you kid. Is it a big class?"

"Pretty big."

"Tell you what. This is the back entrance to the place. Tell the guard at the door over there that you got lost. He'll let you in, just hop right back in with your class, you'll be fine."

"You think?"

"Easy peasy. No problem."

"Thanks. How much is it?"

"Ah, don't worry about it. You gotta do me a favor though, chief."

I opened the door and started to slide out. "What's that?"

"Have a Merry Christmas."

# CHAPTER TWENTY-FOUR

Christmas Eve had finally come. I sat on the couch facing our giant, branch-impaired tree, dressed in my Sunday best, listening to the sounds of my father cursing up a storm as he rewired the upstairs bathroom. A few days before the Christmas extended-family invasion, John Doyle went through a brief but alarming period of enlightenment in which he became privy to the reality that two-thirds of the house was still under construction. It was a trying time for all of us.

"GOD BLESS IT! Where's the caulk gun?"

I was doing my best to stay out of his way. I'd done a good job of avoiding trouble in general over the past couple of days, the field trip included. The cabbie had been right. I was able to sneak right back in with my class at the Art Institute. Huge-Blow was oblivious to the whole thing. I gave everyone their money back and apologized about everything, but no one seemed to complain. My moment with Delund at the back of the bus had given me a new reputation. My girls' boots were no longer an issue. All in all, it hadn't been too bad an afternoon. Huge-Blow even forgot about making me stay after school. Even so, two days later, I still couldn't get over the hump. All I could think about was Nintendo.

I'd never considered myself a praying man, but this close to zero hour I was all out of options. As I sat there on the couch, lost in thought, I figured, why not give prayer a shot? I'd seen it work in *It's a Wonderful Life*. It seemed like George Bailey and I were on an even playing field as far as dilemmas go, so maybe it could do the trick for me too. I centered myself, took a deep breath, focused on the Baby Jesus ornament at the center of the tree and offered up a doozy . . .

*Dear God. It's me, Jake Stephan Doyle. How's it going? You'll probably hear more from me in an hour or so at Holy Trinity Church. I'm an altar boy there. Not that I'm bringing that up to score points or anything. You probably already know I'm an altar boy, because you know everything, because you're God. I'm just bringing it up because, well, you know, because I care. I really care about you, God, and your son, Jesus, even though you guys are like the same person. And I care about Mary and Joseph and all the saints too. I guess what I'm trying to say is, Happy Birthday, Jesus. I hope you get all the presents you want. I'm sorry if someone tries to double up on a birthday present and a Christmas present at the same time. Actually, do you even get Christmas presents, Jesus? Or are they all birthday presents? That sucks if they're all birthday presents. Sorry I said* sucks. *Sorry about that. I know it's not a swear, but I shouldn't have said it anyway. Shit. Oh, man. Now I said* shit. *Now I said* shit *twice. God—sorry. Sorry about that. Now I'm really blowing it, aren't I? I'll say a bunch of Hail Marys right after this, I promise.*

*New paragraph. I know this is a new paragraph because if I was writing this prayer down in my school workbook, then this is when a new idea would start. Mrs. Huge-Bl—I mean, Mrs. Hugo, she would make me indent here. So that's what I'm doing in my mind: indenting. I'm getting very good at it. I'm working very hard in school, just so you know. Anyway, I guess what I'm trying to say, God/Jesus, is this: I really want a Nintendo for Christmas. Is there anything you can do to help me? Do you have a line to Santa Claus? I'm not really sure I believe in him anymore, but if you can call him up and let him know my situation, I'm confident he'll get me one. If there's anything you can do, I know you'll do it, because you're a loving God. Father Joe says that all the time. So if you could, please give me some kind of sign that you'll figure this out, some kind of signal that can give me hope. I don't want to sound like Princess Leia or anything, but you're my only hope, God. Please, will you help me?*

With my eyes still closed, I let the question linger there for a second. I felt a slight breeze on my face, then suddenly . . . WHOOSH! I opened my eyes just in time to see the Christmas tree come crashing down on top of me.

"Jake! Did the tree just fall over again?"

"Yeah, Mom."

I crawled out from under the branches, covered in sap and broken ornaments. Some sign from God.

My mom hustled in from the kitchen. "Oh, honey, did it fall on you?"

"Kind of." Luckily the coffee table had broken much of the fall.

This wasn't the first time the tree had fallen over. Thanks to our ancient stand and my father's cutting techniques, it happened about once a year, usually when we were out of the house. We'd come home to find Elwood drinking out of the stand amid broken ornaments and pine needles.

"Did the tree just fall over again?" my dad called out from upstairs.

"Yes, John."

"God bless it!"

He flew down the stairs, covered in drywall. "How many times do I have to say it, Patty? We need a new tree stand!"

"Do you see that trunk? It's cut at an angle. How do you think a tree can stand up straight when it's at an angle?"

"The bottom of the trunk doesn't even touch the ground, it's balanced on the—oh, forget it. What time is it?"

"We have to be at the church in thirty-five minutes."

"Thirty-five minutes! I haven't even showered yet."

"I showered, Mommy." Lizzy was standing on the stairs enjoying the mess.

"Yes, Lizzy, good girl."

"I haven't even finished putting up the socket covers yet, Patty. How long have they been exposed like that in the bathroom?"

"Since you tried to redo them last Christmas Eve. Just forget them, John, and go shower. You need to get ready."

But the old man was already sniffing out another project. He lifted the tree back up and set it in the corner against the unfinished staircase railing. You could see the Bob Vila wheels turning. "Jake. Go get the shop-vac from the garage. And the band saw. The one with the teeth.

Have your sister help you. I wanna recut this banister before we go to Mass. Move it."

Christmas Eve Mass at Holy Trinity Church was always packed. Folks found religion overnight, as my mom was fond of saying. I guess you could liken all the extra people in church to a bunch of fair-weather fans showing up for a playoff run at a sporting event. But the Doyles were no fair-weather churchgoers, no sir. We were there every week, no matter how bad the team was. When it came to Catholicism, my mother was a diehard. She never left the game early to beat the traffic. She never dozed off when things got boring. She always kept score. She always believed. Even as a kid, I respected her for that. That blind faith was probably what also made her such a great Cubs fan. It was her ability, like so many other diehards, to see through that constant fog of disappointment. Doom and gloom were all too familiar at Holy Trinity and the Friendly Confines, but it was the promise of "next year" that kept it all going. Hope without logic, that's what defined each theology. Catholics and Cub fans; in my opinion, they're pretty much the same thing.

My dad, on the other hand, was a realist. He'd given up on both teams years ago. Sure, he still went to Mass with us every Sunday, but it was out of habit at this point. Much the same way he still watched the Cubs in the summer. He certainly didn't *enjoy* watching them, but what else was he supposed to do? Watch the Sox? He'd been a Cubs fan his whole life, a Cubs fan who lived on the South Side, no less. He couldn't switch now, just because they still sucked, just like he couldn't become a

Baptist just because it was a pain in the ass to find a parking spot at Holy Trinity on Christmas Eve. He was stuck.

"Look at this. *Look at this.* Church doesn't start for another forty minutes!"

The Chrysler minivan darted into the already packed lot, weaving around old ladies and children like they were orange cones. Five o'clock Christmas Eve Mass had gotten so popular with the "twice-a-years," as my dad called them, that we now had to show up almost an hour early just to get a seat.

"Easter and Christmas. Easter and Christmas. Jiminy Cricket. What do they do the rest of the year? Huh? They should make 'em pass a test to be able to come tonight. Look at that idiot. That truck's straddling two easy-out spots. COME ON!"

My dad was a big fan of "easy outs," parking spots with direct and immediate access to the exit. He'd almost always back up into the spot so he'd be able to pull out quicker during the home stretch. Leaving Mass in a hurry was a very important part of the process for him. Secretly, I think he loved the thrill of it all. Getting in, securing seats, leaving quickly—these were the only aspects of church he actually had control over. The man had a system.

"Alright, Patty, I'm dropping you at the door. Kids, seat belts off, I want a quick hop out. Go save a row while I park. Let's see a little hustle for once."

He zipped up to the church's front entrance, revving the gas as he waved us out the sliding door.

"Go, go, go."

Securing a whole row was always very important for the Doyles. We had over a dozen family members on their way, and they were almost always late. As an altar boy, I had to head back to the sacristy to get ready for the big show, so my mom and sister took charge initially. My sister wasn't above shedding a few fake tears just to get positioning near the front. But once my dad got back from parking the car, reserving the row was strictly his job. The old man guarded the aisle like a junkyard dog, carefully scanning the entrance for possible threats and emitting grunts of hostility to those who got too close to his turf.

"Excuse me, sir." A family of five approached, attempting to scoot by.

"Seat's taken, Mac," my dad growled.

"Which ones?"

"The row."

"The whole row? You gotta be kidding me."

"Afraid not. Haven't seen you around here before. Just move to Batavia?"

"We've lived here fifteen years."

"And how many times you been to church? Huh? Three? Move along."

Just because my dad hated going to church didn't mean he had any sympathy for the twice-a-years. And why should he? He had to spend every Sunday morning stuck in a pew while they slept in or watched football or did whatever it was twice-a-years did on Sundays. Now here they were on Christmas Eve, prancing around, acting like they owned the place. My dad was not about to sit by and let that happen. Even the regular churchgoers all knew to steer clear of John Doyle on Christmas and Easter. He was a force to be reckoned with.

Luckily, I didn't have to be a part of the seat-saving scene. I had a job to do. I had fires to light with the Grusecki twins. Lighting the massive advent candles at the front of the altar was a dream come true to a nine-year-old pyromaniac such as myself. It was the main reason I'd signed up for the altar boy job in the first place. I'd been fascinated by the candles and their giant lighting stick since kindergarten. As such, it was always a power struggle between the Gruseckis and me to determine who would have the privilege of lighting them. We usually resorted to feats of strength to decide a victor.

"One two three four, I declare a thumb war."

Tommy and I went at it, our thumbs twiddling at breakneck speeds.

"You're bending your hand."

"So."

"So, you can't do that," Tommy whined as he shimmied for position.

"I can do whatever I want. It's war."

"No, you can't, that's illegal!"

"*You're* illegal."

"Ooooh. Good one."

We danced back and forth around the sacristy. Tommy's porker of a thumb always proved difficult to pin. You couldn't just jam it down with brute force; it was too chubby. So my go-to move was the old rope-a-dope. I'd dangle my thumb under his, and then shoot it out counterclockwise just as he pressed his down, resulting in a reverse pin. I took thumb wrestling very seriously.

"Pinned! Pinned! That's a pin!"

"Was not!"

"Was too!"

"Boys. Boys! That's enough." Father Joe pulled us apart. "For crying in a bucket, get ready for Mass. Tommy, bring down the crucifix. Ryan, set up the chalice and the purificator. Jake, go grab the lighter thing."

Hell yes! The lighter thing! Every single piece of tableware and preparatory utensil in the Catholic Church had a specific holy Catholic name for it except the lighter thing. The lighter thing was just "the lighter thing." I loved it. It was more or less just a large metal stick with an adjustable candlewick inside of it, but it required lighting matches, the big kind that could ignite off any surface, including my retainer, which always proved quite interesting. Under no other circumstances, at home or at school, was I allowed to operate such dangerous pyrotechnics, so this was a very big deal. I scurried to the side of the sacristy to fire it up.

As I did, I got my first good look at the Doyle family, now all scrunched together in my dad's row. I could see them pretty well from the sacristy side doorway. Every year they traveled to Batavia from the four corners of Chicagoland to celebrate Christmas Eve Mass and have dinner back at our house. It was a night filled with holiday cheer and repressed Irish/Polish hostility.

There was Uncle Hillard, the cop—he was sitting at the end of the row with his gun and badge holstered on his belt and as many as three different pocket knives secured on his person. You could never be "too armed," according to him. Next to Uncle Hillard was my aunt Anne and their three kids, who were always suffering from some kind of real or imagined sickness or ailment. The youngest, Maggie, was currently in a neck brace with an eye patch over her glasses. She was missing some teeth too, which gave her the unfortunate appearance of a five-year-old pirate. Her older brother, Kevin, was poking her eye patch with a pencil. The middle sibling, Heather, was crying, for God knows what reason. Maybe Kevin had stolen her pencil. I did not look forward to sitting with the three of them at the Kid Table later.

Then there was my other uncle, Dr. Dan, the chiropractor. He had his beeper on, as always, just in case, you know, there was a life-or-death sore back emergency that required his immediate assistance. His two bratty kids, Cole and Donnie, munched on red and green Hershey's Kisses, which they shared with no one. Although they were never scientifically proven to be autistic, they both had an unfortunate likeness to Dustin Hoffman in *Rain Man*. "Definitely" was definitely their favorite word. They yell-whispered in chocolate-mouthed monotones back and forth to each other.

"Definitely thirsty right now."

"Yeah. Definitely need to get a drink."

They were seated between their dad and his second wife, who I once heard my grandma call a trollop, a term I thought meant "smells like cinnamon," due to her heavy perfume use. It wasn't until years later when I called a substitute teacher the same thing that I learned the hard way what it really meant. Not a good day for me.

My aunt Connie and Uncle Jack sat next to my parents. They had the oldest kids in the family, Jenny and Jeff. Jenny was sixteen, basically an adult in my eyes, and the coolest person I knew. She performed death-defying feats daily, like telling her parents to "shut up" or "take a chill pill." She'd been to actual live rock concerts and knew that Sting's real name was Gordon Matthew Thomas Sumner. She dressed in new-wave attire and used about a pound of Aqua Net on her hair. My dad had warned me several times to be careful around her with the lighter thing. Then there was Jeff. He was fourteen. Although Jeff and I didn't really get along, mostly because he was always putting me in a sleeper hold, I admired him a great deal. He could fart on cue, and after one or two

Pepsi's could actually burp the alphabet. He was my role model growing up.

Sitting next to my sister were my grandparents. My grandma Doyle was decked out in one of her famous Christmas sweaters. The original, unintentional hipster, Betty Lou Doyle's wardrobe would later launch thousands of ugly-sweater parties throughout the Midwest. Yuppies and frat boys the world over owe her a great deal of gratitude, I think. Grandpa Doyle sat next to her. He was dressed to the nines, as always, in a suit and tie, quietly judging the congregation. He caught me out of the corner of his eye and gave me a wink. I winked back. I loved Grandpa Doyle.

I lit the match off the counter top and watched it blaze forth before me as I held the wick up to the flame. At the front of the church, a tone-deaf collection of eighty-year-old men, also known as the Holy Trinity choir, began to belt out "O Holy Night." That was our cue. It was time to get this show on the road. I grabbed my stick-o-fire and lined up behind Tommy. Ryan slid in next to me and Father Joe filed in behind us.

"Let's play ball," he whispered.

As we processed down the aisle, I watched with glee as the flame on my lighter thing grew bigger and bigger. I was careful to shield it from Zilinski, who was standing toward the back row with his family. He'd been known to try to gleek it out on more than one occasion.

You could feel the energy in the building. Christmas Eve Mass was unlike any other Mass. People were dressed up, kids were engaged, even the music was better. It wasn't "Jingle Bells" or "Rudolph" or anything, but at least you knew the songs. Anticipation hung in the air. Every kid bubbled with excitement. Depending on what time your parents let you get up in the morning, Christmas presents were only twelve or so hours away. All you had to do now was sit through an hour-long Mass. It was an almost impossible task, but this close to the big day, you did not want to give Santa, God or anyone else in charge any reason to dock you for bad behavior. Throughout the church, tongues were held in check, coughs were covered, shoes were tied, and hair was left unpulled. Every kid was at their best.

The Gruseckis and I bowed before the altar and took to the stage. This was my big moment. Every eye in church would be on me as I lit the four Advent candles. They were front and center, surrounded by a huge Christmas wreath. It was almost like lighting the Olympic torch. I had to be steady, I had to be strong, I had to give 100% concentration on what I was—

Holy cow, Ciarocci was sitting in the front row!

Was I dreaming? Nope. There she was, not ten feet away from me, wearing some kind of hippie Christmas skirt thing. Did she have . . . ? She did indeed. She had garland in her hair. She looked beautiful, like an angel, a sweet, smiling, hippie art-teacher angel. And she was smiling right at me. At *me*! Immediately I began to sweat. My hands shook beneath the weight of the lighter thing. I steadied myself and gave her a smile back.

What was she doing here? I'd never seen her once before in church. I'd never even seen her outside of school, period. Running into a teacher in real life was always a shock to the system, but running into a teacher you're madly in love with on Christmas Eve? That was almost too much to handle. She just kept smiling at me. Apparently the whole "I hate you" thing had blown over. I lit the first candle and managed to give her a little head nod. She gave me a tiny wave. We were communicating now.

My hands were trembling. I lit the second candle and let my gaze wander to the tips of her pretty fingernails . . . And that's when I saw him. His arm draped over the back of the pew behind her. He was wearing a gray suit and a dopey Christmas tie. His hair had been gelled and his glasses were now without their ever-present duct tape. It was Mr. Murphy, HC Wilson's fifth grade teacher. He was whispering in her ear. Her hand rested comfortably on his bony knee. Son of a bitch.

Seriously? Mr. Murphy? This was a real thing? Mr. Murphy could barely shoot a basketball. I'd seen him. He sometimes subbed for Mr. Vlahos, our gym teacher. The man was a dweeb. He was from Eau Claire, *Wisconsin*. He was a *Packers* fan. How could this be happening?

The congregation seemed to be in agreement with me, because I began to notice a slight murmur coming from the front rows. What did she see in him? He wasn't artistic. He wasn't cool. He was *Mr. Murphy*. If he gave you a pat on the back, you got "Murphy germs." Didn't she know this?

The murmur grew. It felt like the whole church was on my side now. They had to be. Surely they were seeing what I was seeing. Mr. Murphy with Miss Ciarocci? It was an injustice too big to ignore. This was infuriating. I couldn't take it. My eyes began to blur. My face was getting hotter and hotter. Even more chatter rose from the congregation, growing louder and louder. You see? You see? That's the spirit! Mr. Murphy and Miss Ciarocci? Impossible! Words were beginning to form from within the crowd. They were all with me now, all in agreement. Murphy had to go! Heat was spewing out of them. Anger.

Rage. Panic, even. I could see it in their faces. I heard myself cough, once, twice, then—

"FIRE!" It was Lizzy, yelling through the crowd. "FIRE! JAKE!"

Holy God! The wreath was on fire! The wreath was on fire! Jesus Christ, I'd lit the wreath! The crowd was yelling at *me*! You idiot, Doyle, you're about to burn the whole place down! Smoke began to billow out of the wax-covered pine needles. I had missed the third candle entirely and lit the holy Advent wreath! Flames were leaping from branch to branch. A Catholic inferno was raging before me. The entire poinsettia-dressed altar was in danger of going up in smoke. Had I not been in such a state of shock I might have enjoyed the view. But instead, as I was told later, I just started screaming like a little girl.

"Jake! Look out!" The Gruseckis were running toward me with pitchers of holy water. Father Joe was already batting down the flames with his chasuble.

My arms and legs began to flail about wildly. Oh my God! My robe was on fire! The bottom of my altar boy robe had caught fire! Quickly my mind flipped through the hundreds of public service commercials and Cub Scout warnings I'd been subjected to over the years. What was the thing you were supposed to do when you lit yourself on fire? Tell a friend? No. Tell a grown up? No. Just say no? No, that wasn't it. Come on, doofus, think. It was a three-parter, a rhyme or something . . . It was coming to me now. The first word was a command. That's it, a command.

STOP.

I froze right there on the altar. Stop. That was the first part. What came next? I just stood there like an idiot as people rushed around me. Come on, Doyle, pull yourself together.

DROP.

I dove on the ground, knocking over the manger and a few microphone stands, my face planted on the cold marble. Oh God, what was the third part? What was the third part? It didn't rhyme with stop or drop, it was, it was . . .

ROLL.

Aha! Of course! ROLL. Immediately, I tucked into a barrel roll, the kind I'd perfected on the grassy hill at the back of my grandparents' house, and I rolled. I rolled and rolled and rolled. Through the manger, down the steps of the altar, past the baptismal font, down the aisle—I just kept going. Nobody ever actually explained to us exactly what we were supposed to accomplish by rolling, or when, if ever, we were allowed to stop, so I just kept rolling. The crowd called out my name. Arms and hands reached out to slow me down, but I just barreled right though them—rolling and rolling and rolling, snot and drool and groans emerging from my body. I made it all the way clear to the back of the church before an usher kindly put his foot out and brought me to a halt.

"You can stop rolling now, kid. The fire's out."

I looked up, out of breath. The room was swirling. I could smell smoke. All eyes were on me.

"You alright?"

I nodded.

And then I puked all over him.

On the bright side, in the history of the Catholic Church I was probably the first guy to both puke and light himself on fire in a two-minute span. That's two thousand years of history, so there's something to be said for that. But in actuality I felt about as low as I'd ever felt in my life. It took half an hour or so for the fire department to come and give us the all-clear to finish Mass. The Advent wreath was totally charred, most of the manger animals were broken, and I reeked of burnt vomit. Merry Christmas, Jake Doyle.

The rest of the Mass was a blur. I just wanted to go home, but my dad wouldn't let me. I had a job to finish, he told me, and I had to tough it out. I wasn't burned or hurt, the fire on my robe had been hardly more than a little spark. I was okay. So I carried on as best I could with the ceremony. I tried not to look at Ciarocci. I washed Father Joe's hands when they needed washing, I cleared the altar when it needed clearing, and much to the congregation's relief, I let the Gruseckis handle the candles for the rest of the service.

As I sat on my altar boy chair while Mass was winding down, I took stock of my situation. So far this Christmas season I had single-handedly destroyed two mangers, burned a wreath, forced my friends to sell all their best baseball cards, prayed to God and gotten hit by a tree, lost my retainer and my sister, lied to my parents, skipped out on a field trip, cried in public and puked in church. There was no WAY I was getting a Nintendo for Christmas now. Neither my luck nor my behavior warranted one. Heck, I'd be lucky if I even made it to Christmas morning at this point. All I wanted to do was to go home and go to bed.

Mass ended without any further incident. Father Joe told me I could keep my robe if I wanted to, since it wasn't much use to anyone else anymore. I decided to throw it away. The Gruseckis tried to cheer me up and told me I could come over to their house anytime and burn their encyclopedias, but I wasn't laughing.

I trudged through the parking lot as everyone filed out of the church. Walking out of Christmas Eve Mass into the cold night air had always been one of my favorite moments of the Christmas buildup. It meant I was home free, that there was nothing else standing in the way between me and presents except a restless night's sleep. There was something about that night air that always calmed me down and made me feel at peace. But now, that feeling had been replaced with disgrace and embarrassment. I could tell everyone was staring at me as I headed through the crowd, even my own family. It was a walk of shame.

"Way to go, Smokey." Uncle Hillard slapped me on the back, laughing hysterically. "Remember, only you can prevent church fires."

Hilarious, Uncle Hillard. You know what you can prevent? Being a jackass.

"See ya at home, fireball." He jogged off to his car.

I just kept walking. Miraculously, my dad was still waiting for me, patiently revving the motor in his easy-out spot. I was just about to open the sliding door when a hand touched my shoulder.

"Jake?"

I turned around. It was Miss Ciarocci.

"Are you feeling any better?"

"Uh, I'm okay," I lied.

"You were very brave up there tonight, I thought. You remembered to stop, drop and roll. That was very important."

"Yeah," I said. I was sick of talking to her already. Mr. Murphy was hovering a few yards away, giving me one of his cheese-dick head nods. Ciarocci bent down to my eye level and reached inside her jacket pocket.

"I brought you something."

She gently grabbed my hand and placed a little wrapped package into my glove. I opened it up. Inside were two of my macaroni Wise Men. They were a little beat up, but they were still intact. She'd saved them from the wreckage.

"I thought you might like them." She smiled, her hair beautifully backlit by the headlights and falling snow.

"Thanks."

"You're welcome. Have a Merry Christmas, Jake. I'll see you in a couple weeks."

She stood up and turned to walk away.

"Hey Miss Ciarocci?"

She turned back and brushed her hair behind her ears. "Yes, Jake?"

"Would you like one, one of my Wise Men? You know, that way we can both have one?"

"I'd love one."

I handed her a Wise Man and she gave me a hug.

"Look, Phil, Jake gave me one of his Wise Men."

"One of his what?"

She put her arm around me. "His Wise Men. See?"

"Oh, oh yeah, cool. Good work there, little buddy."

Don't patronize me, Murphy. I stared him down. He blew into his hands impatiently, still keeping his distance in his bright yellow Green Bay Packers' jacket.

"Come on, hon." He nodded to Ciarocci. "Let's get going." He turned to head back toward his car. Only then did I notice the large black and brown marks on the back of his coat.

"What happened to Mr. Murphy's jacket?"

"Oh, that? Well, he tried to put out the fire with it."

"You mean I ruined his Packers' coat?"

"I guess you did." She smiled slightly. "And between you and me, I'm kind of glad. I hate that thing."

I stood there by the van as the two of them walked toward his car. Smiling a secret smile, I watched as charred bits of green and yellow nylon flaked off his shoulders and fluttered into the night.

Jake Doyle: 1. Wisconsin: Zip.

# CHAPTER TWENTY-FIVE

The house was alive with activity. Cousins ran up and down the stairs. The California Raisins' *Claymation Christmas* flickered away on the TV. My mom and my aunts bustled around the kitchen while Elwood and my grandpa sat by the window calmly solving the world's problems over a glass of scotch. It was Christmas Eve on Watson Street, the holiest of all holy nights in Batavia.

Packages upon packages rested haphazardly under the tree. They were all guarded by the stern and often torturous warnings of my grandmother, who would not allow us within fifteen feet of them for fear of us detecting what was inside. We had been warned that even touching a present before present time would result in the loss of a gift. No one really believed her, but no one really wanted to test it out either.

"Get away from those presents, Jeff!" she yelled from the kitchen.

"I'm not touchin' anything, Grandma, jeez. I'm just looking."

The fifteen-feet barrier was the hallway outside the living room. A steady stream of cousins would line up at the edge of the double doorway and peer into the Christmas abyss, obsessively trying to decipher what was what.

Little Maggie was doing her best to see through her one good eye as Kevin continued to try to poke it out with a pencil.

"Quit it! I'm trying to see. Quit it!"

"Make me."

"Mom!"

Cole and Donnie plowed through their unending bag of Hershey's Kisses, robotically munching away as they took stock of the pile below the tree.

"Definitely a shirt box right there. Definitely a shirt box for you, Donnie, not me."

"Definitely not a shirt in that box, definitely not. Probably Legos, not a shirt."

"Shirt box. Definitely."

As for me, I was on the stairs in a headlock, compliments of Uncle Hillard. He was telling my dad another one of his insightful cop stories. The man both talked and looked like a cross between one of the *SNL* Superfans and Dennis Franz from *NYPD Blue*. You couldn't get more Chicago than Uncle Hillard.

"So I get to the house, I don't know: One, who's coming for backup? Two, what kind of yahoos are inside? Tree"—he meant three—"what the hell is going on?"

I was gasping for air under his armpit. "This hurts."

"It's supposed to." He clamped down harder. "Go ahead. Try and get away."

"No."

"Come on."

"No. Let me go."

"Say, 'Uncle Hillard.' Say it."

"Uncle Hillard."

"I can't hear you."

"Uncle Hillard!"

"Don't make me read you your rights, boy."

"UNCLE HILLARD!"

He released me and I scampered off down the hall. "Heh, heh." He grinned at my dad. "You got a whiney little kid there, John. Anyways, where was I?"

"You were wondering what the hell was going on."

"Oh yeah, right. So I says to the lady who opens up the door, ya know, what's the problem? I'm thinking domestic abuse of some nature, which I will 'handle,' thank you very much. Ends up, she's got raccoons."

"Raccoons, huh." My dad was now discreetly sanding a banister.

"Raccoons. Several dozen, loose in her apartment. I don't know, one, how they got there; two, what I'm supposed to do with them; tree, what the hell is going on. I call the Department of Health, they send me to Animal Control, who sends me to the Humane Society. Humane Society asks if any of the raccoons are injured. I says no, they are not, to my knowledge, injured. Guy says, well, officer, we can't help you then. I hang up. Click. I pick up my gun. Click. I take aim. Bang-a-bang. I pick up the phone again. Ah, yes, Humane Society? Why yes, there does appear to be an injury here with one of the raccoons. Tra-la-la, dip-dee-doo, thank you very much."

"You sure showed those raccoons, Hil."

"You betcha."

"Dinner's ready!" my mom yelled from the kitchen doorway.

Two dozen Doyles shot up and clamored toward the

smell of turkey and canned cranberry sauce. Christmas Eve dinner was here at last.

The foremost dynamic to the American extended family dinner is one of positioning and posture, dominated by two distinct and segregated groups. They are universally known as the Grownup Table and the Kid Table. Your position at either of these stations is only advanced by death or divorce. Ranks are never to be broken. There is no buying your way up a notch, no bargaining for position. You're stuck where you're stuck. Only Father Time could grant release from a crowded card table in the kitchen to the spacious, adult luxury of a dining room spread. With the size of the Doyle family, some of my cousins and I would be married and in our late twenties before we actually got called up from the Kid Table to the big show.

The food at a Doyle Christmas was pretty standard. Turkey, cranberry sauce, mashed potatoes, corn, some of those perpetually bottom-burned Pillsbury crescent rolls—it was basically the exact same meal we'd eaten at Thanksgiving four weeks earlier. You'd think we could have mixed it up a little bit, but no.

The lone difference between Thanksgiving dinner and Christmas dinner was the addition of a gourmet Doyle delicacy known as NutraSweet orange Jell-O. Our family loved the stuff. We savored it the way other families might savor caviar or imported wine. And since Aunt Connie only made it once a year, (even though it came straight out of a box), we looked forward to it like the Second Coming. It was like dessert for dinner. A creamy, off-colored, gelatin dreamsicle of sorts, it tasted like a combination of sherbet and Big League Chew. I couldn't get enough of it. I would have gladly substituted orange Jell-O for turkey as the meal's main course. I plowed through the stuff at the Kid Table like a Hungry Hungry Hippo, often leaning in and sucking it straight from the plate.

There were nine of us kids now scrunched together at the kitchen table; a few in booster seats and high chairs, each of us actively protecting our plates from any number of Kid Table attacks that we might be subjected to. There were no rules at the Kid Table. It was every man for himself. My cousin Kevin was inconspicuously spooning peas into his sister's milk, while Jeff entertained us between gulps and burps of Pepsi. He was in the middle of the alphabet, belching up the "L-M-N-O-P" section, which, as everyone knows, is the trickiest part.

Jenny put on her earphones. "That's totally disgusting, Jeff."

*Burrrrp*. . . "Q-R-S, *you're* totally disgusting"—*burrrp*—"T-U-V"—*burrrrp*—"W-X, Y and"—*burrrrp*—"Zeee!"

The whole table applauded, even my sister. The kid had real talent.

"Thank you"—*burp-burp*—"thank you very much. Alright, let's get down to business. What do we got out there?"

We all knew the drill. For years it had been a Kid Table ritual to skip the small talk and systematically divulge as many Christmas gift secrets as we could come up with. Figuring out what your parents were giving you for Christmas was always tough, but figuring out what your parents were giving your cousins, well, that was a manageable task. Our Kid Table had become a well-orchestrated unit of little spies all working together throughout the year in various sibling splinter cells, gathering information and intelligence for our big Christmas Eve meeting.

I sat up and went first. "Jenny, Lizzy and I saw that my parents got you a tape of a band."

"What band was it?" She took off her earphones.

"I think it started with a D. My mom came in the room before I could get a good look at it."

"Depeche Mode? They're so hot."

"No, that's not it."

"Def Leppard? They are so hot."

"No, it wasn't them."

"Flock of *Dorkheads*?" Jeff burped. "They are soooo hot."

"Shut up, Jeff. Was it Duran Duran, Jake?"

"Yeah. That's it. Duran Duran."

"Oh my God, yes! They're totally the hottest."

From there we went around the table for the next ten minutes, revealing the contents of practically every carefully wrapped package under the tree. Despite the cloak-and-dagger aspect of it all, it usually wasn't too hard for me to figure out what I was going to get from my aunts and uncles anyway. The Doyle family was pretty predictable.

You had my uncle Hillard and aunt Anne. They were the king and queen of the two-for-one sale. So their gifts directly correlated to the gifts they were already giving their kids, who, unfortunately, were way younger than me. That meant that I always ended up getting baby crap that I wouldn't be caught dead using. This year was no exception.

"My mom got you the *Boxcar Children* books," said Heather. She was six. "It's stories about kids who live in a boxcar. It's my favorite."

"Neat."

"They also got you a *Sesame Street* sweater."

"Ha ha!" Jeff laughed in my face. "Books and clothes! Books and clothes!"

Then there was my uncle Jack and aunt Connie. Their gifts came from wherever they went on family vacation the previous summer, as if they just *had* to show you how great it was that they went to Iowa or the majestic falls of Douglas County, Wisconsin. Not only that, but their gifts were also very bizarre, items that no kid in his right mind would ever want.

"My parents got you a birdhouse from Phoenix," said Jenny. "It's for both you and Lizzy. It's very ornate, by a very famous Pueblo artist."

"Yeah," burped Jeff. "It sucks ass."

"Mom!" Heather yelled. "Jeff is swearing at the dinner table!"

"Don't make me come in there!" eight dining-room voices called out in unison.

My grandparents of course got us presents too, but we didn't have as much access to figuring out what those might be beforehand. It wouldn't have mattered. They got us the same stuff every year. The dreaded "stuff we needed" versus "stuff we wanted." Did I *want* a new winter coat? Not really. But did I need one? Probably. So that's probably what I was going to get. One thing I could be sure of was that there was no way in hell Grandma Doyle thought I *needed* a Nintendo Entertainment System. That was bound in ironclad certainty.

"Well, what about Dr. Dan?" I asked Ronnie. "What did your dad get me?"

Dr. Dan was my only hope left this year at getting a Nintendo. He was the lone wild card in the bunch. Rich, adventurous—with no regard for parental concerns whatsoever—Dr. Dan was the dream uncle when it came to presents. He once bought my cousin Jeff a BB gun that looked exactly like a Glock nine.

Dr. Dan did all his Christmas shopping on December 23rd, in one hour, on his lunch break, with his secretary. It was a game to him. How fast could he get all of his Christmas shopping done? Could he beat last year's time? Could he get everything on everyone's list in one store? Could he buy everyone the same gift somehow? Price was of no concern to him. It was all about speed.

He was also an exceptionally oblivious shopper. I knew for a fact that he wouldn't have heard about the recent ban on video games in Batavia, and even if my parents had told him of their disapproval of Nintendo he would have paid very little attention. Dr. Dan was going to buy what he was going to buy. If it was in the store and it was on my list and he didn't have to go searching for it, he was going to get it for me. Which is exactly the reason I had mailed him my Christmas list months ago. And exactly the reason I had kept it short and sweet. It read simply:

NINTENDO
(And no clothes)

And that was it. That was the whole list. I'd typed it at school on one of the library's new Apple IIE computers to look as professional as possible, something I thought a man of his stature would appreciate. I was banking on Dr. Dan coming through.

"Hey. Ronnie?" I asked again with baited breath. "What did your dad get everybody this year?"

Ronnie was putting the finishing touches on a snowman made of mashed potatoes and Hershey's Kisses on his lap. "Savings bonds, from the bank," he said, without making eye contact. "Definitely Barris Bank. It took him sixteen minutes. He said it was a new record."

"Yeah, definitely a new record," chimed his brother.

The whole table groaned. *Savings bonds?* From Dr. Dan? That was worse than clothes. That was nothing at all—a useless piece of paper that you'd have to make a trip to the bank on a Saturday just to get rid of. This was the worst year ever!

For a brief moment the Kid Table was quiet. Kevin tossed another pea into his sister's milk, Jenny put her headphones back on, and I worked my way through the remnants of a turkey–Jell-O salad I'd mashed together on my plate. My faint glimmer of Nintendo hope would have to hang on till Christmas morning now.

Fat ladies standing by quietly warmed their vocal cords.

# CHAPTER TWENTY-SIX

There are few tasks more difficult in the life of a kid than trying to fall asleep on Christmas Eve. You could rank it right up there with attempting to fly or meeting Michael Jordan at Jewel-Osco. I'd never been a big fan of sleeping in general, so on Christmas Eve you could forget about it. I was wide awake.

At this point in my increasingly pessimistic Christmas career, I was pretty sure I did not believe in Santa Claus anymore. That was the popular line of thinking in third grade anyway. But that night, lying under my covers, listening to the desperate sounds of our house creak with the wind and the cold, I could think of no one else on Earth who could help me. I *had* to believe in Santa now. There was no other choice.

After all, believing in the big fella was the key to any number of great Christmas stories. I'd read *The Polar Express*. I'd watched *Miracle on 34th Street*. I'd even sat through friggin' *Prancer* with my sister multiple times. Believing in Santa Claus was the key to a happy ending in every single one of them. If you didn't believe, you were doomed.

Maybe, I thought, if I believed hard enough and I managed to stay awake late enough, then maybe I could talk to the man. Maybe I could convince Santa to give me a Nintendo. He had to have extras on his sleigh, or at least some kind of go-to elf floating off in the atmosphere somewhere with a bunch of emergency toys ready to go. I was a pretty convincing guy. I could convince Santa to give me one, right? Heck, with a cap gun and the Mahoney brothers, I had almost convinced little Jimmy Yong from three doors down to lick yellow snow last winter. That took some doing, so maybe I could do the same with Santa. All I had to do was stay awake and listen for him.

A train whistled in the distance. My Chicago Bears clock ticked away on my wall. I laid there, eyes and ears open, and I waited . . .

Tick, tick, tick . . . Ten o'clock. I tried organizing baseball cards in my head, thinking of new and revolutionary ways to sort them based on batting averages and moustaches.

Tick, tick, tick . . . Eleven o'clock. I had little conversations with my GI Joes and He-Men, introducing them to each other. "Orko, this is Shipwreck. Shipwreck, Orko. Here's a topic of conversation: annoying sidekicks. Ready, discuss."

Tick, tick, tick . . . Midnight. I rubbed my blankets together, shooting off static electricity in the dark. I recited the "Super Bowl Shuffle" lyrics in my head, I threw Creepy Crawlers at my wall, anything to keep me awake.

Tick, tick, tick . . . Another half an hour passed. I was still awake, but my eyes were beginning to get a little heavy. I was starting to realize that not being able to fall asleep and trying to stay awake were two entirely different things. Elwood had given up on me at this point and was now lying beneath my bed, dreaming of chasing rabbits and pooping indoors. The house was completely silent. Even the wind had died down. Watson Street was fast asleep and there was still no sign of Santa. I rolled over and concentrated on the window, searching the skies. Tick, tick, tick . . .

*Scrape, scrape, scrape.*

The noise was soft, but it was enough to wake me up. My eyes shot open. The clock read two thirty. Oh no! I'd been asleep for two hours! Had I missed him? Had I missed Santa? I sat up in bed.

*Scrape, scrape, scrape.*

The noise was real. I wasn't imagining it. It was coming from outside. I tossed off the covers and rushed to the window. My heart was pounding. Could it be? Was it the sound of reindeer landing on houses up and down the block? It made sense. I mean, I was in full-blown believing-in-Santa mode right now, what else could it be? I looked out the window. More snow had fallen but there were no tracks, no signs of life, no disturbances to any of the roofs on my block.

*Scrape, scrape, scrape.*

There it was again. It was coming from the other side of the house. I could barely make it out. I stood still and listened. It was a pattern of sorts. A familiar sound, somehow, but I couldn't put my finger on it. Where had Elwood gone off to? Maybe he was downstairs with Santa right now. Maybe he was hanging out with the reindeer in the backyard at this very instant! I had to get down there.

Quietly, I slipped into my imitation LL Bean slippers and grabbed my robe. I knew the rules about getting out of bed on Christmas Eve—there were serious repercussions, including, but not limited to, being banned from presents for life. But this was a risk I was willing to take. My Nintendo fate rested on getting to Santa now, no matter what the cost.

"Dance of the Sugar Plum Fairy" eerily scored the scene in my head as I felt my way down the hallway in the dark. Like my mad dash home from school without a coat on, I knew that this mission was a big one. I had to get downstairs without being detected by my parents, a feat I had never even attempted before. This was going to be tricky.

I crawled past their doorway to the top of the stairs and looked down. The stairs were always the toughest section to maneuver in my house. They creaked like an old ship, and you had to balance your weight evenly on either side of them to keep them quiet. I gently hopped from step to step in the dark, careful not to touch the railing, which my dad had said he was going to varnish before going to bed. I could tell that the Christmas tree lights were still on, illuminating the family room below. Cautiously, I crept to the landing and made my way to the hallway. I tiptoed around the corner and peeked into the room.

Rats! Santa had come already. There was a fresh mound of presents under the tree. Never before in my life had I actually been upset to see presents. I'd missed him. I'd missed Santa. The cookies and milk were gone, and so were the pickles that Lizzy had left for the reindeer (we were out of carrots). For a moment I just stood there, looking over the scene, trying to think of what to do next.

And then I saw it.

It was off by itself at the back of the tree, a present far bigger than the rest. It was thick and rectangular. It looked heavy and solid. Could it be?

*Hello Jake.*

My heart skipped a beat. The Kevin Spacey voice was back. I felt myself floating toward the tree. Before I knew it, I was picking up the package and holding it in my shaking hands. The tag on it read exactly what I hopped it would. "To Jake. Love, Santa." It was a Nintendo. It had to be.

*Up a little late, aren't you, Jake?*

"Are you for real?" I heard myself asking the package out loud.

*Do I feel real?*

"Yes." I lifted it again. It felt like about the right weight. I shook it. It was solid. No moving parts, no Legos rattling around. I put it up to my nose. Cardboard. I could smell it right through the wrapping paper. I pushed at it harder. It felt like Styrofoam underneath, another good sign.

My gun-shy mind fired through the possibilities. There were no other toys this size that I'd ever expressed interest in. There was no way this box contained clothes. It wasn't a train set or a GI Joe hovercraft. There were no random cardboard boxes that would fit a present like this. This was a Nintendo. As sure as I lived and breathed, it was a Nintendo. And it was all mine.

I had done it! I began running around in circles, sprinting from one side of the room to the other, silently screaming at the top of my lungs. Santa had come through! Everything was going to be okay! I could go on living! Come tomorrow morning, I would bask in the 8-bit glow of flying turtles and sideways-running mushrooms. I would shoot fireballs from my eyes and smash bricks with my head. I would get to the last level in *Super Mario Bros.* and not have to worry about waiting my turn or having to go home for lunch. I would be a Nintendo owner! Dreams really do come true! I dove headfirst onto the couch and kicked my feet wildly in the air. Ha-ha! I jumped on the coffee table and danced around like a moron, trading high fives with an entire imaginary starting lineup. Nintendo-my-friendo! Nintendo-my-friendo! You can put it on the boaaaaaard, YES!

I was so caught up in the moment that I barely registered the back door opening and closing shut. By the time I heard the footsteps coming down the hall, it was too late. I crouched down and saw my dad's profile walk into the doorway. He was wearing his work jacket. He looked cold, like he'd been outside for a while. Elwood was with him. I tried hiding behind the coffee table, but the dog went straight for me.

My dad jumped. "Jesus, Jake. You scared me half to death. What are you doing up?"

"Uh . . . nothing. What are you doing up, Dad?"

"Uh . . . nothing."

We were at a standstill. I'd never heard my dad answer "nothing" before. This was weird. Maybe he had just seen Santa. Maybe that's why he was outside.

"I thought we told you never to get up on Christmas Eve, Jake."

"I heard a noise. I, uh, I was looking for Elwood. Did you . . . did you just see Santa?"

He paused for a second, like he wasn't sure if I was

asking him for real or if I was just yanking his chain. "Yeah," he said finally. "I saw him. He told me he knew you'd snuck downstairs and I should send you back to bed before your mom finds out. He seemed like a pretty cool guy, actually."

But I was already halfway out of the room by the time he finished the sentence. There was no way I was going to blow this opportunity now, not with a Nintendo sitting right there under the tree. I flew up the stairs and dove into bed, already envisioning all the games I was going to buy and not share with anyone. If it was hard falling asleep before, then there was no way I was falling asleep now.

A few restless hours later, I was standing in the pitch-black hallway outside my parents' bedroom watching Lizzy pace back and forth. It was still dark; the sun had yet to come up. We were counting down the minutes until it was safe for us to wake our parents to let us go downstairs.

"Now?" she asked, shaking with excitement.

"Not yet."

Waking up our parents on Christmas morning was a very exact science. It had to be done with just the right timing and just the right mixture of excitement and subtlety. If you went in too early and too loudly, you could get yelled at, but if you tried to wake them up too quietly, you ran the risk of not seeming excited enough and you were sent back to bed without really waking them up at all. I'd learned that sending Lizzy in to do the dirty work was a much smarter move. She was cuter than I was. My dad had a hard time telling her no.

"Now?"

"Not yet, Lizzy, just a minute. We have to wait until seven or they'll send us right back to bed."

"What if we just change their clock?"

Man, Lizzy was a pistol. "No, we're not changing the clock. We don't want to get in trouble on Christmas morning, dummy. Just wait."

"Alright, alright, gosh."

Elwood wandered into the hallway, his tail wagging from side to side. Even he seemed excited. Lizzy gave him a great big bear hug.

"It's Christmas, Elwood!"

"*Shh.* Quiet, Lizzy, jeez."

I stared daggers at my father's digital alarm clock resting on his bedside table, silently willing it to turn from 6:59 to 7:00. It was the longest minute of the year.

"Now? Now?" Lizzy was practically crawling on me.

Finally, it ticked to 7:00. This was it. It was officially Christmas morning.

"Yes, Lizzy. *Now.*"

Lizzy's plastic-footed pajamas pitter-pattered into my parents' room.

"It's Christmas! It's Christmas!" She dove onto the bed, jumping up and down between them. "It's Christmas! Wake up! Wake up!"

My mom rolled over. "Merry Christmas, Lizzy, dear."

"Merry Christmas, Mommy. Dad. Dad! Wake up, it's Christmas!"

"Christmas is canceled," he groaned.

"Daaad."

"No Christmas, it's too early." He put the pillow over his head.

"Can we go open presents now?"

"There are no presents."

"Pleeease, Dad. Can we pleeeease go downstairs. We waited until seven."

I stuck my head into the room and gave Lizzy a thumbs-up. She was doing great.

"Pleeease, Dad." She dug her head under his pillow. "Pleeeease."

"Oh, alright . . . I'll put the coffee on, Patty."

Christmas morning in the Doyle house always started off with a painful series of delays. It was worse than a space shuttle launch. First you had to wait until seven before you could wake my parents up. Then you had to wait until they went to the bathroom and brushed their teeth before you could line up on the stairs. Then you had to wait at the top of the staircase until they got their coffee and let the dog out before you could go downstairs into the family room. Then you had to wait until everyone was seated and somebody got the garbage bag for all the wrapping paper before you *then* had to wait your turn before you could actually open a stinking present. It was torture.

Lizzy and I jostled for position at the top of the stairs. For some reason, being the first one downstairs was very important to us, just in case maybe there was a present down there without a nametag on it and somebody had to call dibs first.

"Can we come down yet?"

"Ask your father!" my mom yelled. "He won't let me in the room either."

"Can we come down yet, Dad?"

"Just hang on a minute."

One minute. Got it. *One-one thousand, two-one thousand, three-one thousand,* I was counting down the seconds.

Lizzy couldn't wait that long. "Can we come down yet?"

"Hang on."

"How 'bout now?"

"Hang on, will ya!"

I was crouched down in a runner's position, straddling the top two steps like they were starting blocks at a four-hundred-meter dash.

"Okay," my dad yelled, finally finished with whatever grossly unimportant thing he was doing down there. "Come on down!"

I threw two big elbows and took off like a shot.

Running downstairs on Christmas morning was an unparalleled feeling. Those two or three seconds of sheer joy always proved to be the absolute pinnacle of the kid year. In that moment anything was possible. I hopped the stairs two at a time and slid across the hardwood floor into the family room, almost knocking down my father and the bizarre apparatus he was now operating. It was a brand new video camera.

"Say cheese!" He grinned from behind the tripod. It had a ribbon on it and everything.

My mother, who had just wandered into the room, was practically speechless. Video cameras were very expensive. "A video camera? John, when did you get this?"

"Relax, Patty, I won it in a hockey raffle. I'm gonna record the whole morning. Isn't that great? We're all on tape right now!" I'd never seen the old man so excited. "Everybody say Merry Christmas!"

Lizzy just stared at him. "You know the red light's supposed to be on."

"God bless it!" He fiddled with the controls. She was right. Nothing had been recorded. He'd missed the entire opening scene. "Go back upstairs and do it again. Run back down the stairs again. Everybody. On the double!"

With the video camera now in the mix, this year's Christmas delays were prolonged even further due to technical difficulties. The next thirty-five minutes were spent sitting on the couch watching my dad try to figure out how to work the camera's maze of controls and buttons. We were not allowed to open a single present until he did so. I was practically foaming at the mouth.

"I think you're supposed to press the red button, John."

"I just pressed it, Patty."

"Well, what does it say in the manual?"

"Half of it is in Japanese, how the heck should I know."

"I think that's the translation of the English half, dear."

"Oh, you speak Japanese now? Up, up, wait." He closed a flap and the VHS canopy whizzed and clicked. "I think I got it. There! I got it!" The red light blazed forth. It was working. "I did it! Ha! Lizzy, say something cute."

"Gimme a present!" she rasped.

"Are you having a good Christmas so far?" He zoomed the camera in closer.

"A present! A present!" she yelled again. Elwood was barking too; he could barely stand it either.

"Just let her get a present, John."

"Okay, okay. Lizzy, you're Santa this year. Go ahead and pick one out for yourself first."

For reasons I could only see conceived as a means to inflict agonizing pain on me, my parents always let Lizzy play Santa. This meant that she was in charge of my supply of presents. She dictated the entire operation. Not only was she extremely slow in selecting and distributing the gifts, she was also quite adept at finding the crappiest presents to give to me first. I usually had to sit through two or three rounds of shirts and sweaters before I got a toy, and this was no accident.

"Let's see . . . " She was sifting through the mound for her gifts. "I'm gonna pick this one for me first." She sat down and tore into a Cabbage Patch–sized box with a gleam in her eye, only to be disappointed by a Barbie Ferrari.

"Wow, look at that, Lizzy." My dad zoomed in closer. "A car for Barbie."

"Yippee."

I was up next. The Nintendo box was still under the tree. I'd made darn sure of that the second I ran down the stairs. I did my best to drop hints to Lizzy to give it to me. Subtle ones like "Hey, look at that big present for me behind the tree, why don't you give it to me first?" She handed me a shirt box instead and smiled.

It went on like this for some time. Packages were selected and passed out. There were "oohs" and "ahhs," "thank yous" and "you're welcomes." Discarded paper was thrown directly at the camera whenever possible. My dad was already turning into a regular Scorsese behind the lens, setting up different angles and demanding more emotion from his actors. My mom sipped her coffee and smiled, every once in a while picking up a discarded bow and placing it in her bathrobe pocket for next year. Slowly but surely, I ate away at the remaining presents. There were a few He-Man action figures, a couple of books, the sweater my mom had picked out for me weeks ago at Water Tower Place, but nothing of any real significance. I kept my eye on the prize the whole time.

"Okay, Dad, your turn." Lizzy handed him a thin, record-sized present.

"What's this?" he asked, turning the camera around.

"It's from me and Lizzy," I said. The two of us had spent the better part of half an hour wrapping it. There was a considerable amount of tape involved. The old man inspected it closely. He was a painfully careful opener, as if he were uncovering a fossil or handling a piece of broken glass. He used his thumb and forefinger to pull apart each individual section of the paper, unwrapping it in one big piece. Eventually he got to the gift inside. It was a large black-and-white cardboard cutout of an old man's face.

"Who's that?" my mom asked, leaning in to get a better look. The cut-out man had an enormous forehead and a pained expression on his face, as if someone had just punched him in the stomach or asked him for money.

"That's Bill Wirtz," my dad scoffed. "Owner of the Blackhawks."

"It's for your dartboard in the garage!" Lizzy exclaimed. "We cut it out of the newspaper."

My dad smiled widely, staring down the face of his enemy. It might have been his favorite gift all year. "Wow. Thanks, guys. I love it." He gave Lizzy a hug and shot me a wink. "Hey Jake, why don't you hand Lizzy that present to the left of the tree over there."

Toward the back of the tree was a crumpled-up package wrapped in newspaper, no doubt the handiwork of my father. I handed it over to Lizzy. I was pretty sure it was the doll. Even though we hadn't spoken a word about our infamous Aurora mission since it went down, I knew the old man had been hard at work getting the doll in fighting shape.

Sensing the magnitude of the moment, and perhaps feeling a plastic face underneath the newspaper, Lizzy tore open the gift with one large rip.

"A Cabbage Patch!"

It was indeed a Cabbage Patch, in the rudimentary sense at least. Apparently my dad's dye job hadn't gone exactly according to plan, because the doll's hair was now bright purple. She was also clothed in nothing more than a child's size Chicago Bears T-shirt, which I was pretty sure used to belong to me. I shot my dad a look to see if he would offer some kind of excuse or explanation but he just brushed me off. Lizzy didn't seem to care one bit.

"A Cabbage Patch! A Cabbage Patch!" She was clutching the doll to her chest. "Smell her, Jake, she smells like a newborn baby!" I took a whiff. It smelled a lot like food coloring to me, but I let it slide.

"Yeah, mmm, smells good."

"I'm going to name her Dawn Rebecca!"

"Okay, sounds good, Lizzy. Why don't you hand me my present now." There was only one present left under the tree. It had been sitting there patiently for over twenty minutes. I hadn't taken my eyes off of it once. Lizzy had gotten what she wanted. Now it was my turn.

Lizzy ran over. "Mom, look at how beautiful Dawn Rebecca is!"

"Oh, she's gorgeous, Lizzy. We'll have to dress her up and find some—"

"Hey!" I yelled, bobbing up and down on my knees in front of the tree. "There's still a present left with my name on it. Can I grab it or what?"

"Don't interrupt your mother," my dad barked from behind the camera.

"Sorry, Mom."

"That's okay. Lizzy, hand your brother his present."

Lizzy trotted over to the gift and slid it across the carpet toward me. Her eyes widened at the size of it. She too could tell what it was. Her mouth opened a little, and for a second it almost looked like she was happy for me.

"Look at how big this is, Jake," she whispered.

"I know."

"It feels like it's—"

"I know, Lizzy, I know." I slid the package farther out into the room and sat down behind it, facing my family. I wanted everyone to have a good view. I read off the tag. "To Jake. Love, Santa." I smiled devilishly. "I wonder what it could be?"

Below me sat the product of hundreds of man-hours of plotting and scheming. Now that it was finally here, I hardly knew how to go about opening it. I placed my hand at the edge of a fold and closed my eyes. I'd later read of Olympic athletes training their entire lives for one ten-second moment. This was it. This was my moment.

Carefully I peeled back a corner of the paper and took a peek. All I needed was a little sign to make sure it was a Nintendo, just a little visual confirmation. One inch, then two inches, then . . . there it was! A small patch of an outer-space backdrop shone through the red-and-white wrapping paper. It was just like the Nintendo box I'd seen Kleen unwrap months earlier. Praise be to God! Halleluiah Santa Claus! A Nintendo Entertainment System at last! An electronic *RBI Baseball* crowd roared in my head. The *Mario Bros.* invincibility star pulsed through my veins. *Double Dribble* cheerleaders danced all around me. This was it! It was time to break out the pop! It was time to sit in front of the TV all day and do nothing but play Nintendo! I pulled back further on the paper, overjoyed to finally read the eight letters I'd spent months dreaming about. My eyes sped across the logo at top of the box. In big red print and in clear, beautiful English it read . . .

L-I-T-E B-R-I-T-E.

"Lite-Brite?"

Lite-Brite. The world suddenly came to a grinding halt. Oh God, NOOO! Not Lite-Brite! Anything but that!

"You've got to be kidding me!" I yelled out loud.

I wasn't looking at a space scene on the box at all. I was looking at a bunch of glowing plastic peg-lights. Santa Claus had not brought me a Nintendo. Instead, the son of a bitch had brought me the shittiest of shit presents in all of Shitville: *fucking Lite-Brite!*

An 8-bit Mike Tyson socked me in the face. My *Rad Racer* car exploded into flames. Two hundred and seventy-six *Kung-Fu* elves began kicking me in the groin. Lite-Brite wasn't a toy or a game or even a *thing.* It was in a monumentally bad category of its own. It was a crappy plastic box that you plugged into the wall and stuck little light bulbs into through construction paper, like you were some kind of retarded savant. Its annoying commercials had haunted Saturday morning cartoons for years. They were filled with preppy-looking six-year-olds staring in slack-jawed wonderment at illuminated ballerinas and clown faces. It was a baby's toy. Even its jingle was terrible. "*Lite-Brite. Lite-Brite. Turn on the magic of colored lights!*" Getting a Lite-Brite instead of a Nintendo was like asking for a ten-speed for Christmas and receiving a three-legged mule. Was this some kind of joke?

"It looks like it's the deluxe edition, Jake," my mom pointed out proudly.

It was indeed the deluxe edition, that's why it was so big and that's why it felt like a Nintendo box. I'd been duped. Santa had played me like a game of Uno.

"Think of all the neat projects you can make."

I couldn't speak. I wanted to cry but I was in a state of shock. I just sat there staring at the box with my mouth open. Lizzy plopped down next to me and put her hand on my shoulder. Elwood nuzzled my chest. They both knew I'd just lost the war. As I slowly tried to grasp the situation, I began to fear that I might never recover from this. That this was a tragedy so great that I would never go to prom, never go to college, never get a job, never leave the house. I'd be a thirty-year-old balding man sitting in his parents' basement making elaborate pictures of Zelda with his Lite-Brite. Christmas was dead to me now.

# CHAPTER TWENTY-SEVEN

I spent the rest of Christmas morning curled up under the TV watching *Anne of Green Gables* on VHS with my sister. That's how depressed I was. *Anne of Green Gables* was the story of a young orphaned girl who, despite her "humble beginnings," charms everyone in town with her "fiery spirit" and lives "happily ever after." It was set at the turn of the century in Canada, and in the opinion of this nine-year-old boy, was probably the worst video ever made. I hated it with a passion. But I was so distraught that I didn't care. I watched the whole thing.

After months of Nintendo disappointment, it was almost like I'd gotten used to the pain. It was almost as if I enjoyed it. I sat through Christmas lunch without a word, picking at leftover Jell-O and turkey. My dad asked if I wanted to go outside and throw the football around like we'd done last Christmas, but I declined.

At noon I received a phone call from Zilinski. All

around town, despite the panic, levelheaded grandmothers had come through and three-fourths of my friends had received a Nintendo for Christmas, even Zilinski himself. By nightfall countless kids across Kane County would go to bed sporting throbbing headaches and blistered thumbs from a full twelve hours on their new Nintendos. It was a tough pill to swallow.

I wandered around the house in a daze. I fed the gumdrop head of my macaroni Wise Man to Elwood. I even offered to take down all the Christmas decorations, a chore that in years past had been a death sentence. But I didn't mind. I wanted Christmas over with. I was sick of it. The holiday had brought me nothing but trouble and heartache. I counted the minutes on the clock. Day turned to dusk. Dusk turned to night.

"Are you packed yet, Jake?" my mom called up to my room, where I'd been pouting in seclusion for hours. Every Christmas night we loaded up the van and drove up to St. Paul, Minnesota, to visit my mom's side of the family. A normal person could drive it in about seven hours. My dad usually did it in five. That's why we waited until Christmas night to leave. He didn't want to hit any traffic. Where exactly this "traffic" came from, we could never be sure, as Christmas was one of the least congested days of the year, but my dad wanted to avoid it just the same.

"I'll be down in a second!" I yelled back. I tossed a few more He-Men figures into my suitcase and brought it downstairs. The pile of luggage in the kitchen had been growing all afternoon. My mom was not exactly a light packer. She stood next to the mound with my sister, quietly trying to stay out of my dad's way as he sputtered back and forth between the kitchen and the garage, packing the car. If there was one thing the old man hated more than traffic, it was luggage.

"We're going to Minnesota for four days. You've been in the car before, Patty. I've seen you. How much room do you think we have in there?"

"It's mostly gifts."

"What do we need gifts for? How many Christmases do we have to have, for crying out loud?"

"Why don't we just leave in the morning, John, you'll feel better then."

"I'm not hitting traffic!" He carried another three bags out the door past my sister. She was bundled up in her pajamas and coat, already prepared for the long drive ahead. She held Dawn Rebecca tightly.

"Mom?" she asked. "Do you think I can bring Dawn outside when we get to Grandma's?"

"Yes, Lizzy, dear. Maybe we can find her a little hat to keep her head warm."

"Yeah, she's gonna need it. Her hair . . . " She leaned in, covering the doll's ears. "It's an embarrassment."

"Jake. Grab your coat and get out here," my dad called from the garage.

Oh, great, now what? I put on my new, and decidedly hideous, London Fog jacket that my grandparents had just given to me and I trudged outside. My dad was standing at the edge of the garage holding a shovel.

"Here." He handed it to me. "There's a ton of poop out there. I want it all cleaned up."

"Now?"

"Yeah, now. You've had all week to do it."

"But it's Christmas, Dad."

"I don't care. I want it all cleaned up before we leave.

Now, get going."

Reluctantly, I swung the shovel over my shoulder, catching a cool whiff of poo as I pulled it toward me. Of course I had to pick up dog poop on Christmas. Of course I did. It was the perfect end to a perfectly crappy Christmas.

I grabbed a garbage bag, zipped up my coat and stomped through the snow toward the back of the house.

"And don't forget to do the other side of the house behind the shed," my dad called out. "You haven't been back there in months."

"Yeah, yeah," I muttered under my breath. Elwood trotted alongside me as I made my way across the yard toward the shed. My dad was right. I hadn't picked up a single piece of poop back there since probably September. There was poo as far as the eye could see, all the way to the tree line bordering the neighbor's lawn. I sat down on an overturned garbage can and watched my breath.

The stars were already out and the sky was clear. I heard a distant hum of a plane flying high overhead. It was a beautiful Christmas night in Batavia. Sitting there in the cold, I began to play back all the scenes that had taken place over the past few weeks. I thought about the Salvation Army Santa Claus and my missing retainer. I thought about the cute checkout girl and Mrs. Huge-Blow. I thought about Mr. Murphy's burned coat and Miss Ciarocci's smile. I thought about Dan Delund and Timmy Kleen. I thought about my girls' boots and the man in leather pants. They were all steppingstones that I'd imagined were supposed to lead me to a glorious Nintendo victory. But in reality, all they'd done was lead me here to this sad moment. I was alone on Christmas night with a shovel and a garbage bag, staring into a yard of frozen dog poo.

My mind wandered to thoughts of the cab driver, that gruff old pro with all the answers. Maybe he was right. Maybe I'd blown it. I hadn't so much as said Merry Christmas to a single person all year. I'd ruined a perfectly good Christmas, and for what?

Elwood sat down at my feet and stared out into the yard with me. Despite the moon and the stars, it was still pretty dark out. My dad had forgotten to turn on the floodlights. How did he expect me to do a decent job if I couldn't even see? What was he doing right now that was so important? Why couldn't he come out here and help me?

"Hey Dad!" I yelled back toward the garage. "You forgot to turn on the flood lights!" There was no response. I tried again. "Hey Dad! The lights!"

Suddenly, the lights flicked on and a wave of brightness fell over the backyard, making every inch of snow sparkle and every piece of dog crud even more apparent. I rose slowly and looked up toward the trees for the first time.

And then I saw it . . .

There, high above the frozen dog poo that had become the bane of my Nintendo-less existence was the most beautiful structure I had ever laid eyes on.

"Whoa . . . "

It was a tree fort—a glorious, two-level, solid-wood tree fort. Freshly painted, with a rope ladder and a red ribbon on its roof.

"Whoa . . . " I gasped again. It was all I could get out. I stood there awestruck for a moment. Cautiously, I looked around to make sure I hadn't accidentally wandered into a neighbor's yard by mistake. I hadn't. I was still on Doyle soil. I dropped my bag and shovel and made my way toward the tree.

Oh, it was breathtaking—rows and rows of wood slats descending from high up in the snowy branches, gracefully separating in the middle for a large window with two red shutters. And it was high in the air too, very high, high enough to keep out bullies and kid sisters, that was for sure. As I got closer I noticed a little note tied onto the rope ladder. I turned it over. "To Jake. Love, Santa," it read. Sure enough, this tree fort was for me. It was all mine.

Slowly and steadily I climbed up the ladder, carefully ascending past branches and needles. There was a trap door at the top, one that could be opened and closed from the inside. Perfect for secret knocks and last-minute escapes. I pulled myself up through the hatch and stood up on the floor. It was even more beautiful on the inside. The fort was fully enclosed from the elements, with the trunk of the tree running smack dab through the middle of the floor and up through the roof. A few feet up toward the ceiling was another level, almost like a loft. There were pegs nailed into the trunk so you could climb up there. And there was even another little hatch in the loft itself that led to the roof, perfect for a periscope or a squirt-gun lookout post.

I ran my fingers over the fresh varnish on the walls and took it all in for a minute. This was a better Christmas gift than I'd ever hoped for. Better than a trip to Disney World, better than a Cubs' World Series, better than even a Nintendo. Way better. I couldn't believe it.

By the time I looked down into the yard below, my family was already standing there watching me. My dad had his hands in his coat pockets. My mom held Lizzy in her arms. I could tell they'd been there for a few minutes.

"Wow-ee, Jake!" Lizzy called out. "Mom, can I go up there?"

"You have to ask your brother, Lizzy."

"Just let him be," said my dad. "It's his fort."

"Did you see this, Mom?" I yelled down. "It's from Santa!"

"Yeah, looks pretty neat, Jake! Maybe you should ask Santa to build us a new kitchen next year." She smiled at my dad.

I was hardly paying attention. "It's got a trap door, Dad!"

"Yeah, I see that. Careful by those shutters, the paint still looks wet."

"Why don't I go get the camera, John?"

"Nah. You two should go inside. It's getting cold."

My mom set Lizzy down and held her hand. She gave my dad a kiss on the cheek and patted his chest. "Come on, Lizzy, let's go back inside, it's freezing out here."

My dad walked across the yard in the snow and stood below the rope ladder. "Mind if I come up there to check it out, Jake?"

"Sure, come on up."

He climbed up through the hatch and swung his legs up with precision. "You know," he said, "if we got a big enough basket and maybe some pulleys, I bet we could rig up an elevator to bring Elwood up here."

"You think?"

"Yeah, you'd have to help me, though."

"Okay."

He walked around the fort for a minute, touching the walls and checking the strength of the pegs on the trunk.

I'd never seen him like this before. He was calm and open, like he was out for a Sunday drive without a car on the road. He put his hands on the windowsill and took a deep breath.

"You smell that, Jake?"

"Fresh air?"

"That's right. Smells good, doesn't it?"

I nodded and peered out the window next to him. "It's just like in *Swiss Family Robinson*."

"Yeah, I guess it is. You'll have to keep a lookout for pirates."

I laughed. "Maybe we could bring the movie up to Grandma's and watch it while we're up there."

"Okay," he said, hardly able to contain his smile. "Sounds like a plan. Come on. Let's get going. It's getting cold and I don't want to hit the traffic."

I followed him to the ladder as he climbed down. It was only then that I noticed the smudges of paint on the collar of his coat, red paint, just like the kind on the shutters. My nine-year-old mind slowly put the pieces together.

From that moment on, I saw my dad a little differently. He was more than a guy who drove too fast and could never quite finish remodeling the kitchen. He was a magician. He was a hero. *He was Santa Claus.*

I climbed down the ladder to where he was waiting for me on the ground. He grabbed me by the waist and slung me over his shoulder. As he carried me back toward the house through the snow, I looked back at the fort, still lit up by the floodlights. Peacefully, my mind unfolded all the tree-fort adventures that undoubtedly lay ahead. Ghost-story campouts by flashlight, weeklong snowball battles, and round-the-clock sky gazing for Soviet spy planes.

"Hey, Dad?"

"Yeah?"
"Merry Christmas."
"Merry Christmas, Jake."

## ABOUT THE AUTHOR

A native of Batavia, Illinois, Kevin Jakubowski is a film and television writer best known for the Sundance Film Festival hit *Assassination of a High School President* and for his work on the Comedy Central series *Brickleberry*. He has written and co-written scripts for Warner Brothers, Paramount, Lionsgate, Sony and Fox and is currently developing his own animated series at Nickelodeon. *8-Bit Christmas* is his first novel.

kevin-jakubowski.com

CPSIA information can be obtained at www.ICGtesting.com
Printed in the USA
BVOW05s0840151215

430328BV00004B/474/P